Berkley Prime Crime titles by E. J. Copperman

NIGHT OF THE LIVING DEED
AN UNINVITED GHOST
OLD HAUNTS
CHANCE OF A GHOST

Night of the Living Deed

E. J. COPPERMAN

BERKLEY PRIME CRIME, NEW YORK

THE BERKLEY PUBLISHING GROUP
Published by the Penguin Group
Penguin Group (USA) Inc.
375 Hudson Street, New York, New York 10014, USA

Penguin Group (Canada), 90 Eglinton Avenue East, Suite 700, Toronto, Ontario M4P 2Y3, Canada
(a division of Pearson Penguin Canada Inc.)
Penguin Books Ltd., 80 Strand, London WC2R 0RL, England
Penguin Group Ireland, 25 St. Stephen's Green, Dublin 2, Ireland (a division of Penguin Books Ltd.)
Penguin Group (Australia), 250 Camberwell Road, Camberwell, Victoria 3124, Australia
(a division of Pearson Australia Group Pty. Ltd.)
Penguin Books India Pvt. Ltd., 11 Community Centre, Panchsheel Park, New Delhi—110 017, India
Penguin Group (NZ), 67 Apollo Drive, Rosedale, North Shore 0632, New Zealand
(a division of Pearson New Zealand Ltd.)
Penguin Books (South Africa) (Pty.) Ltd., 24 Sturdee Avenue, Rosebank, Johannesburg 2196,
South Africa

Penguin Books Ltd., Registered Offices: 80 Strand, London WC2R 0RL, England

NIGHT OF THE LIVING DEED

A Berkley Prime Crime Book / published by arrangement with the author

PRINTING HISTORY
Berkley Prime Crime mass-market edition / June 2010

Copyright © 2010 by Jeffrey Cohen.
Cover illustration by Dominick Finelle.
Cover design by Judith Lagerman.
Interior text design by Kristin del Rosario.

ISBN: 978-0-425-23523-2

BERKLEY® PRIME CRIME
Berkley Prime Crime Books are published by The Berkley Publishing Group,
a division of Penguin Group (USA) Inc.,
375 Hudson Street, New York, New York 10014.
BERKLEY® PRIME CRIME and the PRIME CRIME logo are trademarks of Penguin Group (USA) Inc.

PRINTED IN THE UNITED STATES OF AMERICA

10 9 8 7 6 5 4 3 2 1

To my brother,
Charlie,
the other writer in the family.

ACKNOWLEDGMENTS

It would truly have been impossible for this book to exist without the incredibly talented and dedicated Shannon Jamieson Vazquez, the editor who took a wisp of an idea and helped it become an actual book, and then a much better book. My sincere thanks.

And none of that would have happened had it not been for my agent, Christina Hogrebe of the Jane Rotrosen Agency, whose inexhaustible energy and belief in my work warm my heart and boggle my mind.

Special thanks to Luci Hansson Zahray, "The Poison Lady," for figuring out what would be needed to dispose of three unlucky people.

Thank you to the generous authors who read this work in an earlier form and offered kind words, many of which you'll find on these pages. The camaraderie of mystery authors is a powerful force, and one that I think is quite rare among people who could see one another as competition.

And finally, thanks to my family, my friends, those who will read this book and hopefully enjoy it. Encouragement is a powerful drug, and luckily, a legal one. It is greatly appreciated.

One

"I don't get it, Mom. If this is our house, why are other people going to live here?" My daughter, Melissa, nine years old and already a prosecuting attorney, looked up from the baseboard near the window seat in the living room, which she was painting with a two-inch brush and a gallon can of generic semigloss white paint. Never use the expensive stuff when you're letting a fourth grader help with the painting.

"I've explained this to you before, Liss," I told her without looking down from the wall. I was trying to locate a wooden stud, and the stud finder I was using was being, as is often the case with plaster walls, inconclusive. Using a battery-operated gizmo to find a stud and failing: I tried not to dwell on its metaphorical implications for my love life.

"Other people aren't coming here to live," I continued. "They'll be coming here when they're on vacation. We're going to have a guesthouse, like a hotel. They'll pay us to stay here, near the beach. But we've got to fix up the place first."

"Mr. Barnes says these houses have history in them, and it's wrong to make them modern." Mr. Barnes was Melissa's history teacher, and at the moment, he wasn't helping.

"Mr. Barnes probably didn't mean this house. Besides, we're fixing it up the way it was meant to be. I mean, no one would want to live in the house the way it looks now, right?"

Our hulk of a turn-of-the-last-century Victorian house was not, by the standards of anyone whose age was in double digits, livable. Sure, the house had once been adorable, maybe even grand, but that was a *long* time ago. Now, the ancient plaster walls downstairs were peeling and, in some places, crumbling. There was a thick coat of white dust pretty much everywhere, and as far as I could tell, the heating system was devoid of, well, heat. The October chill was already starting to feel permanent in my bones.

However, it was clear that *some* work had been done by the previous owner, though by my decorating standards, he or she must have been demented. The living room walls had been painted bright bloodred, and the kitchen cabinets were hideous and hung so high Shaquille O'Neal would have a hard time reaching the cereal. Luckily, the upstairs walls had been patched and painted, the landscaping in the front of the house was quite lovely (although the vast backyard had been untouched), and the staircases (there were two) going upstairs had been refinished beautifully. It was a work in progress. Slow progress.

"*I* would live here," Melissa said, and went back to painting. That settled it, in her view.

"You *do* live here," I answered, not noting that there was no furniture, and that we were both sleeping on mattresses laid directly onto the floors of our respective so-called bedrooms and living out of suitcases. Why remind her of all the things we'd left in the house in Red Bank after the divorce? Melissa's father, Steven (hereafter known as The Swine), hadn't wanted the furniture, but he *had* wanted half the proceeds when I sold it all to help make the down payment on the house. The Swine.

Besides, now the house was a construction site, and any furniture would have been prone to disfigurement or worse while the work went on. As soon as the house was in shape, the new furniture I'd ordered (and, in some cases, collected from consignment stores) would be delivered.

I'd decided to open a guesthouse after my last job—bookkeeper at a lumberyard—hadn't worked out. Mostly, it hadn't worked out because my boss had a habit of forgetting his marriage vows when he walked over to my desk to discuss the company's finances. Luckily, there had been multiple witnesses when he'd tried to put his hands in the back pockets of my jeans, so he didn't press charges after I decked him. But I decided to sue, strictly on principle. And because the guy was a jerk.

We settled the case for an amount that had seemed like a lot of money, but once I'd done the math on paper, I realized it would last Melissa and me only about two years, and even then, only if we were very frugal in our lifestyle. The alimony from The Swine wasn't much, and living in New Jersey, a state with some of the highest real-estate values—and property taxes—in the country, wasn't going to be easy on "not much."

So I'd decided the thing to do was to take the money and put it into something that could start me off in a business capable of sustaining us for years. And that was when I thought of a guesthouse.

I'd always wanted to own and run a guesthouse here in Harbor Haven, the town where I'd grown up. I liked the idea of people coming in and out, of helping them enjoy the area I loved so much, and of restoring and maintaining one of the majestic beach houses that all too often faced a wrecking ball these days. Developers are everywhere on the Jersey Shore, even in rough economic times. History was being wiped out in favor of expensive vacation condos, and I hoped I could save at least one beauty from extinction. Now, knee deep in it and feeling like I had taken on too much, I was still loving it.

The New Jersey Shore ("down the shore," to us locals), contrary to the popular notion of the state, is absolutely gorgeous, and a wildly attractive vacation destination. Harbor Haven had not yet been discovered by teenagers and families with young children, which meant there were no thrill rides, no hideous souvenir shops and no boardwalk here. (All things I had sorely lamented as a teenager, but whose absences I now considered serious advantages.) The only thing I really missed was the saltwater taffy, but you could get that in nearby Point Pleasant.

In other words, the only tourists who came to Harbor Haven were quiet and wealthy. The perfect place to open a guesthouse . . . assuming I could get the shambles around me to look like a palace in the next few weeks. My real estate agent, Terry Wright, had told me people often booked their next summer vacations right after the previous season ended, especially in November and December. If I wanted to get color brochures and Internet advertising going before people started making their summer vacation plans—and I did—I'd really need to get cracking.

I hadn't put down a drop cloth where Melissa was working because I was going to paint the rest of the wall after I'd made my repairs, and the wall-to-wall carpet in the living room was among the first things I'd decided to remove when I first saw the house. Giving Melissa woodwork to paint was going to be little help in the long term, but mostly it was a good way to keep her busy.

I went back to concentrating on the wall. If it were a modern wall, I could knock a hole in the drywall and look inside, then patch it back up, and by the time I was finished painting, nobody would ever know anything had happened.

But not in this house. These walls were the original plaster, which afforded them a smooth, gorgeous effect (among many other features) I was planning to exploit for a higher per-night price. But repairing plaster is not easy, much more an art than a science, and the only people who really knew how to do it had died out at about the same time that drywall became popular. If I breached the wall by more than a small crack, I'd end up having to replace the whole wall, and that would be bad.

So, I steeled myself and let my father's voice ring in my head. "Alison," he'd say, "you know perfectly well that no contractor is going to care as much about doing it right as you will. So stop feeling sorry for yourself and just get it done." Dad had taught me everything he knew about home improvement, which was a lot. Not exactly a general contractor but more of a handyman, he'd spent decades learning about what makes houses—especially old ones—work, and he'd taught me what he knew "so you'll never have to rely on some man to do it." He was never as proud as when I'd worked at HouseCenter and was teaching some guy how to install a lock or regrout a bathtub.

It hurt a little to think of Dad; it had been four years since he'd died, but you don't stop missing someone you love—you just stop obsessing about it. When their memory comes flooding back, it still has the power to wound.

"Is this good, Mom?" Melissa roused me from my flash of depression to show me the completed baseboard. As I'd expected, there was a good slick coat of paint on about the first four inches of carpet away from the wall, and another one about four inches up above the molding (impressive, considering that it indicated multiple brush widths), but the baseboard itself was indeed freshly painted, and Melissa had done a nice, careful job for a nine-year-old.

"Very good, Liss," I answered. I took a few steps over to examine the work more closely. "You have the touch."

She beamed. Melissa is always looking for approval,

and usually deserves it. "Would you do me a favor and go get the ball-peen hammer from the kitchen?" I asked her. I didn't really need the hammer, but if I'd reached over and carefully removed the two brush hairs from the baseboard while Melissa was in the room, she'd have seen it as a failure and been upset.

"Sure." She got up and ran into the kitchen. Nine-year-olds never walk; they either run like they're being chased or shuffle like they're being dragged. There is no modulated speed.

As I reached over to pull off the first brush hair, which luckily had fallen only partially on the wall (so I might leave no finger marks), I heard something heavy fall to the floor behind me. But Melissa was in the kitchen, in the other direction entirely.

I turned, but there was nothing disturbed. Well, old houses creak. Hopefully, this particular noise was not caused by something that would require skills beyond what I knew how to fix.

The first brush hair was easy, but the second one, now that I was under time pressure, would be more difficult. But I had tweezers in my shirt pocket (always be prepared), and lifted the hair gently even as Melissa called from the kitchen.

"I can't reach the hammer!"

Now, it didn't matter a bit whether I got the hammer, but that was odd, so I stood up and walked toward the kitchen.

"What do you mean, you can't . . ."

I stopped short in the doorway. Melissa was standing in the center of the (mostly) empty kitchen, cabinet doors removed and countertops missing from their spots. That was normal in our current state of repair, so it didn't bother me in the least.

But what did worry me was that every drawer in my

roll-up toolbox was open, and every tool appeared to have been flung around the room. One backsaw was hanging precariously from a nail near the ceiling. Hammers, screwdrivers, wrenches and sockets pretty much covered every surface. If it's possible for a construction site to look especially messy, that was what I was staring at now. *That* bothered me.

"It's too high up," Melissa said, pointing at it, sitting on top of the window molding.

"Melissa, what did you *do*?" I launched myself into the room and started picking up tools.

"Nothing! I thought *you* did it."

Oh, please. "Why would I throw my tools around like this?"

"Why would *I*?" she asked.

"Come on, Liss. You know I didn't leave the tools like this, and there's nobody else in the house." Although I had to admit, that hammer hanging from the window was awfully high for her to manage. Did she just fling it and get lucky?

"Well, I don't know! This was how it looked when I walked in." She stuck out her bottom lip in a gesture of defiance.

I forced her to look me in the eye. "Really?" I asked.

Melissa's gaze never wavered, which was unusual. "Really," she said.

Swell. Now I was beginning to believe her. "Well, then, how . . ."

I never managed to finish the question, since I was interrupted by a loud groan of wood and what sounded like hailstones hitting the floor in the hallway just off the living room. That was followed by a loud crash. I was out the kitchen door before Melissa could even turn her head, but she still ran faster than I did. We arrived in the living room at the same moment and stopped dead in our tracks.

The very wall I'd been agonizing over now had a gaping hole at least three feet tall, right down its center. My visions of retaining the period detail and integrity of the room had been literally destroyed. I wanted to cry.

"Why did you do *that*?" Melissa asked.

Two

"These walls are real plaster." Terry Wright, the unbearably upbeat real estate agent, had been especially proud of that fact when she'd shown me the house for the first time. "They don't have that bland feel that wallboard gives you. This could be a real selling point for your bed and breakfast."

"I'm not opening a bed and breakfast," I'd told her, deciding not to comment on her suggestion that people would choose whether or not to vacation here because of the walls (I came around to the idea later). "I'm opening a guesthouse. I'm not going to serve food."

"Oh," Terry said, her usually unbreakable glee momentarily dampened. "Well, that will keep more of our restaurants busy, won't it?" From zero to cheerful in less than three-point-two seconds, a new record. Terry, maybe five years older than I am, obviously took good care of herself and was at exactly her proper weight, with blonde hair and a beatific smile. It's a wonder she didn't work at Disney World.

The house was exactly what I had been looking for, but I couldn't let Terry know that. It had a real sense of dignity, but without stuffiness: three of the seven bedrooms had wood-burning fireplaces, as did the living room; the ceilings were twelve feet high; the overall feeling was one of comfort and ease. It had been built as a residence, not a vacation home, so it was insulated, and Melissa and I could live here all year long.

I'd known something about the house before I'd started searching. The people who had lived here for years, the Preston family, had had a lot of kids, the oldest of whom I'd gone to school with. They'd moved on about a year and a half ago, and there'd been another owner since then. The house seemed to have held up reasonably well overall, but while it was obvious *some* recent work had been done, this was no in-move-in-condition house. I'd have a lot of work to do. Which was also what I wanted (I couldn't afford a perfect house, and I would have missed the challenge), but I didn't tell Terry that, either.

I put on a pensive face and stroked my chin a little. "Well, I don't know . . ." I began.

Melissa, behind me, practically burst out of her skin. "Come *on*, Mom!" she bleated. "This is *exactly* what you've been talking about!" The girl had a lot to learn about negotiation.

I turned to look at her. "Not *exactly*," I said, and made significant eye contact.

My daughter, enthusiastic but astute, nodded, looked around the room, and tilted her head. "Yeah," she said. "The fireplace does look kind of crooked."

Damn! It actually did. I hadn't noticed that. Would I be able to repair it, or would it become "part of the charm of the place"?

"Oh, I don't think so! I think it's darling," Terry said. Her voice, directed at Melissa, dripped condescension and syrupy child-speak. "It looks fine to me."

"Is there any way to find out if the fireplace has been maintained properly?" I asked. Show doubt; maybe bring down the price a little.

"It'll all come out in the home inspection, but I'll check my file. I have two copies of everything on my computer," Terry said. She was so organized I had to fight the urge to punch her.

"I'm not sure," I said, back in my scorched-earth-negotiator mode. "I'm a little spooked by the fact that the house has been on the market for eleven months."

Terry waved a hand to dismiss that fact, and her voice took on a false confidentiality. "Everything's staying on the market for months these days," she said. "It's the economy." Uh-huh. "I'm telling you, with seven bedrooms, four baths and that kitchen, this is *the* place for a bed and breakfast."

I looked at Melissa, who rolled her eyes. Then she stared off into the distance, as if something really interesting were suspended from the ceiling. "Somebody died here," she said in a faraway voice.

I sighed a little. Melissa does that kind of thing sometimes when she thinks she can put one over on a grown-up. She doesn't like it when she's talked to as if being a kid equals being stupid.

"Knock it off," I hissed at her.

"Actually, someone *did* sort of die in the house," Terry said. I tried not to imagine what "sort of" dying could mean. Terry was doing her best not to stammer, but the effort was clearly difficult. "The previous owner of the house passed away here last June."

Of course, I already knew about that; it was why the house was for sale. Terry had mentioned it as a sales point ("the estate is *really* motivated to sell") when we'd first met at her office.

"I'm okay, Mom," Melissa said, noticing the way I was looking at her, and tried to wink. But she can't wink just yet, so to Terry, I'm sure it looked like a grimace of pain. I could use that.

"I think maybe we'll go home and think about it," I told Terry.

"They'll drop the price another ten thousand," she said immediately.

Really? "Make it twenty," I countered.

"Done."

"I'll have my lawyer call you," I told her, and took Melissa, who had given up on her audition for a séance and resumed her normal expression, by the hand. I needed to get back to the car *before* I had my inevitable panic attack.

Terry looked positively triumphant when we left. Maybe I should have held out for a thirty-thousand-dollar reduction.

But I hadn't walked into this transaction blind. I'd done my research: Even in a down economy, a house on the Jersey Shore could more than pay for itself as a vacation rental, and one that allowed for five sets of guests at once (seven bedrooms minus one each for me and Melissa) meant I could make enough in a decent summer to pay for the rest of the year and put some money away for Melissa's education.

"You bought Patty Preston's house?" Jeannie Rogers asked in a disbelieving whisper on the phone. Jeannie, my best friend since the sixth grade, was talking quietly because she was at work. "Isn't that kind of creepy?"

"What's creepy is that you still think of it as Patty Preston's house, despite the fact that neither of us had ever set foot in the place before I went to ask about buying it, and besides, I hear she lives in Colorado now."

"You have no appreciation for the past," Jeannie said.

"If I had no appreciation for the past, I wouldn't be buying a house that's over a hundred years old," I pointed out. "I'd bulldoze it and get myself a McGuesthouse."

"No, you wouldn't," Melissa said, her eyes wide. "Mr. Barnes says . . ."

I put my hand over the phone. "Nobody's knocking the house down," I told her. Then I took my hand off the phone and said to Jeannie, "You know I'd do it."

I could hear Jeannie look heavenward. We know each other too well.

She didn't respond, so I went on: "Listen, if this deal does go through, I'm going to need an expert's advice. Talk to your husband." Jeannie's husband, Tony Mandorisi, was an expert contractor and the man I asked for advice whenever I was taking on a project I hadn't tackled before. Besides, I introduced Jeannie and Tony, so they both owe me. Tony is a good guy, something I discovered back when I was working at HouseCenter and he returned an extra pallet of drywall I hadn't counted, knowing the overage would've come out of my paycheck. He wasn't my type (I mentioned he was a good guy, no? I tend to end up with men I'll eventually call The Swine), but we'd chat whenever he came in for supplies, and eventually I suggested he might be interested in meeting my friend Jeannie. They were married a year later.

"Consider him on alert," Jeannie said.

We hung up, and I looked over at Melissa. She was smiling, but an unusual smile that made me grin back at her.

"What are you thinking about?" I asked her. Mothers can do that, I've decided. From anybody else, it's annoying.

"It's going to fun be living in that house," she answered.

Three

"A hole just opened up in the wall by itself?" Tony Mandorisi, general contractor extraordinaire, good friend, and Jeannie's husband, sounded tired on the phone. Guys who work with power tools love to sound tired—it conveys the message that they labor hard, physically, all day. "Was there any sign of instability before that?"

"No." I sat on a lawn chair in my bare living room, nursing a bottle of Rolling Rock. "I hadn't even touched it yet. I was trying to figure out how to preserve the plaster." I had spent a few hours priming the living room walls for painting, and now had to decide on a color to replace that alarming red. And I had looked into repairing that crooked fireplace and decided that the amount of work involved translated into an amount of money that meant the fireplace's quirkiness was quaint and should be preserved just as it was.

"I guess you don't have that problem anymore," Tony said. Thanks. "But I don't get it. How does a wall demolish itself? It doesn't make sense."

"Yeah. I'm telling you, I'm afraid the upstairs will come crashing through the ceiling and become the downstairs."

Mentally, I could see Tony close his eyes and push his Yankees cap down on his head. "Are you sure this house is something you can handle? You need to get that B and B running soon if you want to make your mortgage payments."

"It's not a B and B," I told him for the nineteenth time. "It's a guesthouse."

"And the difference is?"

"I'm not going to serve breakfast."

"So it's not a B and B," Tony admitted. "It's just a B. And I'm still worried that you're in over your head."

That was not what I needed to hear. "You were the one who encouraged me to open a guesthouse," I reminded him.

"Yes, *a* guesthouse. Not *that* guesthouse."

"What's wrong with the house? I got it for a great price and I can fix it up for not too much more."

"I just don't know that you can do it all by yourself, Alison. The trouble is, you're swinging for the fences on your first try."

"My *only* try. How many houses do you think I can afford?"

"Maybe you should have gotten a smaller house," he tried.

"Then I couldn't accommodate as many guests, and it would be ten years before I'd be able to turn a profit. I don't have that kind of time."

Tony hesitated; he knew that already. "Or . . ."

"Or?"

"Or I'm right, and you shouldn't have tried to do the repairs all by yourself. You know, there's no shame in hiring help."

I burped, a window-rattler. I never have to worry about being ladylike around Tony, thank goodness, and luckily

Melissa sleeps like a rock, or she'd have heard that one all the way upstairs. "No, there's no shame in it, but there is expense, and I can't afford it."

"And that's your problem," Tony said. "Your margin for error is too narrow. If you don't get this house in order, and I mean soon . . ."

"I will," I said. And I left no room in my tone for argument. In my mind, sure, but in my tone, not at all.

Tony made a grumbling noise. "I'll come by and take a look tomorrow," he said. "See if there's anything I can do to help."

"Can you make walls stop self-destructing?" I asked.

"The least I can do is watch," Tony said. "I've never seen one do that before." He chuckled.

"You're a gem, Anthony," I told him.

"Tell that to my wife."

"I *introduced* you to your wife."

"I'll come by tomorrow."

It's good to have friends.

At one in the afternoon the next day, I was alone in the house. Melissa was at school until three, and Tony had called to say he'd be in after he finished the tiling job he had scheduled.

I don't mind being alone, especially when I have things to do; it helps me focus and keeps me on task. The quiet is nice, too.

But today, I kept hearing things, even when they weren't there. Creaks. Snaps. Crackles. Pops. I had to wonder if I was under siege by breakfast cereal.

I was on a small, three-step ladder, sealing a small hole in the kitchen wall with joint compound from a giant fifty-pound bucket resting on the top step. Fixing a gap like this is a study in a steady hand and judicious use of compound. If the hole is small enough, you can get away without plaster, and besides, there would eventually be cabinets over this part of the wall. I was doing this one mostly as a test for other, more prominent patches.

And maybe it was also a way to get a little something done before Tony arrived and kill some time without having to make any decisions about larger things, like the gaping hole in the living room hallway wall.

The iPod dock in the corner was playing one of my favorite oldies, a Creedence Clearwater Revival song, "Bad Moon Rising." I allowed myself to sway a little, but just a little, on the ladder, in time to the rhythm.

And of course, that was when I dropped the knife I was using to spread the compound.

Now, you have to understand. I *never* drop a tool. Not ever. But this time—there's no other way to say it—I could have sworn it was knocked out of my hand. I know, I know. But that was what it felt like.

I stood there for a moment, baffled. But there was nothing to be done but climb down and pick up the wide knife, which was currently stuck to the floor with joint compound.

This was the kind of week it was shaping up to be.

Grumbling about what a klutz I seemed to have become, I stepped onto the kitchen floor, littered with newspaper (which I'd spread everywhere except exactly where the knife had landed—compound side down, of course), nails and sawdust.

John Fogerty of CCR was warning me not to go out tonight as I reached down to get the knife from the floor. Then I heard something from above me, and I looked up just in time to see the bucket of compound slide itself off the top step of the ladder.

And fall directly toward my head.

I don't actually remember anything for a while after that. Honestly, I couldn't tell you how long I was on the floor. I *do* remember that I felt incredibly sleepy, and my head really, really hurt.

So what if the rapidly spreading joint compound was all around me? I was sitting, and not lying down. That was what was important, I decided.

It was obvious my head had taken a decent-sized hit, and when I put my hand up, it came back with blood on it. Swell. Which was what I also assumed was happening to my head.

I grabbed a roll of paper towels that was within arm's reach and blotted the spot on my head that hurt the most. The blood was already beginning to slow down. Head wounds bleed like crazy at the beginning but stop quickly. I held the towel wad there, wishing I had the strength to get up and walk over to the cooler I'd left in the living room. A cold beer would be almost as good as ice on the wound right now.

My mind began to clear as the desire to sleep for six or seven weeks was overtaken by pain. I took a vote in my mind and came down against touching my head where it hurt again. I didn't want to know how much it had swollen. And then my breath caught again, but for a different reason.

Standing in the kitchen, on the other side of the ladder, were a man and a woman. He was in his mid-thirties, like me. He was also tall and looked powerfully built, like an athlete, but with an incongruous goatee.

The woman was smaller and younger, maybe late twenties, and would have been beautiful if she hadn't been scowling. She wore a pair of cargo pants and a tight t-shirt that read, directly across her breasts, "What're YOU lookin' at?"

But it wasn't just the presence of two strangers in my kitchen that was bothering me. The really disturbing part was that I couldn't see them clearly.

Great, I thought. *A concussion. Just what I need.*

"What did you do *that* for?" the man barked at the woman. He had an accent of some kind. I couldn't place it.

But then, my head was in another time zone. "You could have killed her!"

"Well, that would have stopped her too, wouldn't it?" the woman responded, with almost no inflection in her voice.

"Excuse me," I said, my voice sounding very far away. My head was starting to throb. "I don't want to pry, but who are you and what are you doing here?"

They both stiffened as if struck by electricity and turned to stare at me.

"Uh-oh," the man said. "I think she sees us."

Four

"Of course I see you," I said, still sitting on the floor with a wad of paper towel held to my bleeding head. "But I can't see you all that well, really. Something hit me in the head. Sorry."

"Don't be," the man said. "*We* should be sorry. Is your head okay?"

I wasn't so sure; I still had a King Kong–sized headache. Of course, my having been clobbered on the head with a blunt instrument could account for that. I wondered what lobe of my brain had been damaged.

"I'm not sure," I answered honestly. "I'm just going to sit here a minute. Who are you, and why are you in my house?"

"Her house," the woman snorted. "You hear that?"

"Shut up," the man answered, and moved in my direction. "I'm Paul Harrison, and my . . . companion here is Maxie Malone." He didn't turn around to look at the woman when he spoke to me. Where was that accent from?

My head was starting to clear, and the paper towel was coming down almost bloodless now. But I could feel the cold joint compound soaking through my jeans. "How did you get in here?" I asked. "I had the doors locked. I'm pretty sure."

"We heard something fall, and we thought someone might be hurt," Paul told me.

I experimented with standing up, but my head was not pleased with the attempt. I just wanted to make it to the cooler and get some cold water (I'd given up on the beer). My butt was stiff with wet joint compound. But my mind was clear, and what it was telling me was not what I wanted to hear. "No, that's not what happened," I told Paul. "Paul, right? I remember, you were yelling at her." I indicated Maxie. "You said she might have killed me."

Paul's eyes widened in an "uh-oh" sort of way for a flash, and he clearly avoided the urge to look quickly at Maxie. "I wasn't talking about you. I was talking about our dog."

"Your dog."

Paul nodded. "Yes. Maxie left our dog in the car with the windows closed. In this heat . . ."

"Heat?" I asked. "It's October. It's maybe sixty degrees out. What heat?"

His stammering got worse. "Dogs feel the heat more than we do," he said. "All that fur . . ."

"I got hit on the head," I told Paul. "It hurt, but it didn't make me stupid."

Maxie laughed. "Good one," she said.

I turned to Maxie. "Don't look at Paul," I said. "What kind of dog do you have?"

She wasn't chewing gum, but she should have been. "We don't have a dog," she answered.

"Then what's going on?"

"We're dead." She cocked her head defiantly.

Paul looked aghast. "Maxie!"

I opened and closed my mouth a few times. It was worse than I thought. I wasn't just woozy—I was hallucinating. I decided to lie down and close my eyes for a moment.

And when I woke up, I was in the hospital. I could tell by the water marks in the dropped ceiling, the blank TV monitor bolted to the wall and the plastic tubes sticking out of my left hand. And Tony, standing to one side of the uncomfortable bed on which I was lying.

"I suppose asking, 'Where am I?' is too clichéd," I said. Well, croaked, really. My voice wasn't exactly firing on all cylinders just yet.

"You're in the hospital," Tony said. He was talking slowly and loudly, as if I weren't just beaten up, but hard of hearing as well. I started to understand how foreign tourists must feel when asking for directions to Times Square.

"No kidding," I tried to joke. "I thought the curtain around the bed was mosquito netting."

"No, it's to separate the beds." That sounded like Jeannie's voice, but she wasn't where I could see her. "You're in recovery."

"I knew that, Jean," I told her. "I was kidding. Where's Melissa?"

Her little face popped up on the left side of the bed. "Here, Mom."

I reached over to hug her. The tube coming out of my hand—saline drip, I guessed—restricted my movement a little. Maybe they gave me something else for the pain. I hoped. "It's okay, baby," I told my daughter. "Mommy's all right."

She turned toward Tony. "It's worse than the doctor said," she told him. "She thinks I'm three."

Tony didn't answer her, but he leaned over my bed. "I came by to look at that wall you were telling me about, and I found you on the floor in the kitchen and brought you here. They said you had a severe concussion. That's the kind where you pass out."

"Felt pretty severe," I agreed. "I hallucinated."

That seemed to stump him. "Really?"

"Yeah. I thought there were other people in the kitchen with me, fighting over whether or not they'd killed me and if we were all dead. I didn't know either one of them. But the guy was sort of cute," I said. Too late, I realized that I probably shouldn't have mentioned death or hallucinations around Melissa, but thankfully she didn't look scared.

Jeannie appeared at my feet, smirking. "That figures," she said. "If *I* hallucinated, I'd probably see snakes."

"What'd the doctors say about me going home?" I asked.

It was Melissa who spoke up. "They said it depended on when you woke up, and the doctor was here just a little while ago. I can go get him, if you want." She has an uncanny ability to see what needs to be done and offer to do it.

"I want," I assured her. Melissa was out the door before either of the other two adults in the room could consider stopping her.

"Hallucinations?" Tony asked.

"I certainly hope so," I told him. "They said they were dead."

"They talked, too?" Jeannie asked.

"Yeah. The girl was sort of surly, but the guy has this lilt to his voice. Almost like a British accent, but not really."

"That's it," Jeannie answered. "I'm definitely subscribing to your hallucinations."

Melissa appeared at the open door, dragging in a beleaguered-looking doctor, an older gentleman maybe in his late fifties.

"Ms. Kerby," he said. "I'm Dr. Walker. I see you're awake."

"You can't ever be sure, Doctor," I said. "I might just be dreaming you."

He didn't react. I got the impression he never reacted. It would be undignified. "Do you know what today is?"

"Your birthday?" I tried.

"What day of the week," he answered without a change in facial expression.

"It's Friday," I said.

"Do you know your name?"

"You called me 'Ms. Kerby' when you came in," I said. "Isn't that sort of a giveaway?"

"Alison," Tony admonished.

"Now he's given me the rest of it," I complained to the doctor. "Alison Kerby, right?"

"Mom," Melissa said. "Stop fooling around, or they won't let you go."

Dr. Walker made a point of looking me in the eye. "She's absolutely correct," he said.

Well, that was different. "Okay," I said. "Fire away."

After correctly answering questions about the time of year, the construction of my family and the President of the United States, I was given permission to leave with a prescription for acetaminophen with codeine for pain "if needed." I chose not to tell the doctor about my hallucinations, as I didn't see that information helping me leave the hospital anytime soon.

Standing up wasn't all that easy, but since Dr. Walker was watching, I was careful about not giving in to the pounding in my head. At least my vision had cleared up—no one in the room was the least bit fuzzy.

Given all the proper paperwork and a sample of my prescription to start me off, I was wheeled to the front door at the doctor's insistence. Once you're outside, they couldn't care less if you can walk or not.

Jeannie insisted that Melissa and I spend the night at their house in Lavallette, and I offered little resistance. I was really tired and not really ready to face the site of my hallucinations just yet.

Jeannie made dinner and Melissa was very happy with the macaroni and cheese, but I wasn't in a mood to eat and didn't feel up to making very good conversation, either. I kept asking Tony about how to fix the plaster wall, and he said he really hadn't had time to make a decent evaluation, what with having to pick me up off the floor and cart me off to the emergency room while getting Jeannie to pick Melissa up from school. I commended his priorities, but my head was starting to feel like it weighed about two hundred pounds, and I just wanted to lie down. I went to the spare bedroom, but I couldn't sleep.

How much of what I remembered could I trust? I stared at the ceiling for hours pondering that one.

What had been a truly hideous evening got just a hair worse when my cell phone rang a little after midnight.

The news didn't improve when caller ID showed my mother's phone number.

Now, don't get me wrong: I love my mother. Much of the time, I even *like* my mother. But she has one fatal flaw that is destined to drive me completely and totally over the edge and will possibly end in violence.

She thinks everything I do is *wonderful.*

I know what you're thinking. Sounds nice, right? Sounds like the ultimate extension of parental approval—a mother who truly supports and adores everything you do. But it's not really like that. It's more a case of a woman who is incapable of seeing the flaws no matter how obvious they might be: If I deliberately burned my mother's house in Manalapan to the ground, she would stand outside and marvel at my ingenuity in bringing my own kerosene, and then point out to her neighbors how evenly the flames were engulfing her living room.

This left me with a discouraging choice: I could ignore the call, in which case Mom might actually show up at my door to make sure I hadn't died, or I could talk to her now, which might make me wish I had.

"Hi, Mom."

"Oh, thank God you're all right!" she gushed. "I was terrified!"

"Who called you?" I asked.

There was a catch in my mother's breath; she'd been found out. "I'm not supposed to say."

"Spill, Mom. I'll find out anyway, and you'll be a shred of your former self when I'm through."

"You're so silly," she giggled. Honestly, the woman may be in her sixties, but she still giggles. "Melissa called me."

So I'd been ratted out by my own daughter. "Melissa," I said.

"She didn't want me to worry."

"Neither did I, which is why I didn't tell you anything."

"I know," Mom said. "You're so thoughtful that way."

See what I mean?

"I'm fine, Mom," I told her. "Just a bump on the head. I have some Tylenol"—I didn't mention that my prescription also had codeine in it—"and it doesn't even hurt."

"What happened?"

I told her the story, leaving out the questionable elements like the people who weren't there, as I thought that might fall into the category of "Bad Information to Tell Someone after You've Been Hit on the Head."

She was completely aghast. "Alison! You could have been killed!"

"Don't overdramatize, Mom. I know what I'm doing."

"Of course you do. You're very capable." Sometimes I can make it work for me.

"So don't worry. I'll be fine. In fact, I'm going right back to work on the house tomorrow." I knew even as I was saying it that I shouldn't, but it came out anyway.

"Tomorrow!" my mother exclaimed. "Is that wise?"

"I'm very capable, remember?"

"I know, Ally." No one else—*no one*—gets to call me

"Ally." And even my mother only gets away with it under duress. "Will you be there around noon?"

Oh no. There had to be some way to head this off at the pass. "I don't know, Mom. Don't plan on coming over just yet. The place isn't in shape."

"I'll keep my eyes closed. I just want to see *you*, and make sure you're all right."

"I promise I'll let you know if I'm not. But I have a *lot* of work to do in the house."

"And you'll do it brilliantly," my mother interjected. Any opportunity will do.

"Thank you. But I don't have time to give a tour yet, and there's really nothing to see. I promise I'll get Melissa to take a picture of me and e-mail it to you, okay?"

"Oh, don't be silly," Mom answered. "If you don't want me to come, I won't come yet."

"It's not that I don't want you to come. It's that I promised Melissa the place would be ready by Halloween, and that means I don't have much time." I'd made no such promise, but it had been a vague goal of mine.

"I completely understand," Mom said.

Never breathe a sigh of relief when talking to your mother. She's always going to follow up. I should have learned by now.

"But you'll need something for lunch, won't you?" she asked.

Sometimes, there is no escape.

Even with the drugs coursing their way through my bloodstream, I still couldn't sleep after I hung up with Mom. So I pulled my antiquated laptop computer up onto the bed with me and plugged in the wall connection to the Internet. Tony and Jeannie don't have Wi-Fi in the house.

I admit it: I couldn't shake the images of Imaginary Paul and Imaginary Maxie, but that seemed strange, because you usually dream about people you've at least heard about. I wondered if perhaps there were such people, and I'd dreamed about them for a reason. Google is a great way to waste time and not sleep.

So I started looking for Maxie Malone, but got no hits. I figured "Maxie" must be a nickname, but for what? I tried "Maxine" and got no responses. Then I tried "Maximus," "Max," "Mackie," "MacArthur" and "Moxie"—hey, my head was really foggy—and got nothing that went with "Malone."

A few more tries, for obituaries (Maxie *had* said they were dead, after all) in the *Asbury Park Press* or even the *Star-Ledger*, which doesn't really cover the shore area, turned up fruitless. And the meds were starting to kick in—I was finally getting sleepy.

I decided to give just one more news source a try; I had completely forgotten about the *Harbor Haven Chronicle* (it had no Web site of its own, but its content is incorporated into a regional news site, downdashore.com), the local weekly. And that was when I found something that made my head start to hurt again.

There was a mention of my address and two bodies being found on the premises in a half-page article. It identified no police sources, but referred to a Detective Harold Westmoreland visiting the scene.

The headline read, "Two Bodies Found in Local House."

I realized my jaw had dropped. I was shaking my head. I was breathing through my mouth. How could I have known that there had been two people who died in the house? Had the information been in the file, and I'd missed it? Somehow, I doubted that.

The next morning, I left a message on my mother's voice mail telling her to push back lunch for a day.

I told myself it was because I hadn't gotten much sleep.

I thanked Tony and Jeannie for their concern and their hospitality and, since my head was feeling better even without rest, laughed off their offers to drive Melissa to school. I gathered up my daughter, dropped her off where she needed to be and drove to my new house/business/project.

And when I opened the door, the same two people were standing there, as if they hadn't moved all night, and even though my vision had cleared up, they still seemed somehow vaguely transparent and fuzzy.

I shut the door and ran for the station wagon. Then I drove to Dunkin' Donuts and called Jeannie to ask if I could stay there one more night.

Five

"So. How much do you know about ghosts?"

Tony and Jeannie looked first at each other and then at me. The dinner I'd "made" (I'm better at ordering than cooking, mostly because my father taught me to fix houses, and my mother taught me that I was perfection incarnate) as a thank-you gift for the two nights in their house was suddenly going untouched, which would no doubt be a disappointment to the proprietor of the Golden Sun Szechuan House. Melissa could barely hear me, engrossed as she was with her friend Wendy at the far end of the table discussing Halloween costumes, since the candy-and-mask date was a little more than three weeks away (the consensus was *NO DISNEY PRINCESSES!*), and little girls don't spend much time listening to adults when given a choice.

Suffice it to say, Tony and Jeannie were being remarkably hospitable.

"You mean shadows left behind by paintbrushes?" Tony asked hopefully.

"No," I said. "I mean real ghosts. You know, people who are dead but don't go away."

Jeannie's eyes narrowed. "Is this about your hallucinations?"

"No!" I insisted. "Of course not. I just was watching this movie last night, and it got me thinking about ghosts."

Looking relieved, Tony and Jeannie went back to work on the sesame chicken and veggie lo mein. "Good. I was starting to plan a trip back to the emergency room, only the mental health wing this time," Tony said after swallowing.

"What movie?" Jeannie asked.

"What?"

"What movie were you watching that got you thinking about ghosts?"

Oops. I hadn't quite thought this plan through. I'd figured if I could start a conversation on the topic, then drop in that odd things had been going on in the house, I might be able to gauge Tony and Jeannie's opinion on whether I was, you know, crazy. But now that I'd gotten a suspicious reaction on my first foray (which, admittedly, had been clumsy), I instinctively backed off.

"Um . . . what's the name . . . ?" I had no idea where I was heading. From somewhere in the deep recesses of my mind, I was hoping to conjure up a nonthreatening ghost movie, but I really didn't want to use *Casper* if I didn't have to. "You know, the one with the really benign ghosts. A man and a woman." Why not? It would make the lie easier to remember.

"*Topper*?" Tony asked.

"That's right!" I pointed at him like a game show host. "It was *Topper*." Had I ever seen *Topper*? "It got me to wondering why ghosts are usually supposed to be so dangerous. I mean, not all dead people are going to be pissed off and violent, right? Some of them might just like hanging around the old neighborhood for a while."

Jeannie laughed. "Only you would see things that way, Alison. Ghosts are scary."

"So you think there *are* ghosts?" My best friend was leaving the door wide-open for me, the dear girl.

Jeannie almost spat out a mouthful of soy-covered noodles. "Of course not!" she said. "I'm talking about in movies, books, stuff like that." She swallowed and chuckled low. "Do I think there are ghosts? You kill me, Alison." I *could* have, at just that moment.

"Oh, I don't know." Tony was looking thoughtful, which he does better than most, because he's actually thinking. "I've heard some stories that make you wonder. Friend of mine swears she heard the voice of her husband on the day of his funeral. And she says six friends of hers called her that night to tell her they'd heard it at the same time."

"It's silly," Jeannie gave back. "People just don't want to let their loved ones go. When someone they love dies, they don't want to admit the person's gone forever. So they comfort themselves with a story about spirits and ghosts hanging around, giving them a chance to have a conversation with a loved one who can't say anything except what they want them to say." She waved a hand to declare the whole subject absurd.

"Well, what if it's not a loved one? What if the person thought they saw, or heard, someone they'd never met before?" I had no emotional stake in seeing Paul Harrison or Maxie Malone, after all.

Tony cocked an eyebrow. "Did this 'person' have a big ol' bucket of joint compound fall on her head recently?"

I stuck out my lips in rebellion. "What did I say when you asked me that question the last time?" I asked.

"Name one actor who was in *Topper*," he countered.

"Oh, Tony, seriously," I folded my arms across my chest. "I'm not playing this game." Not when I didn't have immediate access to IMDb, I wasn't.

This time, Jeannie *did* rescue me. "Stop it, honey," she

told her husband. "Alison's had a rough couple of days."
She had no idea. "Don't tease her."

"Look, fortune cookies!" I said, reaching for the five
cookies we'd left in the center of the table and trying hard
to change the subject.

"Just take one!" Jeannie warned. "It's bad luck for someone else to hand you your fortune."

"Oh," Tony teased. "So you don't believe in ghosts, but
fortune cookie luck is scientifically provable, huh?" Jeannie didn't answer.

Melissa must have heard our conversation, because she
turned her head toward me and narrowed her eyes. Wendy
kept talking about getting wigs that matched.

To change the subject, I took one cookie and gestured
that everyone else should do the same. Wendy walked over
to get one, and Tony and Jeannie were reaching as I opened
the little plastic bag with my teeth. Jeannie always orders
from Golden Sun because they have the chocolate fortune
cookies we both adore.

"Hey! 'Your smile illuminates the lives of those around
you.'" Jeannie grinned beatifically. "What do you think?"

"I think you got my fortune cookie," Tony answered,
and read from his own. "This one says, 'You are a good
and stalwart friend.' Now, how is that a fortune? That's
just a compliment." He shook his head. "How about you,
Alison?"

I broke open the cookie and pulled out the little slip of
paper.

It read, "New acquaintances need your assistance."

I looked at Melissa. "Would you mind if I took your
cookie?" I asked.

Six

Wendy's mom, Barbara, had invited Melissa for a sleepover on a Saturday night because Barbara thinks I'm a single mother who needs time off to have a social life. Silly Barbara.

So, on my second night in Jeannie's guest room, right before exhaustion won the battle with anxiety, I decided I'd go to the house the next morning and confront my fears.

Mostly, that meant I'd be tackling the furnace to see why the heating system was so sluggish. But if there happened to be some out-of-focus imaginary people who claimed to be dead on the premises, well, as the owner of a respectable guesthouse, I'd certainly have to confront that, too.

That morning, after a decent amount of sleep and home-made pancakes (Tony is a good cook when he sticks to the basics), I thanked everyone yet again, hopped into my trusty Volvo station wagon around nine a.m., and drove to my home away from home—HouseCenter—where I dropped even more of my money. Then I stopped for some coffee. Then I drove to Oceanside Park and sat on a bench drinking the coffee. Read the paper. Did the crossword puzzle. Went and got some lunch.

But it wasn't like I was avoiding my responsibilities at the house. I got there about two, I'd say.

I took an extra-deep breath before unlocking the back door leading into the kitchen. And when I walked inside, I exhaled with relief.

There was no one there.

I took off my old denim jacket and dropped it on the floor. There was no point in looking for a clean spot—every surface downstairs had the same coating of dust. The jacket was used to it.

Okay. The nightmare was over. I could start in on the furnace (probably another nightmare in the making). But maybe I should get my feet wet with something a little less complicated. There was still that wall-to-wall carpet to pull up in the living room, and the woodwork was certainly dry enough by now.

It felt like—and I know this is a cliché—an enormous weight had been lifted off my shoulders. I was downright jaunty as I ambled into the living room, hammer and screwdriver in hand.

And there were Paul and Maxie, actually floating about a foot off the floor. Just as transparent as they'd been yesterday. And the day before.

"Alison!" Paul shouted, sounding worried. "Where have you been?"

"You are not there," I said. I decided that would be my mantra. "You are not there."

"Of *course* we're here," Maxie said disgustedly. "What we want to know is where *you've* been."

"They are not there." I changed the mantra to make it even more definitive. If I didn't acknowledge them, they weren't there. It was that simple.

"This is hopeless," Maxie said, presumably to Paul. I

wasn't looking. Instead, I began pulling at a loose corner on the carpet near the door.

"Alison!" Paul shouted. "I know you can hear me. Stop it! We need your help!"

"You're not really there." Oops. I'd forgotten not to answer.

Paul sounded irritated with me. "Oh, we're really here," he said.

"You're not. I read about you in the paper. You're dead. So clearly, you're not here, and I'm not going to talk to you anymore." I had the cutout by the door almost entirely carpet free, and started pulling up the padding beneath it. After all the carpet was up, I could go around the perimeter with the screwdriver and hammer and pull up the tackless molding that had held the carpet in place. I bent down.

Paul walked over to me and knelt, or dropped, down so that he was looking directly into my face. "We know we're dead," he said calmly. "But we're here."

It was just too much. I was biting my lip so hard I tasted blood. But I wouldn't look.

"Look at me," he said slowly. "I'm here."

My eyes started to tear. My jaw was quivering. I couldn't look. And then there was a strange sensation, like a warm breeze, right in the vicinity of my chin. I looked down and saw his finger trying to raise my chin up to face him.

"Look," Paul said.

I couldn't hold it in any longer. "No!" I practically wailed. "Don't you understand? If you're really here, then I'm either crazy or I'm hurt much worse than I thought, and I can't face that now. I have too much . . . my daughter needs me, and I . . . you *can't* be here."

And then I did the dumbest thing I've ever done in my life. I looked Paul straight in the face.

He *was* there. He was fuzzy and kinda see-through, but he was there. And my stomach dropped to the floor. He looked so terribly sympathetic, like he wished he wasn't there, just so I wouldn't be so upset.

"I'm sorry," was all he said.

But with those words, with that tone, with that accent (Canadian? English?), came a terrible, terrible truth—these two people *were* here, they *were* dead, and they *were* in my new house. So this was what a concussion could do to you.

"I am crazy, or seriously hurt," I said. "I have a brain injury."

"No, you're not," Paul told me quietly, in a soothing tone. "There's nothing wrong with you. There's something wrong with *us*. We're dead."

"I don't understand . . . anything," I said.

"Neither do we," Maxie responded. That wasn't much help.

"It's true," Paul said. "We don't know what happened to us. We don't understand what's going on. But we've been stuck here in this house for almost a year. And when you started in last week with the repairs and the construction, we thought you might be able to help us."

I closed my eyes. "So one of you dropped a bucket of compound on my head to get me to *help* you?"

There was loud knocking on the kitchen door, and through the window I could see Tony standing on the back stoop. Paul and Maxie both turned and looked.

"Who's he?" Maxie asked. She grinned, which was kind of scary. "He's cute."

"He's taken," I answered reflexively. "Besides, you're dead."

"Doesn't mean I can't *look*."

"Get rid of him," Paul hissed. "We need to talk."

"What do you *mean*, 'get rid of him'? He's here to help me." I figured Tony could also prove my sanity—if he saw the two ghosts, then I wasn't crazy.

I walked to the door and unlocked it. "Thank goodness you're here," I told Tony.

"More self-crumbling plaster?" he asked.

"He's *better* than cute," Maxie said.

"Calm down," I warned her.

"I'm perfectly calm," Tony said. "I was just joking about your plaster."

"He can't see or hear us," Paul told me, hovering next to Tony. "Only you can."

I stared at him. "Why?"

"Because you asked me to come here and look at some wall with a big ol' hole in it, and this time, I'm happy to say, you're awake and not bleeding," Tony said. "That's why."

"How am I supposed to know?" Paul answered. "You think they give us a handbook? We died, and when we woke up, we were here. There's no welcome wagon."

"What?"

"Is your head okay?" Tony asked. He looked at it like a large neon sign reading "INJURY" would present itself. None did.

"Tell him you're fine and to come back later," Paul said. "Or I'll let Maxie loose on him." Maxie looked very interested. She walked right up to Tony and ran her finger down his spine. He shivered, turned to look, then turned back to me. "Chills," he said. "Maybe you need to fix the furnace first."

"I was thinking that, too, but I can look at it myself," I told him. Paul was right—I had to get Tony out of here before Maxie did . . . something. Oh, damn: I was thinking of my two apparitions as real.

Maxie licked her lips in a way that suggested something other than hunger. For food.

"You'd better go," I told Tony.

"What? Don't you want me to look at that wall for you?"

"No! I mean, yes, I want you to look, but not now. I . . . have to go pick up Melissa at Wendy's." Yeah. That was it.

Tony chuckled. "So go. I can't look at a wall by myself?" He started toward the living room. Maxie was following him. Closely.

"No," I told him. "I don't ever want you left in this house by yourself."

Tony turned and considered me. "You're serious."

"You bet. Insurance. Anything happens and I'm liable. So come back later. I'll call you."

"If you hadn't stopped me to tell me to go away, I'd be gone already." Tony turned and, not waiting for a response, walked into the living room despite my protests.

Maxie tried to follow, but I held my ground in the doorway and hissed at her. "Step back."

Surprisingly, she did.

"Wow." I could hear Tony from the next room. "You weren't kidding about this wall. The plaster just fell down by itself?"

Maxie picked up a small rubber mallet from my toolbox and stroked it. She grinned at me nastily.

"Yeah," I said. "Spooky, huh?" I snarled, and Maxie put the mallet down.

"Could be trouble," Tony said, walking back into the kitchen. "All the best plasterers are dead."

"Who isn't?" Maxie said.

"What do you think I should do?" I asked Tony.

"I don't see how there's a choice," he answered. "You've got to take the whole wall down and put up drywall. Maybe in the whole hallway, and possibly into the living room, depending on how it goes."

For a second, I forgot about the deceased people in the room, and thought only about my house. "Oh, Tony," I moaned. "I *love* the plaster walls. They give the place character. I can't make that room look like every other one built in the last fifty years."

Tony shook his head. "I don't see an alternative. But let me ask around. Maybe someone knows someone."

Maxie licked her lips and moved closer to Tony. She reached a hand in his direction again.

"Tony." My mind cleared—I had to get him out of here. "I'm not so sure I should be driving yet. Can you pick Melissa up and bring her home?"

"You drove over here this morning." Now Tony was going to argue with me.

"And I probably shouldn't have. I'm just a little tired now. Please?"

Paul nodded silently, as if Tony would have heard him even if he'd screamed at the top of his lungs.

"Sure," Tony said. "But I'm calling Jeannie and telling her to check up on you, too."

"Yes," I said, staring in Maxie's direction. "That'd be nice. Tell *your wife* to call me."

Maxie yawned.

"*I will*," Tony answered, matching my tone. Then he left, shaking his head, probably wondering if it was safe to go off and abandon someone as crazy as me in an empty room.

Empty.

As soon as I heard his truck pull out of the driveway, I turned to Paul. "Okay," I said. "Explain yourself. Why did I just hustle my friend out of here so we could talk? What do we have to talk about?"

"We need you to help us," Paul said, much in the same tone he'd said it before. Like it was a foregone conclusion, and anyone who questioned his word must be demented.

"What do you mean?" I asked. I should have known better than to ask, but my head was still a little fuzzy.

"We need you to find out who killed us," Paul answered.

Seven

"Let me get this straight," I said. I sat back down in the lawn chair, having cleaned off the dried compound from days before, and remembering fondly the jeans I'd worn that day, now forever at the bottom of a contractor's trash bag. "You almost crush my skull with a fifty-pound bucket of compound, and then you think I should help you find out who killed you?" The fifty-pound thing was an estimate, but I thought I'd made my point.

"Geez," Maxie said, rolling her eyes. "Are you going to hold that against me *forever*? I *said* I was sorry!"

"Actually, no, you didn't."

She sneered, probably involuntarily. I got the feeling Maxie sneered a lot, and it had become second nature.

"It's tremendously important," Paul said. "And it seems you're the only one who can help."

"Help you do what? Why don't you know who killed you? Weren't you there when they did it?" I closed my eyes.

Another headache was coming my way. And I was pretty sure it wasn't related to the concussion.

Paul smiled in an ingratiating way. "It's really very simple. Sit down."

"I am sitting."

"Right," he began. "Here's what happened, as far as Maxie and I can tell. Maxie here was the most recent owner of this house before you bought it," he said.

I stared at her. "*You're* the one who painted the walls the color of blood?"

I thought—but couldn't be sure—that I heard Maxie mutter, "It's *my* house," under her breath. If she had breath.

"But as soon as she closed on the property and moved in, strange things started happening," Paul continued, either unaware of Maxie's comment or ignoring it.

"Strange things?" I asked. "Like plaster walls that I can't replace coming down all by themselves?" I glared at Maxie for a moment, but she didn't flinch. And it was my best glare, too. My glare couldn't beat her sneer.

"No," Paul jumped in. "She started receiving strange e-mails, phone calls, and . . ."

"You don't tell it right," Maxie interrupted him. Paul spread his hands, giving her the floor. "So, some creep starts sending me messages about how I had to leave the house or I was gonna die." She snorted. "Guess he was right."

I turned to Paul. "How did you get involved?" I asked him.

"I am . . . I *was* a private investigator," he said. "Maxie contacted me when the threats started getting serious."

"I wasn't scared," Maxie interjected. "I was pissed off."

"Of course," I told her. "Who wouldn't be?"

Paul jumped back in. "Less than two days after I started investigating, we both ended up . . . like this."

"Yeah, good thing the retainer check never cleared," Maxie said. "Some private dick you turned out to be."

"It wasn't . . ." But Paul couldn't finish the sentence. He didn't *know* if it was his fault or not. I could see it clearly in his eyes. What bothered me was that I could see the window behind him just as clearly.

I didn't have time to answer because just then my phone vibrated (another unfortunately accurate metaphor for my romantic life). I looked down and saw Jeannie's number. "I have to take this," I said.

Paul frowned. "Don't you realize how . . ."

"If I don't answer, she'll send the rescue squad. Besides, you're not alive and I am, so I outrank you." I opened the phone. "I'm fine, Jeannie," I said.

"That's not what Tony told me," she answered. "He just called me from the truck. He says you were too tired to drive Melissa home, and you're talking like a crazy person."

"And how is that different than usual?" I asked.

"Normally, you're not that tired."

"Normally, I'm not just out of the hospital with a head injury," I reminded her.

Jeannie sighed. "Exactly. What am I going to do with you?" she asked.

"I don't know," I said. "But let me get going, because I'm two days behind on my repairs." Not to mention a lot of dried compound on the floor in the kitchen that wasn't going to clean itself up. We said our good-byes, and I moved toward the kitchen.

"If we can avoid any more interruptions . . ." Paul started.

Oh yeah, ghosts in the room! "What do you want *now*?" I asked. "Can't you see I have a crisis on my hands?" And on my kitchen floor, now that I remembered that.

"*You* have a crisis?" Paul demanded. "We're trapped in this house for the rest of eternity, and *you* have a crisis?"

I ignored him (partly because I didn't want to think about them being trapped in *my house* for eternity), and walked into the kitchen to survey the hardened white mess on the floor. I could break it up with a hammer, but that would mean sanding and refinishing the whole floor afterward. Another day and a half of work. "What do you mean, 'trapped in this house'?" I asked. "Can't you leave the house? Go roam the countryside?" I looked at Maxie. "Haunt a punk-rock biker bar?"

Maxie picked up the mallet again and took a step toward me, but Paul stopped her. "Humph," she said, and scowled off into the living room. I made sure she didn't have the mallet with her this time.

"We can't seem to leave the grounds," Paul went on as if nothing had happened. "Every time we try to get past the sidewalk in front or the fence in back, we just can't move."

"Is this one of those things where you have some unfinished business here on Earth and have to get through it before you can enter the afterlife?" I asked.

Paul shrugged. "I have no idea," he said. "Remember? No handbook."

There was no sense in denial anymore—they were here, and they very much appeared to be ghosts. "Okay," I sighed. "Tell me what happened and what you want me to do."

"All right, then." Paul seemed pleased at my apparent cooperation. "The night . . . the night Maxie and I . . ."

"*Died*," Maxie shouted from the next room. She sounded disturbingly happy, and I chose not to dwell on why.

"That night," Paul continued, trying to pretend he hadn't hesitated, "Maxie and I went to a meeting of the Harbor Haven planning board. Actually, Maxie went to the meeting, and I went as her bodyguard."

"Another bang-up job," came the comment from the living room. Paul ignored *that*, too.

So did I. "Who needs a bodyguard to go to a planning board meeting?" I asked.

He took a deep breath—which was interesting, since I doubted he needed the air anymore—and re-boarded his train of thought. "There was a proposal to condemn this property and sell it to a developer. The only place you can be assured of making money on real estate is near the shore. Maxie was there to defend her claim on the house."

"They can do that? Just take the house out from under the owner?" How come I hadn't heard about any of this when I was buying the place? I'd have to get on the phone to Terry Wright the minute I was finished hearing the sad story of these two freeloading displaced spirits.

"Yes," Paul answered. "Assuming it gets approved by the various levels of the municipal government. But Maxie spoke up at the meeting, and the plan was rejected that night."

"I don't understand what that has to do with your . . . circumstances," I told him.

Paul frowned. "Neither do I," he said. "All I can tell you is that after we went out for a celebratory dinner, we came back to the house, and I was just about to leave for the night when we both collapsed."

"Collapsed from what?" I heard an ominous scraping noise coming from the living room. But I wasn't willing to deal with it at that moment.

"I don't know," he answered. "Something hit us very suddenly, because one minute we were fine, and the next, we were . . . like this. Here. And we couldn't leave, so there was no one here but us for days."

"So, what did you die of?" The heck with Miss Manners. You could tiptoe around the word only so long. They were going to be dead a long time; Paul might as well start getting used to it. Maxie seemed to have moved on emotionally, assuming she had emotions.

"I have no idea," Paul told me. "Our physical bodies weren't here when we became conscious. Well, *aware*."

"Well, you might have died of natural causes, then," I said. "Food poisoning. Some kind of fever. Swine flu."

From the living room came a flat, moist sort of sound. I guess Maxie didn't agree with my reasoning.

"We were definitely murdered," Paul said, his tone leaving no room for argument. "After the threats, and immediately after that meeting, it doesn't make sense otherwise. But since I can't get past the front walk, I need you to find out who did it and why. Alison, please. You can't imagine what this means. It's the last wish of a man who's already dead. You're special—you can see and hear us. You're the only one who can help."

There had to be a way to avoid a reply to that. "Where are you from?" I asked instead, stalling. "I can't place your accent."

"London, originally," Paul said. Damn! I'd thought Canada. "But my family moved to Toronto when I was six." Aha!

In the driveway, I heard the sound of tires on gravel. Perfect! "Tony is back with my daughter," I said, not to anyone in particular. "We can't talk in front of her."

I turned to walk to the back door. Paul moved toward me and reached for my arm. "Alison, stop," he said.

His hand passed right through my forearm. It wasn't an altogether unpleasant sensation; I would have expected it to feel cold, but instead it was a little like a warm breeze. I looked up into his eyes.

"Please," Paul said. His eyes were desperate.

Melissa opened the door and stuck her head in. "Tony says let's go out to the diner," she said. "He's buying." And then she turned and walked back out to Tony's truck. She knew I wouldn't turn down that deal.

"Please," Paul repeated.

The answer was a no-brainer. "No," I said, and went to walk out the front door.

On the way out, I saw that Maxie had picked up a box cutter and carved "WITCH" into the wall next to the hole she'd created with the mallet.

"Alison!" Paul called after me.

I got out as fast as I could.

Eight

That first night back in the house was difficult, although I didn't see the ghosts when Melissa and I returned from the diner. I still wasn't 100 percent convinced I wasn't suffering the effects of a severe blow to the head. In fact, I *wanted* to believe I had injured myself severely enough to see things that weren't there. But the headache was gone, the bump had pretty much subsided, and when I'd called Dr. Walker's office to follow up, he'd actually gotten on the phone, asked me about symptoms, and told me I sounded completely recovered.

Okay, so I still hadn't told him about the hallucinations. The man was so busy; why trouble him?

Sleeping wasn't easy, particularly when I could've sworn that just as I closed my eyes, I saw Paul's head peeking in at me—through the bedroom ceiling. I resolved not to open my eyes again until morning, and fell asleep not long (maybe just an hour) after.

Melissa was grumpy and uncommunicative the next

morning, which was not terribly unusual—she's not a morning person and she hates Mondays. I didn't even ask her whether she wanted me to cook breakfast; I knew she'd just glare at me and eat one of the small, single-portion cups of cereal I'd bought to use until I could get the kitchen into some kind of shape. After a wordless breakfast, she went upstairs, dressed, and came down to get a ride to school. I reminded myself for the umpteenth time to attend a board of education meeting and demand a school bus route.

"Is something wrong?" I asked her on the way. She's always quiet in the morning, but not *this* quiet.

"No."

There are few species on the planet less communicative than nine-year-old girls still coming off divorces. Especially before school. I regrouped. "Maybe it's something I can help with."

"You wouldn't want to," Melissa said as we pulled up to the John F. Kennedy Elementary School. I could see her friend Wendy waiting on the sidewalk. Melissa ran over to her without so much as a backward glance, and the two of them hugged as if they hadn't seen each other in months.

I smiled ruefully, thinking about how, when Melissa was three, she'd refuse to let go of me whenever I dropped her off at day care. I used to call her "the Velcro baby" because she couldn't be pried off my leg.

You pay a price for such sentimental reminiscences, and today was no exception. Before I could drive away, a woman with a superior-seeming smile leaned into my open window. I fought the impulse to hit the gas.

Kerin Murphy (seriously, can't anyone be named Karen anymore?), whose daughter Marlee was in Melissa's class (Liss said Marlee was "stuck-up"), was the head of every parent-involved committee at the school, and still somehow had time to work out diligently, chauffeur her three children to Everything lessons after school, and hold down a job at the local hospital as a birthing coordinator, when not volunteering at a soup kitchen or raising money to fight drought (how do you pay clouds to rain?) in Africa.

"Alison!" Kerin always spoke in exclamation points. "Have you donated to the PTSO's SafeOWeen program yet?" *PTSO* is the twenty-first-century PTA, and stands for "Parent-Teacher-Student Organization." I'm sure they would have added the custodial staff into the acronym, too, if they could've.

"SafeOWeen?"

"Sure! It's a way for the kids to go trick-or-treating without having to go door to door!"

I must have raised my eyebrows. "Isn't going door to door the whole point of trick-or-treating?"

Kerin's look indicated she thought I was speaking Klingon. "We set up stands in the school's playground, and each one gives out a different kind of healthy snack. So the kids can come here, all see each other, and get lots of wholesome treats without any danger."

Now, I should have known from past experience that it was futile to argue with Kerin *or* the PTSO, but if I'd actually ever learned from my past experiences, I'd be back in college now getting an accounting degree instead of trying to restore a ghost-infested house.

"I understand the intention," I told her, "but that doesn't sound at all like fun for the kids."

"It's *tons* of fun!" Kerin countered. "We'll have music playing, and bring in some cars with their headlights on to light it up. The kids will love it!"

There were at least six different arguments I could have used, not the least of which was questioning the entertainment value of all the vehicles that would need jumpstarts afterward, but instead I took the coward's way out and just gave Kerin five dollars. Sometimes, there's just no point.

Once again, I should have just put the car into drive and

hit the road, but a very attractive man walked over and stood next to my window, and that doesn't happen every day, so I stopped again.

"Are you Melissa Kerby's mom?" he asked.

It's always nice to be recognized as a person in your own right. "Yes," I admitted.

"I'm her history teacher, Mr. Barnes," he said, and he had such nice eyes I really didn't care that he seemed to have no first name. "I missed you at Back-to-School Night."

Mostly, he'd missed me because I hadn't been there: Back-to-School Night had occurred on an evening when I'd really needed to sweat some copper pipe in the upstairs bathroom. "I'm sorry I couldn't make it," I said, and at this moment, I actually *was* sorry. If I'd realized then that Mr. Barnes was a good-looking guy under sixty, I might have made more of an effort. "Is there a problem with Melissa?"

"Oh no!" Mr. Barnes seemed astonished at the very idea. "She's a terrific student. I actually wanted to ask about your house."

A regular man magnet, that place was. "My house?"

"Yes. Melissa says it's over a hundred years old, and I'm very interested in the area's history. I'm wondering if I might come by sometime to see it."

That was a new one, all right. "It's not a historical land-mark, or anything," I said. "It's just a house."

Barnes looked disappointed. "I understand," he said. "It was a little forward of me, I guess."

I felt like I'd just told him he couldn't have a puppy for Christmas. "No, it's fine," I said, smiling. "Come by any-time. But I have to warn you, the place is under construc-tion to restore it, and there's a lot of dust."

His face brightened. "That's great," he said. "I can't wait to see it."

"The dust?"

"No, the house." Okay, so I couldn't be my usual hilarious self with him. "Oh, I see what you mean." He chuckled.

"We'll work out a time," I said. "Send a note home with Melissa."

Barnes nodded, shook my hand like a business associate, and started back toward the school.

Had I just made a date? It was hard to tell. I put the car in gear and took off before anyone else could stop me.

When I got back to the house, the ghosts were still there. Paul (in different clothing, which was interesting—when, how and especially *why* does a ghost change clothes?) was pacing in front of the picture window in the living room, and I could hear Maxie, somewhere out of sight singing an Elvis Costello song.

Paul's head snapped to attention, and his body (or the image of it) followed suit when he saw me. "Alison!" he shouted. "Thank God you're back!"

"Of course I'm back, you figment of my imagination," I answered. "I own the place."

"Have you reconsidered?" He looked positively stricken. "Will you help me find out who killed us?"

"Not a chance, dead boy." I started unpacking tools from the box. Today would be devoted to the kitchen cabinets. I'd taken them down, but I wasn't replacing them: It would be more economical—and tons more work—to strip the cabinets and refinish them, something closer to the oak shade they had once been. Then I'd add new wooden doors and hang them at a less beanstalk-like height.

"Alison." Paul's voice dropped to a seductive tone that I'm sure must've worked nicely with the ladies when he was, you know, breathing. "I would do this myself if it were possible. But I can't leave these grounds, and no one else can see or hear us. You're the only one who can help."

I had to sound unmoved. "I have cabinets to strip."

"You're letting a murderer go free," Paul tried.

I turned to face him. "Okay, let's say you were murdered. If I find out who killed you, will you come back to life?"

He probably would have blushed if he were solid. "Of course not."

"The person—or persons—who you think killed you would probably be of a violent nature, yes?"

"I can only assume." Paul's eyes narrowed as he saw the trap beginning to ensnare him.

"Then I don't see the point to getting violent people mad at me when it's not going to do you any good in the long run. Sorry, Paul. I'd like to help, but I really think it's a lousy idea. Besides, as I believe I've pointed out, I'm trying very hard not to believe you're real, and you're not helping." I put on the mask to work with paint stripper. You don't want to smell that stuff full-on, and it can damage your lungs. Use the mask. You should wear goggles, too, and rubber gloves are an absolute must. The last thing you need is paint stripper on your hands.

Paul started a few sentences, but didn't finish any of them. I began spreading the stripper on the first cabinet, on an inside door, to test. If any real damage was done, it wouldn't be visible after the work was completed.

Maxie must have been getting closer, because I finally recognized the song she was singing, in a clear, but definitely creepy, alto.

"A-li-son, I know this world is killing you."

The paint stripper was doing its job without damaging the wood, which was good news. I wiped it down with a rag from one of the mountains of them I had in the house. You shouldn't ever be without rags, in my opinion. I concentrated on the work.

Well, I *tried* to concentrate on the work. Maxie, who appeared in the doorway from the main hall, continued to slowly croon the chorus of the song, the part with my name and a veiled threat in it. Over and over.

"What's your problem?" I asked her. Then it hit me. "Did *you* put up these cabinets?"

She just kept singing.

"I can't help it if they were too damn high. And ugly."

On went the chant. I gave up trying.

It went on like that for a while. I had gotten two whole cabinets stripped down to bare wood and drying in a corner on the floor, and Maxie continued with her chant, which was becoming more intolerable with every repetition. I found myself clutching the paint scraper so tightly in my hand that I expected to find that I'd made indentations in the handle where my fingers gripped it. I'd have gotten very upset if there were any, though, because the scraper had been a gift from Dad, handed down to him from my grandfather, a housepainter.

By the time I'd gotten the door on the third cabinet free of paint, Maxie's singing had brought me to the breaking point. On her thirty-fourth chorus, she caught me glaring in her direction, and smiled beatifically.

Just when I was looking at the scraper and considering using it on myself, there was a knock on the back door. I hadn't even heard a car in the driveway.

The singing went on and on. It was maddening.

I flung open the back door and threw my arms open. "Mom!" I shouted. "Am I glad to see you!"

My mother smiled at the welcome, and accepted my embrace, but looked confused. At least she did until I got my arms around her and held on like I hadn't since she'd tried to put me on the bus for the first day of kindergarten. Family lore has it that she'd finally ended up driving me to school and sitting in the back of the room all day. But only for the first week.

"Alison," she said now. "Are you all right?" She dropped her backpack (Mom carries a backpack, as if she were in the ninth grade) and held on. I didn't let her go for a while.

I made her stay in the kitchen for the rest of the day until Melissa got home.

When I got up the next morning, the cabinets had all been painted a shocking pink.

Nine

It went on like that for the next ten days. Every morning I'd go downstairs to work on the house and find that some new vandalism had taken place overnight. Paul would spend his time moping in one corner, mooning at me, and Maxie would glare daggers at me and do something—anything—guaranteed to drive me insane.

When I turned up my iPod to drown out her singing, Maxie would throw my tools and supplies into the garbage. When I put them in a locked tool case, she would pick up whatever I had been using from the floor and do damage with it. The day she got hold of a screwdriver and started taking down all the interior doors in the house was an especially jolly one, I can tell you.

It was becoming increasingly difficult to believe that none of this was happening, and I was considering a visit to Dr. Walker—because if this *wasn't* happening, there was something very wrong with me.

Meanwhile, Melissa was absolutely livid with me for,

as she put it, "hitting on" her favorite teacher. I tried to explain that Mr. Barnes had asked *me* about seeing the house, but she wouldn't hear of it. Strangely, however, no note came home about a visit, and I started to wonder if I would have found small bits of torn paper at the bottom of her backpack if I'd bothered to look.

But I didn't have time to worry about that. I was still under siege by the two spirits, who appeared to be real and were growing more insistent with each day. Paul emerged from his dark corner to make another impassioned plea while I was steaming wallpaper off the walls of Melissa's bedroom. "I'm a detective," he said. "How will it look if my own death goes unsolved?"

"I honestly don't think it'll hurt your business that much," I told him. "It's possible your reputation isn't a huge issue anymore."

"You don't understand," Paul told me for what had to be the six-thousandth time. Yet, I was fairly sure I understood perfectly. "I can't spend eternity wondering what happened to us. I'm not asking you to do anything dangerous. All you have to do is a little legwork, a little research, so I can figure out what it all means."

"No sale," I answered. "I have a nine-year-old daughter to think about. I don't want to get involved with people who might be inclined to make her an orphan."

"She has a father." Maxie, standing in the doorway, puffed up her lips. "I'll bet he's hot, too, because the kid's a lot better-looking than you are."

"He's a swine," I said. "But if you want to look him up, he's in California. I can give you an address. Tell him I said hi. Spend a couple of months."

In response, Maxie started to sing the Beatles' upbeat ditty about a serial killer, "Maxwell's Silver Hammer," but changed the name to match her own.

"Nobody's going to hurt you," Paul went on, ignoring her. "I'll be watching the whole time."

"Yeah, 'the whole time' in this house or its yard," I answered. "I'm not feeling tremendously confident."

This had the capacity to go on quite literally forever, but I had to have the house ready for business by April at the latest, and Maxie's hilarious "pranks" were setting back my timetable considerably.

"Enough," I said. "You've made your point."

"So you'll help?" Paul asked, eyes wide.

"No. But you've made your point. Now, leave me alone while I check my e-mail." I set down the steamer, unplugged it, and reached into my canvas bag for the ancient laptop I keep there. The wireless connection had finally been activated in the house, so I could communicate with the outside world, particularly with Melissa's school when necessary.

By the time the elderly iBook was powered up (it has a "Little Engine That Could" quality that would be really endearing if it could stay powered for more than ten minutes at a time), Maxie had changed her tune, literally. She was on to "Baby Let's Play House," a Buddy Holly tune whose last line she kept repeating.

"I'd rather see you dead, little girl."

Then she vanished downstairs, just lowering through the floor. I turned on my e-mail program and checked the grand total of three messages that had come in to me since the night before—I'm remarkably popular.

One was an ad for a weight-loss program guaranteed to make me stop looking like I had "saddlebags." I deleted that. Another was for Viagra. I deleted that, too.

But the third e-mail, whose sender was listed as 78.394.051, was something else entirely. Normally, I wouldn't even open such a thing, but my spam filter had cleared it, the subject line read "Alison," and I was stupidly intrigued.

Big mistake.

The message read: "Get out of the house or you'll be dead in a month."

I chewed my lip for a moment, and I must have blanched. Paul looked over at me and seemed genuinely concerned.

"Is something wrong, Alison?" he asked.

My voice sounded scratchy. "Tell me again what you want me to do," I said.

Ten

It took a few moments for my heart to stop pounding, but when it did, Paul was already talking. He didn't leave me any time to be terrified. It was the first nice thing Paul had done for me.

"Here's our situation: Maxie was trying to get the planning board to reject the development plan that would have torn down this house. So all the people who wanted the plan to pass were at the board meeting, and the only one on Maxie's side was Maxie."

"And you." I was trying to concentrate on what Paul was saying. It wasn't easy; I hadn't ever gotten a death threat before. I was catching about every second sentence, but I was trying.

"I was just the bodyguard," he reminded me. "I wasn't advocating for her. She'd only called me two days before, said she'd found my name online and she liked my picture."

"So what happened at the meeting?"

Paul reached into his pocket and pulled out a reporter's

notebook that was just as transparent as he. He flipped a
few pages until he found the one he wanted. "The developer
is a man named Morris. Adam Morris. He spoke about the
benefits to the town if this development went through—
construction jobs, increased tax revenue, retail businesses
moving in, an influx of tourists . . ."

"*I'm* starting to want them to condemn the property,"
I said.

"And I think the board was going to go that way. The
mayor was there. Do you know the mayor?" Paul's feet were
about six inches off the floor. He wasn't paying attention to
his appearance. His shoes changed color three times.

"Bridget Bostero? I've seen her around town a couple of
times, but I don't think we've ever spoken to each other."
If I remembered correctly, the mayor was a former beautician who had taken on the party's candidate and won on
a "Beautify Harbor Haven" campaign. You have to love
New Jersey.

"Well, she was very much in favor of the plan until Maxie
started talking about the parking problems, the increased
traffic, the need for road improvements, sewer improvements, utility upgrades, beach erosion prevention . . ."

"Wow. Now I *don't* want them to pass it." Maxie must
have been really persuasive at that meeting. I wouldn't have
thought she had it in her.

Paul looked at his notes again. "And neither did anyone else. Including the chairman of the planning board,
and three of the four members." Paul closed his eyes,
thinking.

"How did Adam Morris take the news?"

"Well, considering," Paul said. "He told the board he
thought they had made a mistake, but thanked them for
their time and left."

"So that leaves us with a whole board full of prospects,"
I said. I sat flat on the floor. This was going to be harder
than I'd thought.

"We haven't even scratched the surface," Paul went on. "After the meeting we went out for dinner at Café Linguine. Every member of the planning board was there, as well as the mayor, again. I think that's when someone must have poisoned us."

"Why?"

"Maxie and I both collapsed at about the same time, as soon as we got back here," Paul said, but I'm not sure he was talking to me. "There was something in our food—or in the wine, maybe—and that's what killed us."

I took a deep breath. "All right. So let's say—strictly for the sake of argument—that I'm going to help you with this investigation. How—*hypothetically*—would that work?" I confess, I knew that I was getting myself into it by asking the question. There'd be no backing out now.

Paul recognized the moment, too. His eyes lit up almost to the point of physical depth. He grinned and rubbed his hands together. No, really.

"You'd be doing the legwork. I'm the investigator, but I'm not physically able to interrogate suspects or to view a scene, unless it's here in the house or on the grounds." Paul had obviously been giving this a lot of thought. After all, what else did he have to do all day? "You'd have to go out and ask the questions anytime we couldn't get the witness or suspect to come here, which I'm afraid would be much of the time. You'd have to take notes or record the interviews. I want you to take pictures with a camera or your phone when you can. And this is really important: You'd have to do *exactly* what I tell you to do. You're my eyes, my ears and my legs. But I'm the brain in this investigation. I have the experience, and you don't. You can't start believing you're Miss Marple and taking dangerous chances. Understand?"

"Understood," I said. "I have absolutely no desire to take chances. But I have some rules of my own, and unless you agree to them, I'm nothing more than the owner and renovator of this guesthouse. Do *you* understand?"

He put on a face that he clearly thought was suave and so wasn't; the attempt was kind of adorable. "State your terms," he said.

"I have to get this house in shape, and on time, too. So I'm *not* making the PI game my full-time profession. I'll do it when I can, but I won't when I can't. Any further little *pranks* on the part of anybody who . . . exists in this house will just set me back and make the investigation drag on."

"Agreed," Paul said.

"Hold on; I'm just warming up. Next, I'm investigating your deaths, but I'm also trying to find out who's threatening *me*, and that's going to take priority. No offense, but I'm still alive, and I'd like to stay that way. So if it comes down to a choice between your situation and mine, I'm going to opt for mine."

"That's reasonable," Paul said, but he didn't look as happy as before.

"Third—and without question, most important—I will not allow this project of yours to endanger my daughter in any way, shape or form. The *first* time there's the slightest suggestion that Melissa could be in harm's way, I'm finished gumshoeing. That is an absolute deal breaker. Okay?" I looked up at Paul, who was suspended just over the fireplace.

"The last thing I'd want is to put Melissa in danger, Alison. Believe me." But I could see Paul didn't like the idea of *anything* causing an automatic cancellation of my services. He folded his hands across his chest.

So did I. "I'll believe you when you say you agree," I told him.

"Alison. There will *never* be any danger to Melissa in connection to this investigation. I won't stand for it."

I nodded. "Now say that you agree to my terms." He still hadn't committed to the last one. "Say, 'I agree.' "

"You understand perfectly that I have Melissa's welfare . . ."

"Say. 'I. Agree.' "

"I agree," he said.

"Okay." I nodded. "What's my first assignment, boss?"

"They weren't murdered; they committed suicide."
Detective Lieutenant Anita McElone (pronounced "Mack
e-LONE-ee," I'd been told), five-foot-eight and sturdy,
hadn't smiled when I'd introduced myself and was looking
even less happy now. "And frankly, I don't see why it's any
business of yours," McElone said, barely looking up from
her paperwork.

"Are you always this sympathetic, or did I catch you on
an especially sensitive day?" I asked.

She looked up. I guessed she'd been operating on cop
autopilot before, and this was the first thing I'd said that
had captured her attention. "How well did you know these
two people?" she asked.

"I didn't know them at all. I own the house that they
died in."

"So why do you care what happened to them?" McElone
asked. Her face indicated concentration.

I reached into my canvas tote bag and pulled out the laptop computer. "Can I show you something?" I asked her.

"I'm here until five." She sighed.

I hit the power button on the computer and waited the
usual eternity until it booted up. I have the same affinity for
technology that antelopes have for screwdrivers.

Hand tools, I can use. Electric ones, battery-operated
ones, cordless screwdrivers (has there ever been a *corded*
screwdriver?). Dad taught me all about hand tools. I can
hear him now, patiently saying, "It's sharp, baby girl. Don't
ever think you can treat it casually." So I knew about tools.
Things where you push a button and it turns or heats up.
Sure.

But "smart" machines? We have a relationship that is

something less than friendly but just short of adversarial. We simply don't understand each other. Much like with every man I've ever dated.

During the wait, McElone had enough time to finish whatever paperwork she'd been working on, clean off her desk and check a mirror to see if her makeup was smeared (it wasn't). Then she killed some more time getting a new pen out of her desk drawer.

It's possible my laptop is a little old and slow.

When it finally did show signs of life, I clicked—after a little effort—on the e-mail program. And, on cue, the word processor opened. I have a hard time figuring out which little box is supposed to be which.

McElone gave me a withering look and took the computer out of my hands.

"What exactly is it I'm supposed to see?" she asked.

"It's the last e-mail I received," I told her, properly mortified by my lack of techno-skill.

In roughly four seconds, McElone had managed to pull up the proper information and see the threatening message. Her eyes looked concerned, but her voice betrayed no such emotion.

"I don't suppose you recognize the sender's e-mail address?" she asked.

"Yeah. Let's go to his house and arrest him, okay?"

"So you don't have any idea who might be sending you this." She ignored my sarcasm. "Is this the only such message you've received?" Again, no emotion in her voice.

I nodded. "But Maxie Malone, the previous homeowner, was getting the same kind of threats before she and Paul Harrison, the private detective, were killed."

McElone raised an eyebrow. "How do you know?"

Luckily, Paul had anticipated that question for me. "I found Maxie's laptop in the attic," I said. I'd actually found it there because Maxie had directed me to it, saying she "used to go up there to think." (And I believed she still went there occasionally—both of the ghosts would vanish for periods of time, and then return without explanation.) I pulled it out of the tote bag and handed it over to McElone.

"I wish you'd worn gloves," she said. I left it to her to get the second computer working properly. It took a lot less time to warm up than my weathered old laptop.

McElone clicked quickly here and there and came up with Maxie's inbox. "Aha," she said quietly.

"You see what I mean?" I knew, both because I'd looked and because the Dead Duo had told me, that Maxie had received at least eight threatening e-mails in the two weeks before she and Paul had died.

"Yes," McElone said. She consulted the file in front of her. "But the medical examiner's report indicated they'd each taken at least twenty sleeping pills. You can't exactly sneak a dosage that large into someone's food or drink."

"Did anyone come asking when you notified their next of kin?" I asked. Paul had told me he had a brother in Toronto, and Maxie had mumbled something about it being none of my business. But they had no idea if anyone had come to claim their remains.

"May I see your badge?" McElone asked.

"My what?"

"Your badge. You see, I only have to answer questions like that when they're asked by my superiors in the police force or someone from the prosecutor's office. So if you show me your badge, I'll be happy to reply."

"There's no need to be huffy about it," I said, more to myself than to the detective.

"Sure there is." McElone scowled at me. "Look, Ms. Kerby—I'm still new here. I've only been a detective on this force for two months. You're wasting my time over two suicides that have already been cleared by my predecessor, Detective Westmoreland, a man everyone in this building adored."

"Then you won't reopen the case?" I asked. That was

the outcome Paul had hoped would result from this meeting. He wouldn't be pleased.

McElone grunted. "I'll do some looking based on the threatening e-mails, but I still don't think it's murder," she said.

"It doesn't make sense," I told her. "Why would these two people commit suicide?"

McElone shrugged. "Lovers' quarrel?"

I practically spat. "Yeah, right!"

Her eyes narrowed. "*How* well did you know these people?" she asked again.

Oops. "Um, we never met," I said. "I bought the house almost a year after they died."

"Uh-huh. And where were you living at that time?" Great. Paul sends me to open the investigation, and immediately I become the chief suspect. In a double suicide.

"In Red Bank. I was just filing for divorce then."

"I'm sorry to hear it," she said in a voice that indicated she couldn't care less.

I stood up and reached a hand out for my laptop. "Well, I guess I've been wasting your time," I said.

McElone did not offer the computers back. "I don't know that yet," she said. "Until I have this figured out, I'm going to need to keep these."

I blanched. I didn't care what she did with Maxie's laptop, but I relied on my old dinosaur. "That's not possible," I sputtered.

"Sure it is," McElone answered. "Watch how easy it is for me not to give it back." She slipped the two computers into her desk drawer and wrote me out a receipt.

"What's the matter?" I asked her. "Doesn't the department give you your own computer?"

"You've given me evidence that someone is making terroristic threats against you," the detective responded. "Until I determine whether or not a crime has been committed, those computers are staying."

"And how long will that take?"

"It's a small town," McElone said. "We don't get that much crime during the off-season. Shouldn't take more than three or four days."

"Days? My whole life is on that computer!" Suddenly, the separation from my ancient notebook computer seemed horrifying. Okay, so I don't get along with technology, but that doesn't mean I want to live without it. I couldn't get along with The Swine, and . . .

Bad example.

"We have to follow up," McElone said, her voice never showing a hint of emotion. The woman could probably watch *Old Yeller* and not tear up. "I promise I'll call you the minute you can pick it up."

In the end, I had no choice. But then, that was becoming my fallback position on just about everything.

I went to pick up Melissa from school. Maybe I could check my e-mail on her cell phone.

Eleven

Paul had given me explicit instructions to come back to the house and report on my meeting with the police, but I didn't. Instead, I picked Melissa up at school and tried to linger a few minutes, hoping to run into Mr. Barnes. No such luck, but Melissa was in a mood to "work on the house," as she said, and she whined and begged to help enough that I relented quickly. I didn't want my daughter anywhere near the two spirits in the guesthouse, particularly Maxie, but what could I do? It was where we lived, and no matter how many times she could go play at Wendy's or do homework at another friend's house, I really did miss having Melissa pitch in with the renovations (plus, I feel the need to pass on to her the skills Dad taught me). It's not like I could I tell her I'd spent most of my mornings repairing damage done during the night by dead people. And anyway, I didn't want her to be afraid in her own house. Though if there was one thing I'd learned since my knock on the head, it's that you *should* be afraid of ghosts.

They're a colossal pain in the butt.

We were working in the dining room, a large, long space with ornate moldings around the entrance and along the ceiling. Today's jobs were to skillfully fill in cracks in the plaster (me), and *carefully* scrape the paint off the window frames to prepare them for staining later (Melissa, armed with Dad's paint scraper but no chemical stripper).

I didn't see Paul when we entered the house, which was odd—I figured he'd be waiting breathlessly (quite literally) for news of my meeting with Detective McElone. But Maxie wandered in from the kitchen, looking bored, or *pretending* to be bored.

Until she started staring directly at my daughter.

The way Maxie was looking at Melissa was creepier than anything I'd seen since the bucket made its impact with my cranium. And that's saying something.

"Don't do that window first," I told Melissa. "Do this one, closer to me."

"What's the difference?"

"This one's *closer to me*," I said. Maxie smiled a truly bloodcurdling smile.

"Well, I don't see what difference that makes," Melissa protested. "This one looks out on the beach, and all I can see from that one is the house next door, and it's all boarded up."

"*Do this one*," I said, a little too loudly.

Melissa grumbled, but she walked over and started scraping the window next to me, as I began sanding down a small crack in the plaster. Maxie, still grinning that evil grin, moved closer to Melissa.

"If we finish today, this room might actually be ready to be painted, and then we can do the floor, and we'll have a whole room done," I told Melissa, sounding way too cheerful.

Kids can see right through that. "What's wrong?" she asked.

"What do you mean, 'What's wrong?' I just said we can almost have this room finished."

Melissa put the scraper down. "I mean it," she said.

"Nothing's wrong, honey. I'm just tired." You can always tell kids you're tired. They're not familiar with the concept. They never think they're tired, even when they can barely keep their eyes open.

Then Paul walked in. Through the outside wall. I'd never seen that before, and I gasped a little.

"Mom, you're scaring me." Great. I'm trying to keep my nine-year-old away from two deranged ghosts, and *I'm* the one scaring her.

"Alison!" Paul said. "What happened with the police?"

Reflexively, my head swiveled in his direction. And that was when my daughter said the scariest thing I'd ever heard.

"Mom! You mean you can see them, too?"

After all the shouting (mostly from me) died down, I sat my daughter on the folding chair I'd bought to replace the compound-encrusted one and asked her how long she'd been able to see our semitransparent guests.

"Remember the first time we were here?" she asked. "Then."

"Why didn't you *say* anything?" My voice rose about an octave. I could have been singing *Aida*. Not the Elton John version, either.

"Maybe she just doesn't trust you," Maxie suggested. If looks could kill, the one I gave her would have been redundant.

"I *did* say something, but I didn't think you'd believe me," Melissa said. "I thought I'd sound crazy. I didn't know you could see them."

"I couldn't, until *somebody* hit me on the head with a bucket of compound," I told her.

Maxie smiled a little more. "See? There's an upside to everything."

"Upside? My daughter sees ghosts and you want me to see the *upside*?" Too much oxygen in my brain . . .

Paul knelt down to look Melissa in the eyes. "Why didn't you say anything to us, Melissa? I didn't know you could see us all these weeks."

Melissa gave him her best "well, *duh*" look. "I'm not supposed to talk to strangers," she said.

Maxie actually looked thoughtful. "That's very good," she told Melissa. "You really *shouldn't* talk to strangers."

"Yeah, but then how will I ever make any new friends? Everybody's a stranger when you first meet them."

Control. I needed to regain control. I knelt down beside my daughter and looked her straight in the eye. "Okay. You can see the ghosts."

"Maxie and Paul," Melissa corrected me. It was important, she seemed to believe, to be polite to the dead people.

I nodded. "Right. Paul and Maxie. You can see them. Which would indicate that they're not just hallucinations."

"How could you think . . ." Paul began, but I ignored him.

"So you have to know, Liss, that it's *really* important we keep this a secret, right?"

Contrary to popular belief, a mother can usually tell when her daughter is lying, and the nanosecond of panic in Melissa's eyes told me exactly what her words meant. "Oh sure, Mom," she said. "I won't tell anybody."

Oh boy. "Who have you told already?" I asked. Paul frowned.

"Nobody!" It came out much too fast and too loud.

"Come on, Liss. We're in damage-control mode here. Who did you tell? Did you tell Wendy?" Wendy is Melissa's BFF. There are times I believe they'd actually sign up to be joined at the hip if they thought Wendy's mom and I would agree to the surgery.

Melissa looked away. Swell. "Um . . . maybe."

"Maybe? You're not sure whether or not you told Wendy that there were two ghosts in our new house?"

"I can't remember."

"I won't be mad," I said.

Melissa made eye contact with me, her own eyes starting to tear up a little. "You won't?"

"I promise I won't get mad," I told Melissa. "But you have to tell me the truth."

"Don't believe her," Maxie said. "Parents always say things like that, and then they turn on you."

I glared at Maxie. "I really don't have time for group therapy now," I told her. "Go haunt the basement."

Maxie didn't move, but she did shut up.

My daughter took a deep breath. "I told Wendy," she said.

I clamped my mouth shut for a moment, to avoid making Maxie right. Then—admirably, I believe—I smiled, and said, "Okay. As long as it was just Wendy."

"Well, I told Andrea, too." Now that Melissa knew I wouldn't yell at her, she was going to give me every reason to do so.

"Andrea? Anybody else?"

"Just Lenore."

"So you told three girls that you saw ghosts in the house." I was still getting used to the idea that *I* was seeing ghosts in the house, and now it was becoming a spectral chain letter for fourth graders.

"Yeah. But Wendy probably told Sophie, who probably told Clarice, who . . ."

"Who's Clarice?" Wait. What was the point here? "Never mind. Okay. So we can now logically assume that every fourth grade girl in your school has heard this story."

"Clarice is in third grade," Melissa said. Well, that put *me* in my place.

I sat on the floor and held my head in my hands for a moment. My ghostly infestation was no doubt the talk of the elementary school by now, and by logical extension, the town. People were probably gossiping about us behind our backs. They were wondering what kind of mother I was to let Melissa go around telling these bizarre stories. I'd probably have to move out of town again in disgrace, change my name, leave the investment I'd made with my life savings and get a job as a cocktail waitress in a bar with peanut shells on the floor.

"So," Paul said, oblivious. "Tell me about your meeting with the detective."

Twelve

Adam Morris was a very busy man; that was obvious the first time I called his office to ask for a meeting. It took two separate transfers just to get my call to his secretary, who then told me four different times herself that Mr. Morris was a very busy man.

Strangely, however, when he heard that the new owner of 123 Seafront Avenue was calling, Adam Morris managed to put off his very busy-ness and pick up the phone.

"Alison!" As if we were old friends. Already I didn't like the guy. "What a delight to hear from you!"

I was sure the delight was all his, but since Paul was listening on the speakerphone, I'd agreed to be civil, at least. This was a man who might have had a hand in two murders, could be threatening my life and, at the very least, might want to take my home and business away from me.

"Mr. Morris," I said, not giving him the satisfaction of calling him by his first name, "I'm calling because I just found out you'd been trying to . . . acquire my property before I bought it."

"Among others," he admitted. "Are you interested in selling?"

"Actually, I thought it would be a good idea for you to come here. See the house, and what I'm doing with it. You'll see that its value has certainly increased." I figured I'd let him think I was interested in his money, since that's what most businessmen understand. I had no intention of selling the house to him or anyone else, but the purpose of leading him on was twofold: bring him to the house so Paul could get a look at him, and just on the chance that he *was* the person who had killed Paul and Maxie, give him a reason to believe he might be able to get the house from me without having to resort to violence.

A win-win, if you will.

"I'm sure it has, Alison," he said, still taking no notice that I hadn't started calling him Adam yet. "But I don't intend to rent the house out as a B and B, like you."

"It's not a—"

"I was planning to knock it down, in order to make room for Seaside Estates," he went on, undeterred.

"I see," I said, though of course I already knew that. Let him think the bumpkin was now stumped. In the development game, there's nothing like a stumped bumpkin.

"I would offer a very competitive price," he said.

"I'm sure you would," I told him, despite thinking that he would probably try to lowball me just on principle. "But I don't know that I would feel right letting you knock down such a historic property."

Paul whispered, unnecessarily, "Ask him why he didn't buy it after Maxie died."

I waved a hand at him: I was getting to that. "I'm curious—if you're that interested in the land, why didn't you buy it when it was on the market, before I did?"

He hesitated. "I'm not at liberty to discuss that."

"You're the head of your company. You can discuss any-thing you want." I hadn't meant to be rude; it just slipped out—I didn't like the man.

Paul shook his finger at me. "Don't do that!" he shouted. I guess he'd finally realized I was the only one who could hear him.

Morris, of course, answered immediately. "That's right. I can. And I'm not discussing that, Alison."

"Well, I appreciate your picking up the phone," I said. "I'll have to reconsider selling the house. Please give me a few days." I didn't like to think that request was a literal one, but I couldn't be sure.

"A few days," Morris said, and hung up.

"Well, what did we find out?" I asked Paul.

"That you can't follow instructions," Paul answered. "And that you just made an enemy."

"I don't think we ran anything other than that little column-filler." Phyllis Coates, editor of the *Harbor Haven Chronicle*, frowned in thought.

"I thought newspapers didn't print articles about sui-cides," I said. "I was surprised that one was there at all."

Phyllis's office, a throwback to a bygone newspaper age, was filled with actual paper and dust. There was a concession to the twenty-first century in the iMac on her desk, but other than that, you would have expected men in green visors to be yelling, "Copy!" at the top of their lungs in the "news-room" outside, which held old back issues, an unconnected telephone and, at the moment, my daughter. Melissa was examining the bound copies of the *Chronicle* that seemed randomly tossed around. Phyllis hadn't cleaned up for some time, and there didn't appear to be anyone else on staff here.

And I have to admit, every time Melissa looked up or turned her head, I tensed a little, wondering if she was see-ing someone else who wasn't exactly, you know, alive.

This was going to take some getting used to.

"We usually don't," Phyllis answered, bringing me back to the conversation. She was as dated as the office, her face showing every bit of her seventy-something years. I've known Phyllis since I was a papergirl for the *Chronicle* when I was thirteen, and I had renewed the acquaintance when I'd moved back to Harbor Haven. But she insisted she didn't need a papergirl these days, so I'd asked about advertising rates for the guesthouse. Phyllis was still a feisty ex-newspaper reporter and a closet softie, and I really liked her.

Besides, Paul said the local newspaper editor *always* knows more about what is going on in town than anybody else. If anybody knew anything about the "suicides" or Adam Morris, it would be Phyllis. "We only publish on suicides when the person is a celebrity, or if the suicide happens in a public place."

"This happened to civilians in a private home," I pointed out.

"Yes, but we didn't know they were considered suicides right away," Phyllis answered. "And the deaths immediately followed a contentious planning board meeting where one of the deceased spoke. People wanted to know what was going on." She allowed herself a slight smile. "Besides, it was the off-season, and we needed to fill the space."

"Are you sure it was suicide?" I asked Phyllis. "Did you just rely on the police reports?"

Phyllis's voice took on an edge. "Honey, I was a crime reporter for the *New York Daily News* for thirty years before I bought this rag. I don't just rely on the police reports. We reported the incident the week after it happened, and I followed up. Harold Westmoreland, the detective on the case, wasn't exactly Sherlock Holmes, but he looked into it. The medical examiner showed a high concentration of Ambien in each of their bodies, enough for almost a whole jar of pills *each*. Now, you don't get people to take that many pills by pointing a gun to their heads, and you don't take them by mistake. Those people were trying to die."

Through the glass, I could see Melissa close one book of past issues and then turn to look in my direction. I'd told her not to come into the office until I gestured, but she was running out of things to be interested in at a newspaper office. I'd better get to the point quickly.

I bit my lower lip. "Yeah, see, I don't think they were," I told her.

Phyllis raised an eyebrow with interest, not skepticism. I took that as a good sign. "Really," she said.

"Yeah. It seems that Maxie Malone—who owned the house then—was getting threatening e-mails telling her to get out of the house before something happened to her. And then something happened to her. You don't find that suspicious?"

"First I'm hearing about it," Phyllis admitted. "Did the police know about the e-mails?"

"I don't think so, not until I told them. I found Maxie's laptop when I was taking the house apart. I don't think she ever went to the police, but she did hire a private investigator to track down whoever was sending the e-mails. He was the man killed alongside her."

"I know who Harrison was, and so do the cops," Phyllis said. "His brother came down from Canada to identify the body, and he said that Harrison had been depressed before he moved down here. Now, what does that sound like?"

I didn't actually know, but I said, "Like a guy looking for a fresh start, not one about to take his own life. It doesn't make sense these two people who barely knew each other would have an instant suicide pact. And here's the thing—I've started getting e-mails, too."

Phyllis looked up, concerned. "Why didn't you tell me that part?"

"I was trying to prolong the suspense. What do you think, Phyllis? I'm trying not to think about—"

Melissa walked over to the door and knocked, ready to have someone to talk to. I hesitated, considering the topic of conversation, but looked at Phyllis, who nodded, and opened the door for her to come in. Phyllis's mouth twitched from side to side. I guessed she was thinking about the threats I'd been getting, but now we couldn't talk about them.

"Come in, honey," Phyllis said. "You want a hot chocolate? I'm having one."

Melissa nodded shyly, and Phyllis started making hot chocolate on a hot plate she had in one corner.

"Sit quietly for a minute," I warned Melissa, and pointed to a stool in the far corner, which wasn't very far at all. Melissa, who hadn't met Phyllis before, was in her "good behavior" mode and did as I asked.

"You might have a point, Alison," Phyllis said. "But I'd have to check back with the police. You said you talked to Detective McElone?"

"Yes," I confirmed. "I understand that the original detective, Westmoreland, has retired."

Melissa folded her hands in her lap and did her best to look like the best little girl in all the world. Which of course she is.

Phyllis was quiet for almost a full minute. She was clearly thinking, and every once in a while, she'd nod. "Does Adam Morris factor into your thinking?"

Man, she *was* good—I hadn't even mentioned Morris's name yet. "He wanted the house," I said, "and he's been offering to buy me out. I don't know him well—is he the type who would kill to get what he wants?" Whoops. Melissa's eyes widened a little; I'd forgotten myself, and I wouldn't let it happen again.

"Not if he could just pay for it," Phyllis answered. "It's a reach, I know, but he just rubs me the wrong way. All right. Let me see those e-mails." Phyllis got a reporter's notebook from her desk and actually—I swear—licked the end of a pencil.

I exhaled audibly, and sagged into the other chair. "The cops are holding both laptops," I said.

Phyllis didn't miss a beat. "So what? Don't you know the passwords? We'll just sign on from here." She pointed to her iMac.

"I don't know Maxie's, but I can give you mine. May I?" I pointed to the keyboard, and Phyllis nodded.

I punched up my e-mail account and signed on. Phyllis printed out the threatening message I'd received for future study. Melissa got up to look, but I glared her back onto the stool. I turned the screen away from her gaze. The less she knew about the threats, the better.

"How can we trace the sender's e-mail address?" I asked Phyllis.

"I'm not sure we can," she answered. "It's unlikely someone would go out of their way to send anonymous threats through the Internet through their own personal address." I hadn't checked my e-mail since McElone had confiscated my computer, so the slow-loading program kept adding more messages as we worked.

"Maybe he's really stupid," I suggested hopefully.

"That would be lucky," Phyllis said. "The stupid ones are easy to catch." She pointed to the screen. "The address is just a group of numbers—it's probably from a public place, like a hotel or a Wi-Fi café. The police will probably be able to trace it."

She started writing something on the pad in front of her. She looked up only when I gasped.

"What's the matter, honey?" Phyllis asked.

I pointed at the screen. "There's a new one," I said.

The numbers in the address were slightly different this time, but the message was clear and to the point: "Get out or die."

"Well," Phyllis said, "looks like Halloween came a couple of weeks early this year."

Thirteen

I called McElone to tell her about the new message, but she was out. So I drove back to the house, figuring I might as well make it easy for my murderer to find me. I hate waiting.

Since I'd agreed to help Paul and Maxie in the quest for . . . posthumous closure, the little "pranks" that I'd found in the house each morning had ceased, so I'd actually begun to make progress. The dining room was indeed almost ready to be painted, and then I could move on to the two upstairs bathrooms, which were going to require tiling, grouting, painting and some plumbing (the toilet had to be moved about ten inches to the right in one, I needed to seriously unclog the bathtub drain in the other and I had to move some pipes into the master bedroom, where I planned to add an en suite bathroom). Within the next few days, I'd have to find myself an electrician to upgrade the service in the whole house, because that was the one thing I absolutely wouldn't do, Dad's advice notwithstanding.

I'm afraid of electricity, and I'm willing to pay someone to be braver than I am.

That left the furnace, which I'd examined and found mostly sound. So the fact that it was cold in the house was troublesome. I spent a morning bleeding all the radiators, and that didn't make much difference. The Halloween decorations on everyone's lawn but mine (I figured I had enough trouble with real ghosts on my lawn) were reminding me that comfortable weather wasn't here for long, but I hadn't found a flaw to repair yet, so I decided to press on with things I *could* fix. I started with the tiling.

When Paul appeared through the floor, eager for a report on my talk with Phyllis, he was met with questions, rather than answers, and that threw him off.

"Were you depressed before you died?" I asked. Other people say hello. I have my own style.

"No, what . . . Who told you that?" he sputtered.

"Your brother told Phyllis Coates that you were depressed, and he wasn't surprised that you'd killed yourself." Phyllis hadn't actually said that last part, but I felt it was implied.

Paul frowned. "I was . . . upset for a while before I came here to New Jersey," he said slowly. "I hadn't been able to find work in my field. I told my brother I was thinking of giving up. My dream of being a detective, not my life. I think 'depressed' would be a pretty serious exaggeration."

There was a long silence. I felt a little uncomfortable. Okay, a *lot* uncomfortable. Paul had a calm demeanor that seemed unshakable; he could get riled up, but instead of getting angry, he'd just become irritated and, in moments of extreme frustration, he'd simply evaporate in front of my eyes, like he'd shattered into a million pieces too small to see. After about a half hour, he'd be back again, "whole," and never mention whatever had caused him to disappear.

"And I *didn't* kill myself," Paul added.

Another gap in the conversation followed, but he smiled at me as I donned gloves, goggles, heavy work boots and an apron to start removing tiles in the upstairs bathroom.

"Tell me, why did you buy this place?" Paul asked, I think to break the tension left from my last question. He sat down on, or hovered over, the closed toilet. The sad part was, this was the closest I'd come to a date in over a year. Tiling with a dead guy.

"I've told you. I need a sustainable business to keep me in clothes, food and college fund. I'm getting next to bupkus from The Swine, and I've always wanted to run a guesthouse by the shore. I like the idea of creating a place that people could talk about to their friends when they come home from vacation. Is that so hard to understand?" I grabbed a putty knife, a screwdriver and a hammer to start taking down the old tiles, which were, it should be noted, aqua and hideous.

"No, I understand that part perfectly," he replied. "But why *this* house? There must have been a few you could afford."

"In this market, there were more than a few," I admitted. "But this was the only one with seven bedrooms, which means I can accommodate five guest rooms. I need that many to make a profit. And it has three bathrooms, which is about average, but also leaves me able to add more."

"Who was your real estate agent?" Paul asked. "Who sold you this house?" His expression was much too interested; I should have seen it coming.

"Terry Wright," I told him. "Weren't you here when she showed me the house?"

"Oh yes, that's right. You know, she was the agent who sold the house to Maxie, too," he answered, stroking what would have been his chin, if he were there.

"She's a big real estate broker in Harbor Haven. So?" The great thing about taking stuff down before you rebuild is that you don't have to care too much about what damage you're doing—the more damage, the better. So I took a nice, broad screwdriver and drove it into the grout around a tile with a vengeance. Pieces of grout and tile scattered all over.

It felt great.

"*So*," Paul answered, "the threatening e-mails to Maxie—and now to you—have to be related to the house. Not only is the house the only connection between you and Maxie, but the threats are also explicit in wanting the two of you out of here."

"Brilliant, Holmes! But what the hell has that got to do with my real estate agent?" The wall was now almost completely free of the atrocious tiles the Prestons—or their predecessors—had imposed upon it. I could start bringing up boxes of my understated off-white replacements in a few minutes.

"If the source of your trouble is a car, you talk to a mechanic," Paul said. "If it's a dog, you talk to a veterinarian. If it's a house . . ."

"You talk to a real estate agent," I finished for him. "Well, forget it, Kojak. I'm already behind on my work here, and I don't have time to go off and ask a real estate agent why some anonymous murderer wants me out of the house I'm already making mortgage payments on, despite not being able to rent out the rooms I bought it for. No."

"I don't want you to go see Terry Wright," Paul said, smiling a damnably cute Cheshire-cat grin.

"What is this, reverse psychology? You say, 'Don't go,' and I'm supposed to argue with you? How stupid do you think I am, Paul?"

He actually looked alarmed. "I don't think you're stupid." Paul seemed concerned that he'd hurt my feelings. Ghost-as-puppy.

I knocked a couple more tiles off the wall. Make him sweat a little. "I meant that figuratively, Paul. But I'm not going off to interrogate Terry."

"And I meant it sincerely, Alison. I don't want you to go see her." He grinned that grin again. Paul was the most smug-looking specter I'd seen today. Maxie wasn't around.

I was starting to think it was a good thing he wasn't alive.

"I *love* what you've done with the place," Terry Wright said, looking over a living room that could have been more attractively decorated by a hand grenade. The hole in the wall had not become any more filled since the night it had been created two weeks earlier. The floor was covered with dust and drop cloths. A sawhorse sat in front of one window, which had a drapery rod hanging down on one side. Pieces of molding were missing from the dining room (about to become the den) entrance.

"Yeah, it's a work in progress," I told her. Real estate agents are salespeople, and as such will never say anything negative about anything for fear of offending a potential customer. And they see all humans as potential customers.

"But it's got *great* potential, doesn't it, Alison?" Terry had not mentioned she'd be bringing Kerin Murphy with her. I hadn't even been aware Kerin was working in Terry's real estate office, but here she was, with the requisite mauve "TWRE" (Teresa Wright Real Estate) blazer, perfectly tailored over her slim-but-athletic shoulders.

"I certainly hope so," I told her, wondering how the woman found time to sell real estate while heading up every committee in school and, one imagined, giving blood three times a week.

"It will be so lovely when it's done," Kerin went on. "Who's your contractor?"

A chance to show off! "I'm doing the work myself," I said.

Her mouth narrowed. "Oh." It would have been nice to punch her, but I had an interview to conduct and Paul was watching.

Paul's theory had been that if Terry came to the house, he could orchestrate her interview. That is, he could tell me what questions to ask, and hear the answers. I would act, for all intents and purposes, as a PA system. Which was fine by me.

I had asked Terry to come by on the pretense that she might be interested in helping me find full-time tenants for some of the rooms once the renovation was complete. Of course, I had no intention of taking in people on a full-time basis, nor was I even licensed for that, but inviting a real estate agent over to ask about two murders would probably be something of an off-putting experience, we'd decided. (Okay, Paul had decided.)

"This is all going to be the original hardwood flooring, sanded and re-stained," I told Terry, doing my best to ignore Kerin. I indicated the den and living room floors, which were now semi-covered in a wall-to-wall carpet that had probably been sold to the original owners by Ali Baba himself. Terry nodded. You could practically see the thought balloon over her head: "Why is this woman showing me around the house I sold to her?"

"It's going to be gorgeous," she responded. Like she'd say if she thought it would be hideous. "I can't wait to see it."

Kerin simply stared, mostly at the enormous hole in the hallway wall. Leave it to her to find my soft underbelly and gape at it.

"Ask her about the owners before Maxie, the Prescotts," Paul hissed from the dining room entrance. Maxie, sort of floating over the room, did her best to look bored.

"The Prestons," Maxie said. "Get the name right, gumshoe."

"All right, the Prestons," Paul rasped back. "And keep your voice down!"

"Why?"

"The people who owned this place before, the Prestons," I said to Terry, as if there were no conversation going on in the room but ours. "I was wondering about them—I remember when I was growing up they had a lot of children . . ."

Terry nodded. "Yeah, they had nine kids," she said. "Why do you ask ?"

"Their names were on some old documents and letters I found in the kitchen," I lied. "I thought maybe I should give them back."

Terry's eyes lit up like a Christmas tree. "You found old papers in the kitchen?" she asked.

"Yeah, a few." I had, in fact, found nothing in the kitchen, but what could I say—one of the ghosts in the house told me to ask?

"What are you going to do about this wall?" Kerin asked, pointing to the hole. She seemed fascinated by it. I fought the urge to push her in. I'm a professional. I did revel in the look I saw Terry give her and the way Kerin cringed just a little bit when she saw it.

"Ask Terry why the Prestons sold," Paul suggested. No, demanded.

"What were they?" Terry asked before I could get Paul's question out of my mouth.

"What were what?"

"The papers you found in the kitchen." Terry's eyebrows were doing the cha-cha on her forehead. I'd clearly struck a nerve.

"Just letters and some warranties for work on the porch and the roof," I said. "Nothing really interesting. But I'm curious, why did they sell the house?"

"The Prestons? I don't remember."

"When was that, Terry?" Kerin asked.

"Before you started with us," she answered. "I'm not really sure about the date."

A real estate agent who didn't remember a transaction

she had brokered? "I guess they didn't need all the space when the kids grew up, huh?" I said.

Paul scowled at me. "Don't *ever* give them the answer to a question!" he barked. "Now all she has to say is . . ."

"Yeah, that was it," Terry said. I lowered my head in shame. "Something wrong?"

"Oh, it's nothing," I said. "I just have this pain in the neck." I glared at Paul. "All this work."

Kerin strode over from the gaping hole in my pride to join us again. "Do you need the name of an acupuncturist?" she asked, rummaging in her purse. "I think I have a business card."

"No. Thanks," I managed.

"Find out where the Prestons are now," Paul said.

"Where did they move to?" I asked.

"The Prestons?" How many times would she ask that? *No, the Leibowitzes. Who are we talking about?*

"Yeah," I echoed. "The Prestons."

"Why?"

"Because you want to give them the stuff you found," Maxie said. "Geez, this woman is slow!" I hadn't even realized she'd been listening. And I wasn't sure which one of us she was talking about.

I parroted her suggestion to Terry.

"I'll have to look it up," she said. "I could take them with me if you want, forward them along, if that'll help."

"Um . . ." There really were no documents.

Paul finally rescued me. "You'd like to ask them questions about the house," he said.

I told Terry that, and while looking at Maxie, added, "Because I obviously can't ask Maxie Malone for help."

Maxie rolled over on her side, as if sleeping. I'd probably never get used to seeing people float in the air.

"I'll have to look it up and call you," Terry answered after an awkward pause. "But most questions you have about the house I can probably answer myself."

"Of course you can," I told her. "But they have a more . . . emotional connection to the place. I want to hear the stories."

Maxie stuck her finger down her throat. She could be subtle that way.

"I think they're in Eatontown," Kerin volunteered, and Terry shot her a poisonous look. At least I knew I wasn't the only one Kerin could infuriate.

"Okay, then," Terry said, a touch of irritation in her voice. "I'll give you a call with their contact information, and you call me if you have any questions *I* can answer." She snapped her purse shut so hard it echoed through the empty room.

"I'll do that," I said, and before I could blink, Terry had turned on her heel and headed for the front door.

Paul didn't wait until we heard it close behind her. "That," he said, "is a woman who is hiding something."

Maxie yawned. "Which one?" she asked.

Fourteen

"I can definitely recommend the veal parmigiana," said Mayor Bridget Bostero. "I've had it here, and it's excellent."

I looked up at the waiter, who had told us his name was Rudolfo, but was probably Ralphie. After all, this was still New Jersey. I was pretty sure.

Despite having witnessed my crack interviewing skills with Terry Wright, Paul had still suggested I talk to the mayor. I'd called the municipal building to ask if a constituent might meet with the town's chief administrator to discuss real estate futures, and had been turned down flat. But I'd left my name and address, and surprisingly, Mayor Bostero had gotten right back to me (maybe the house was still a political issue) and suggested we meet at Café Linguine, an Italian-French fusion restaurant with delusions of grandeur. Paul had been pleased by the suggestion, saying it would be good for me to see the place, since it was the same restaurant where he and Maxie had eaten their last meal. I hadn't been keen on the idea, since it was also very likely the place where he and Maxie had been poisoned, but I'd been outvoted.

"I'll have the ratatouille," I told Rudolfo, and Bridget scowled a bit. She was clearly used to people doing as she suggested. I was happier to avoid eating anything chosen by someone other than myself, especially here.

The place was light, airy and foreboding all at the same time. In the back was a pizza oven that, according to the sign over the front door, was fired by wood. You could see people in paper chef's hats near the back, making your food right out where they could be observed. (Were the hats a good idea near an open flame?)

"I get a discount," the mayor boasted after Rudolfo had left. "I own a teeny-tiny part of the restaurant." Ever the politician, she scanned the room while trying to maintain the illusion that she was paying attention to me. She was only a local politician, so her technique needed a little work. She'd already waved or nodded to a town council member, a local florist, and a man who I'm pretty sure had only been delivering rolls to the restaurant.

Still, she'd managed to work into the conversation her accomplishments as mayor, such as they were: an increase in revenue (mostly due, I'd heard from Phyllis, to the police ticketing more cars going twenty-eight miles per hour in a twenty-five zone) and the installation of video surveillance cameras in much of the town square, a development that was a little too Big Brother for my taste. But Bridget clearly saw herself as a doer, and I doubted being mayor of Harbor Haven was her ultimate ambition.

"How about a school bus route?" I asked, forgetting my role for a moment. Bridget's eyes widened, and she looked me up and down. I was trying to be careful not to move around too much, so the digital recorder in my purse would be able to pick up our voices with as little background noise as possible.

"You'd be shocked to hear what the insurance would

cost. Shall we have some wine?" the mayor asked. She gave the bartender a wink from across the room, and the poor kid's expression of either embarrassment or total befuddlement spoke volumes.

"Not for me," I said. "I have to use power tools after lunch. I'll stick with water." A drink that, I'd like to point out, doesn't tolerate poison well. It's meant to be clear, for one thing. Flavorless, for another.

"So," the mayor began, "how can I help you?"

"Well, as you know, I'm the new owner of the house at 123 Seafront Avenue."

"Such a lovely old house," she said. "I hope you're doing all you can to restore it to its original beauty." She spotted someone across the room, and waved. But discreetly.

"That's exactly what I'm trying to do," I agreed. "But I'm coming late to a lot of the house's recent history, and I was hoping that as mayor you might be able to fill in some of the gaps for me."

"Oh," the mayor said. She shifted her gaze to look at the chefs.

"I know about the two deaths, Ms. Bostero," I said. "You don't have to worry about that."

Bridget immediately looked back at me, and would have brightened, but she was too busy making a face that indicated her terrible grief at what had happened in my house. "Those poor people," she intoned. "They must have been so horribly sad."

"You really think they committed suicide together?" I asked.

"That's what the police said," the mayor replied. She was interrupted by the arrival of an appetizer of fried mozzarella and *gougères* (to drive the fusion theme home with a jackhammer), which Bridget had ordered without asking my opinion. My opinion would have been that it constituted a lot of cheese.

Once Ralphie had left the table, the mayor continued.

"Have you ever thought of touching up your hair, just a bit?" she asked.

"What?"

"Just highlights, you know," Bridget said. "I'm not saying you're getting gray at all. Not at all. But a few touches here and there . . ." It was possible she'd been happier as a beautician than as a mayor.

"I've never thought of it," I said.

"I could recommend a few things."

"Thanks," I said. "I'll think about it. But getting back to our conversation . . ."

"You never know what's going on in someone else's head," she said with a look that tried to say *sage* and ended up *stumped beauty pageant contestant*. "Some people feel things more intensely than others," she offered. I was no longer sure whether we were discussing possible suicides or hair coloring.

And then the mayor scared the living hell out of me by taking a small bottle out of her purse and administering three drops of liquid into her water glass. Then she *drank* the water.

I must have looked stunned, because she laughed. "It's just a multivitamin," she said. "I can't swallow pills, so my doctor prescribes everything for me in liquid form. Don't worry."

I tried to get back on topic, but after that display, it was difficult. I concentrated on what Paul had instructed me to do: push harder. "These people died right after the planning board meeting where Maxie Malone successfully stopped the plan to raze the house," I said. "I understand you were there. You heard the argument. Don't you think it's possible that someone who was disappointed with the result could have gotten very, very angry?"

Bridget Bostero's eyes widened and her mouth formed a perfect *O* before she spoke. "You think they were murdered?"

"I think it's a possibility," I told her. Paul was going to love this part of the recording.

"Why wouldn't the police agree with you, then?" the mayor asked.

"The police don't have to be corrupt to get something wrong," I said, leaning heavily on Paul's pre-interview coaching. "I'm told that the original investigating officer, Detective Westmoreland, was counting the days to his retirement. He went with whatever the medical examiner told him, and, in this case, was told the bodies had lots of Ambien in them. Ninety-nine times out of a hundred, that'll be suicide or an accidental overdose. There was no way these were *two* accidental overdoses, so they were ruled suicides, and the detective moved on. That's not corruption; it's not even negligence. It's just a failure to question enough."

"You've been thinking about this a lot," the mayor said.

It was time to cut and run. "Yes, but I really wanted to ask you about the development plan," I said. "I know you didn't vote on the proposal."

"That's right. If it doesn't pass the planning board, we don't get to consider the question at all." Bridget seemed proud to show off her knowledge of governmental procedure.

"But I'm told you spoke in favor of the development plan before the vote, but you accepted the decision afterward."

"Yes, I did." The mayor beamed. "I always abide by decisions I don't have to make. And after all, it was obvious the board was moved by the voice of a citizen who deserved her right to speak." Vote for me: the hidden message behind everything any elected official ever says.

"I appreciate that." I looked down and saw that the appetizer, which I hadn't touched, was almost gone. Mayor Bostero must have worked out ten hours a day to be able to eat like that—she had a terrific figure. I started to hate her. "But I'm wondering about the future of my guesthouse. It's zoned properly for what I want to do, but will I have problems with parking, beach access or sewer systems? With fuel prices going up and an ancient heating system, will I be able to have guests during the winter?" That reminded me: I had to do something about my furnace. Really.

"Madeline and David were always working to keep the house going," Bridget said. "The outside, the inside . . . with a structure as old as that one, there's always something."

"Madeline and David?" I asked.

"The Prestons. The people who used to own the house. Lovely couple, you know. I still see them socially every once in a while. They contributed to the campaign."

"The house," I reminded her.

"You think you're in over your head?" Bridget asked, picking up exactly as Paul and I had hoped she would.

"It's possible. I haven't decided yet; I'm still making repairs. But if I were going to sell it, would the town be interested in reconsidering the development plan Mr. Morris had proposed?"

Bridget Bostero took a long moment and looked off into the distance, obviously thinking deep thoughts. "Oh good," she finally said. "Here's our lunch." Rudolfo/ Ralphie appeared out of nowhere with a large tray and a stand and started serving the entrees. "I'm starving," Mayor Bostero went on.

The woman must have had a tapeworm.

Once Rudolfo withdrew, I had to ask my question again; Bridget either didn't remember what I'd asked or was hoping I'd forget.

"That development deal is dead," she finally said. "The planning board won't reconsider unless it's drastically overhauled, and Adam Morris doesn't want to do that. There's no chance for it."

She considered very carefully, and then twirled some fettuccine onto her fork. "You should have ordered the veal," the mayor said. "You don't know what you're missing."

Fifteen

Talking to Bridget Bostero and Adam Morris had yielded little, which Paul informed me was "about par" for a new investigation. But he wasn't the one getting threatening e-mails, and couldn't lose his own life *again*, so I think I felt a slightly more acute sense of urgency.

This was not helped by the fact that my mother still called me every day to ask if my head still hurt (which it hadn't since the day after I'd gotten out of the hospital) and to try to invent more reasons to come over to the house. So far, she'd come only once, and found me engaged in heavy lifting, moving a toilet. She'd quickly remembered an errand she had to run. But I'm sure she thought I'd moved it brilliantly.

I'd also had phone conversations (on speaker, so Paul could hear) with three of the four planning board members, all lovely old gentlemen who recalled that Mayor Bostero had spoken first for the development plan, and then against it, once it was obvious Maxie had persuaded the board.

While they couldn't recall exactly what it was Maxie had said that was so powerful, each mentioned unprompted that she'd looked good while saying it.

The interrogations were taking up a lot of my days while Melissa was in school, but there was still a house to restore before Halloween, now just over a week away. The local houses done up with orange-and-yellow Halloween lights were becoming an unwelcome reminder. Lights are for Christmas, people. That's all I'm saying.

When I told Paul I'd be concentrating on renovations for a while, he got huffy (in a polite, Canadian way) and vanished to other parts of the house when I was working. It took me the better part of the next three days to get the bathroom tiled, but when I was finished, it was a sight to behold. Glistening off-white tile with coral-colored grout gave it just the right seaside touch without making it overly adorable.

Tony and Jeannie stopped by that afternoon to check on my progress, and since Melissa was at Wendy's house, I'd actually been very productive. Tony nodded at the tiling job.

"It's really getting there," he said, admiring the work. "Are you going to tile the floor, as well?"

"I think so, but something a little less plain. A recurring pattern, maybe. I haven't decided."

Jeannie leaned on the bathroom doorjamb and smiled. "You do nice work, Alison," she said. "Do you hire out?"

"If I don't get this house done in time to attract some guests for the summer, I might take you up on that," I told her.

"Come on," Tony said. "Let's take another look at that hole in your living room wall."

We went downstairs and stood, once again, in front of the Delaware Water Gap in my beautiful plaster wall. As ever, it made me want to cry. Tony took on his professional-contractor face and, for the umpteenth time, examined the edges of the gap as if trying to determine how to make the plaster grow back.

"Why can't you just patch it?" Jeannie asked, and again, I explained about the lack of available plaster craftsmen.

"It looks like a regular hole," she said. "I don't see why it's so hard."

Tony picked up a trowel I'd left lying on the floor and offered it to her. "If you'd like to take a shot . . ." he said.

Jeannie just grinned. "Why did I marry you, again?"

"As I recall, at the time you said it was for the sex," I told her. Jeannie blushed. So did Tony.

Maxie appeared through the living room ceiling and, as before, her gaze fixated on Tony. She licked her lips.

"Let's go to the kitchen," I said.

"Why? The hole's here," Tony answered, wrinkling his brow. I think that only made Maxie more ravenous. I didn't know if she had plans for him, but if so, I certainly didn't want to know what they were. "Can we get some more light in here, Alison?" he asked, looking into the cavern.

Maxie swooped down and hit the light switch before I could reach it. Luckily, neither Tony nor Jeannie was looking, because I have no idea how I would have explained that. But Jeannie did shiver a little as Maxie passed by her, as if she'd felt a sudden, cold wind.

Tony could stick his head all the way inside the hole; that was how big it was. With a flashlight in his hand, he looked around the damage. "I don't get how this happened," he said. "There's no sign of weakness around the gap. And look here." He beckoned to me, so I stood close to the hole and looked in. "There's plaster on the floor *inside* the wall. The only way that happens is if something hits it from *outside*."

"Or some*one*," Maxie trilled from up near the ceiling again. If only I could have reached her . . . I still wouldn't have been able to do anything. *Damn!*

"Maybe something *evil* hit it," I said, and Maxie stuck her tongue out at me.

"Yeah," Tony laughed. "Something evil." He thought some more. "Maybe we could build a mold of some sort—take the dimensions of the gap, or better, square it off with a saw, maybe—and then make a mold of the thickness. Then we could just drop the finished plaster mold in, spackle in around the corners and consider ourselves lucky." He looked at me. "What do you think?"

"I think it's better than looking at a hole in the wall," I said. "Let's try it."

"Get me a level, a pencil and a drywall saw," Tony said. He looked positively gleeful. "We'll beat this sucker yet."

"I realize this is fascinating," Jeannie said as I headed for the kitchen, where the tools were, "but I'm going to go out and get some pizza. We could be here awhile. Alison, do you need anything?"

"Can you pick up Melissa from Wendy's? I'll call her mom so she'll know it's not me picking her up."

"Sure." I gave Jeannie Wendy's address, and she was off, ordering extra garlic on her cell phone as she left.

I brought Tony the tools. When he's working, I'm reduced to the role of assistant, and I'm happy to cede my authority. He's the contractor; I'm someone who's good with tools. It's a whole other level. Like the Jonas Brothers should shut up and listen when Stevie Wonder sings. I'm just saying.

Plus, as I hand him tools, I take note of how he does things. So then next time, when he's not around, I might be able to do it myself. Not as well, but well enough.

Tony began by making marks around the hole, using the T-square on the level to assure the lines were straight. He set out to make a square just large enough to touch the studs on either side (to make installing the patch easier) out of what was a jagged oval hole. I didn't say anything while Tony worked.

"Okay, so what's bothering you?" he asked after a minute.

"What do you mean, what's bothering me? I don't want a gigantic hole in my living room wall."

"That's not what I mean, and you know it," Tony answered. And it wasn't, and I did.

"Nothing's bothering me," I said, not even convincing myself.

Tony's head was inside the wall again, so his voice had an interesting echo to it. "Who do you think you're talking to?" he asked.

"Go ahead, tell him," Maxie sneered. "Tell the beefcake that you're seeing ghosts. And make sure you tell him what I look like."

"Why?" I asked her. I had to stop doing that.

"Because I know you well enough to tell when something's eating at you," Tony answered.

"Tell him," Maxie repeated. "He's your friend. If you can't tell him, who *can* you tell?" Now she was beginning to sound rational, and I knew *that* couldn't be good.

"Did you know that the woman who owned this house before me died here?" I said. At least I'd be able to talk to Tony about the murders, I figured.

"Yeah, you told me about that," he answered. He picked up the saw. "Hold that level right there, okay? I don't want to go over the lines at all if I can help it." I did as he asked. "Is that what's bothering you? Do you think the house is haunted or something? Are you still seeing things?"

"You should be so haunted, big guy," Maxie murmured.

"Don't be ridiculous," I said in her direction. "It just bothers me that I'm coming into a place—you know, a place I'm staking a lot of my life on—and it has bad karma."

Tony began to saw, carefully and slowly, on the line he'd drawn. That he can maintain that concentration and hold a conversation at the same time has always astonished me. "Bad karma? If I recall, the woman and her boyfriend killed themselves with sleeping pills or something, right?"

"Boyfriend!" Maxie said. "Tell him I don't have a boyfriend—at the moment."

"That's the thing," I told Tony. "It wasn't her boyfriend; he was a private investigator she'd hired to look into some threatening messages she's gotten. And they didn't commit suicide—somebody killed them."

Tony had made it all the way down the left side and was starting on the right. "How do you know?" he asked. "They pop out of the walls one night, rattle their chains and tell you their sad story?"

"I found her laptop and saw the e-mails. I've been getting the threatening messages, too," I said.

He almost cut outside the line. Almost. "What?" Tony stopped sawing. "Someone's threatening you? Why didn't you tell me?"

"I've been getting crank e-mails," I said. "I didn't think it was serious until I found the messages that had been left for Maxie."

"Maxie? That the private dick?"

Maxie's eyes widened and her mouth dropped open in disappointment. She actually stammered. I have to admit to a certain enjoyment.

"No, that was the woman. Maxie Malone. The PI was Paul Harrison."

"Some great PI if they both got killed on his watch."

"I don't think she told him enough to help," I answered. Maxie sneered. As usual.

"You really have been looking into this, haven't you?" Tony asked.

"Sure. If somebody told you that you were going to die if you didn't leave your brand-new house-slash-business, wouldn't you look into it?"

Tony had been lining up the saw again, but now stopped cold. "You got an e-mail saying you'd die if you don't get out of the house?"

"I believe I just said that."

"Alison. That's more than just a little prank. You've got to call the police."

And I would have told him—I swear, I would have—but my cell phone rang at that very moment. Tony put down the saw as I pulled it out of my jeans pocket.

"Ms. Kerby, this is Detective McElone of the Harbor Haven Police Department." Good to know I wasn't getting calls from Detective McElone of the local Carvel.

"Is my laptop ready to pick up?" I asked.

"As a matter of fact, it is," she said. "And I have a few questions to ask you."

"Me? I don't like the way that sounds, Detective."

Tony shot a look at me when he heard that. I nodded. *Yes, I did call the cops. Happy now?*

"Well, you should know that I traced the source of those e-mails you've been getting." McElone sounded . . . I don't know. Triumphant, maybe? I didn't like it.

"Really? That's great! Have you arrested the guy yet?"

"No. And it's not a guy."

A woman was sending me threatening e-mails? Could Terry Wright really have been hiding *that* much?

"I'm confused, Detective," I said. "Who's been sending me threatening e-mails?"

"Apparently," McElone said, "you have."

Sixteen

The Harbor Haven Police Department's conference room took on an eerie quality once the sun went down, I discovered. It wasn't so much because of the windows—the room didn't have any. It was because this time, I was being treated like a suspect. Sort of.

After giving me back my laptop (but refusing to return Maxie's, which I guess I couldn't argue with, as it was never mine to begin with), then dealing with Tony's relatively heated suggestions that the Harbor Haven police weren't doing enough to protect me, the detective got down to business.

"The e-mail addresses that sent the threatening messages—both on your laptop and on Maxine Malone's, came from public computers," Detective Anita McElone said. "These came from the Harbor Haven Free Public Library."

"So there's a homicidal librarian stalking me after getting Maxie Malone and Paul Harrison?" I asked.

"The cops wouldn't know if they were," Tony mumbled. "To serve and protect. Huh!" McElone wrinkled her brow at him.

Jeannie extended her arm, holding a slice of pizza. "You want this, Alison?" she asked.

Tony and I had run into Jeannie and Melissa, pizza in hand, as we left the house—hurriedly—to come to the police station. So we told them where we were going, packed into my 1999 Volvo station wagon and went off together. When McElone had tried to keep my entourage outside in the waiting area, I had refused to budge without them. Rather than charge me with resisting arrest (especially since she wasn't arresting me—yet), McElone gave up and let us all in.

I shook my head, letting Jeannie know I'd had enough pizza. She then offered the slice to McElone, practically shoving it into her face.

"Whoa!" The detective waved her hand. "Somebody went heavy on the garlic!"

"We like garlic," Melissa said. "It's good for your heart." McElone declined the pizza anyway, and Jeannie started in on it herself.

My cell phone rang and indicated my mother was calling, presumably to ask if my head hurt. I decided this wasn't the time.

"The library," I reminded McElone.

"Yes. The library. They have public computers with Internet access. You go in and sign on and you can do pretty much anything you want. A favorite of pervs, the unemployed and kids who don't have a computer at home, but have homework that requires Internet research."

"What's a perv?" Melissa asked, and McElone looked embarrassed. *Good.*

I ignored my daughter's question. "That's a fascinating civics lesson," I told McElone, taking a swig of the Diet Coke I'd scored off the police department vending machine. "But how does it lead to me sending bloodthirsty e-mails to myself?"

"You can't get access to the computers without getting a librarian to swipe your library card. And on each occasion when you were sent one of these supposedly threatening e-mails, the library records clearly show that the library card used was your own." McElone studied my face closely, no doubt to see if I'd make some telltale mistake that would betray my guilt. I squelched a burp from the soda.

"That's insane," I said. "I haven't had a Harbor Haven library card since high school. I haven't had time to get a new one since I moved back here from Red Bank."

"The library records show one was opened for you about six weeks ago, just about the time you closed on your house. Your public accommodations license was used as a form of identification."

In the back of the room, Tony cleared his throat. "What about the e-mails on Maxie Malone's computer?" he asked McElone. "Even if Alison got a library card six weeks ago, she couldn't have sent those from the library last year."

"No," McElone admitted. "Those were all sent from the Bagel Nook Internet Café in Sea Haven, where you don't need ID, just money, to get access."

"My mom doesn't go to Sea Haven," Melissa said, trying to stand up for me. Bless her heart.

"You don't know what she does when you're in school," McElone said, in what I assume was her "gentle" tone. It sounded more like cast iron being sanded, but it was an attempt, I suppose.

"Neither do you," Melissa shot back. That kid was getting ice cream for dessert tonight. And if she didn't want me to flirt with her history teacher, I wouldn't. A mother's bond with her daughter is sacred. Don't tell my mother I said that.

"I don't think I should say anything else unless you

want to arrest me," I said. "And if you do, I want to talk to my lawyer."

"I'm not arresting you," McElone said. "Not yet."

"Why not?" Melissa asked, downgrading her dessert to frozen yogurt.

"Because I don't have anything except the e-mails." Give McElone credit: She treated Melissa like a person. Most grown-ups talk to kids as if they're mentally challenged trained chimpanzees. "I still think those two people committed suicide, and sending yourself threatening e-mails is crazy, but it isn't a crime. Besides"—she gestured for Melissa to lean in closer, and my daughter did so—"I don't think she did it."

"You don't?" Melissa was now down to Tofutti, and headed toward a brussels sprout sundae.

"No. She bought the old Preston place to turn into a B and . . . a guesthouse."

"So?" Melissa asked, having no impact on her after-dinner options.

"Anyone who'd buy that place isn't smart enough to pull this off."

"That's not a very nice thing to say," Melissa told her.

We headed to the ice cream parlor as soon as McElone let us go.

Seventeen

"They think *you* killed us?" Paul asked the next afternoon.

He was standing in the living room, but his feet, up to the ankles, were sunk into the floor. I got the impression that Paul and Maxie hadn't entirely mastered the art of being ghosts over the past year.

Which was just as well, since they'd have plenty of time to perfect it.

"No," I answered. "They—or at least Detective McElone—still think you killed yourselves."

"That's absurd," he said, shaking his head. "We barely knew each other. Why would we both decide to commit suicide on the same night?"

I rolled my eyes to indicate that I'd already made that point to McElone. Then I got a roll of masking tape out of my tote bag and reached into my jacket pocket for the paint color cards I'd picked up that morning. I started taping them to the walls in strategically selected spots.

Paul looked puzzled.

"I'm trying to decide on a color for this room," I explained. "You tape the cards up to see what the paint color looks like from a distance and in different lights." He nodded.

Maxie's head thrust itself through the living room ceiling. She took a quick look around the room and sneered. "*Man*, you're boring!" she snorted.

I peeled my stomach off the floor—I'm still not used to heads appearing from the ceiling—and scowled up at her. "What do you mean, boring?" I asked.

"That's, like, eight different shades of white. How white do you want your front room to be?"

"They're not eight different shades of white. They're almond, chalk, beige, cream, tan, flax . . ."

"Booooooooorrrrriiiiiiiinnngggg." From upstairs, I heard a giggle.

"Is Melissa up there with you?" The last thing I needed was for Maxie to become a role model for my nine-year-old.

"Melissa *who*?" My daughter's voice came from the upstairs bedrooms. Then she laughed again.

"Melissa Jane Kerby, you get down here this minute!" Suddenly, I sounded like the mother on *Father Knows Best*. Nick at Nite must have been leaking into my brain.

"Oh, Mom!" That was it—this was 1953, and I should have been in a cocktail dress with pearls while I sanded down the windowsills.

"All right, stay up there, but don't listen to a word that . . . spirit says to you!"

Paul looked sincerely amused.

"Eight shades of white," Maxie taunted.

"I suppose you have a better idea? A woman who painted her walls the color of blood?"

"I was going for a different effect."

She floated down all the way through the ceiling as I heard Melissa protest. "Maxie!" The ghost put her hand to her chin, clearly appraising the room and its configuration.

"Every two-bit B and B down the shore does the coral and turquoise," she said. "It's all so beachy. You want to go with white walls? Fine. Make a statement—paint the walls bright white and the molding bright red. No. Blue. Navy blue."

I curled my lip. Who was this ghost to tell me how to decorate my own . . .

Wait a minute. She was right. That would be different *and* classy.

Damn it!

"I don't know . . ." I said, to save face. "I'll have to think about it."

From behind me, I heard Paul stifle a laugh. "You're not helping," I told him.

Maxie took on a look of absolute smugness, said nothing and retreated back to the upstairs. I heard Melissa hoot with laughter a few moments later.

I started taking the color cards down off the walls, purposely avoiding eye contact with Paul. But he went on as if nothing had happened.

"How can we convince them that Maxie and I were murdered?" he said.

"Why don't you go haunt Detective McElone?" I suggested.

"Don't you think I would if I could?"

I got some sandpaper out of the toolbox in the corner and wrapped it around a block. Some of the molding needed sanding before I could repaint it, and it was too delicate a job for an electric sander. I sat on the floor. I would have to work around the window seat, with its grillwork front that housed the radiator.

"Suppose I wrote you a note?" Paul asked.

I looked at him. "You can do that?"

He nodded. "Well, I'm not great at it. It takes me a lot of

time and concentration and, frankly, I'm exhausted afterward. But Maxie's quite good at manipulating physical objects."

"Like she did with the rubber mallet and the bucket of compound," I said. "Among other things."

Paul looked sheepish. "Maxie's a lot better at it than I am," he said again.

"What would the note say? Something like, 'I was murdered' might be a little suspect."

He pursed his lips. "Good point. Suppose . . . suppose . . ."

"Paul," I interrupted. "Who do *you* think killed you?"

"That's the thing," he said after a moment. "It could have been anybody."

I spent the rest of the day in the basement, wrestling with the furnace. Maxie stood over my shoulder, self-satisfied. Now that I'd clearly decided to take her suggestion for a color scheme, she wanted to talk about every detail. I just wanted to replace the thermostat and see if that made my house warmer.

"What are you going to do about window treatments in the front room?" she asked as a drop of sweat fell on my nose. I'd turned the furnace off for this repair, but the work was still hot. "You don't want to go too dark in there—let the windows do their job."

"Thank you, Ms. Stewart," I said. "Or may I call you Martha? I'm not there yet. Let me get the walls in shape first. And since when are you the authority on interior design?"

She pouted. Seriously. Her lower lip actually rolled down over itself, and she frowned. "It's what I was going to do," she said.

I rubbed the drop off my nose and got back to work. "You weren't going to turn this place into a business?"

I asked. "I didn't figure you'd live here all alone. I read your . . . an article about you."

"My obituary," Maxie said without inflection. "What did it say? Can you get a copy online? I want to see it." So much for my attempt at being discreet to protect her feelings.

"I'll try to find it. It said you were a graphic artist and that you are survived by your mother in Ocean Township and a brother in Enid, Oklahoma."

"Yeah," was all Maxie said.

Time to switch gears again. "So, why did you need all this house?"

"I was going to flip it," she explained.

"Flip it? You bought it to fix it up and sell it again?" I just wanted to show her that I knew what *flip* meant.

"Yeah. I figured even in this economy I could make some money with a beachfront property." Maxie stared out the window at the wraparound porch on the house across the street. "I guess this house was valuable enough for someone to kill me for it."

"If you just wanted the money, why not sell to Adam Morris?"

Maxie stared at me as if I were suggesting she set the Louvre on fire. "He was going to knock it down," she said.

After investing so much of my time building up a healthy dislike for Maxie, this was hardly the way I wanted the conversation to go—the last thing I needed was to sympathize with her. The worst thing I could do was *care*.

Ignoring Maxie, I grabbed a paper towel, spit on one corner and rubbed the grime off the glass tube that indicated the furnace's water level. What I had wasn't really a furnace as much as a boiler, and the heating system was run by hot water.

"That's gross," Maxie said.

"You sound like Melissa."

Maxie's face changed in a half second, and she brightened. "That's one terrific girl you've got there," she said.

Oh sure, say nice things about my kid now! Hating Maxie was getting even harder.

"I like to think so," I said, trying to sound objective. "She seems to like you, too. You know, she won't play board games with just anybody." Melissa had said she and Maxie played the Game of Life the night before, which seemed ironic.

"She's ruthless," Maxie said. "That kid will hold you to every rule."

"I know. She told me about your cheating."

"I didn't *cheat*!" Maxie insisted. "I just . . . didn't do what I was supposed to. It's different."

"Uh-huh. That's called cheating."

"You would say that. You're on her side, no matter what."

"That's right," I said. "I'm her mother. I'm sure your mom would . . ."

"*My* mother never approved of anything I did in my life," Maxie cut me off. "From beginning to end, she thought I was a screw-up."

"So I guess you don't want me to get in touch with her."

"No," Maxie intoned.

I pulled the old thermostat out and held up the new one for positioning. Luckily, I'd gotten the right replacement part, and it would fit. In a few hours, I'd know if the change made any difference. "Just, if you wanted me to tell her you're—"

"No!" Maxie shouted. "Which part of *no* are you having trouble with?" Maxie walked through the wall into the side room, which I was planning on making a library. "Geez, you're a pain!"

Now, *that* was the Maxie I'd come to know. And dislike.

Eighteen

"Mom?" Melissa looked out the window of the station wagon. It's nice to drive around the Jersey Shore in the fall. The traffic from the summer visitors is gone, the trees change color and the ocean, although grayer, still has a calming rhythm. "Why don't you like Maxie?"

Living with a nine-year-old can be like living with a combination of an investigative reporter and a district attorney. There's always a question, and you're usually under suspicion. And when I got home, I knew that there'd also be a ghost asking me more questions about everything I'd done today. I was feeling a little picked on, to be honest. "What makes you think I don't like Maxie?" I asked, dodging.

Melissa rolled her eyes. I elicit that response from her on a regular basis. "I can see, and I can hear. That's what."

"Okay, let me ask *you* a question: Why do you *like* Maxie?"

Melissa answered after thinking a moment, but her

cadence was that of a fourth grader reciting a memorized response for a class. "I like Maxie because she's fun and doesn't worry about anything," she said. "And she has good taste in decorating."

"Did Maxie tell you to say that?" It was the "decorating" part that really gave her away.

"A little, but I still believe it. Except I'm not sure about the whole 'good taste' thing," my daughter told me honestly.

"Why do you care whether or not I like Maxie?"

"Why does every question I ask you become a different question you ask me?" Melissa said.

"Because I'm the mom." When you don't have an answer that makes sense, you can always use that one. You're welcome.

The Acura in front of me was enjoying the fall scenery just a little too much, and was therefore driving at a speed of fifteen miles an hour in a twenty-five-mile-per-hour zone. This is what we in New Jersey call a crime against nature. I honked. The car didn't speed up.

"I don't want you to get too attached to Paul and Maxie," I told Melissa, "because sooner or later, we'll figure out a way to get them out of the house."

"*What?*" Melissa demanded. "You want to get rid of them?"

"I'll admit, I haven't read any ghost stories for a couple of decades, but yeah. Isn't that what we're supposed to do? Take care of their 'unfinished business' so they can leave, right?" That Acura was following my route, but before I could follow it myself. Every turn I wanted to make, he made first. And all on single-lane roads. I couldn't pass the Acura, no matter how slowly it crawled along.

"No!" Melissa wailed. "You can't just put them out on the street!"

"These aren't stray dogs we're talking about, Liss. They need to move on to . . . the next stage of existence." I made that part up on the spot. "It's not up to us."

"You're just doing this because you think I like Maxie better than you. I don't, you know."

I turned my head to stare at her. "I think . . ."

And that was when I hit the Acura.

It wasn't a really hard collision; we weren't going nearly fast enough for that. But the sound was still loud and blunt enough to cause an adrenaline rush and some heart pounding. "Are you all right?" I asked Melissa.

Eye-rolling. "Of *course* I'm all right," she said. "You were going, like, five."

I avoided her judgmental gaze and looked at the car in front of me. It didn't look like the damage was very severe. I pulled our station wagon over to the shoulder so traffic could flow by, and the Acura did the same. Then a man got out of the car to assess the damage.

It was Mr. Barnes, Melissa's history teacher. And he was just as attractive as I remembered. I, of course, looked like I had been sanding baseboards all morning. Because I had.

"Get the insurance card out of the glove compartment," I told Melissa. I opened the car door while trying to smooth my hair down, but sea air doesn't really help all that much, even in October.

Melissa handed me my insurance card, and I walked over to the Acura to assess the damage.

"Mr. Barnes! I am *so* sorry," I said. "It was totally my fault."

"That kind of attitude isn't going to be at all helpful in court," he said. "You're supposed to be belligerent. Didn't you know that?" He smiled.

Wow. The blue eyes and the dimples really created an effect.

It took me a few seconds to catch my breath. "I'm sorry. It's my first accident. I'll get better."

"Your first? I'll be gentle." He smiled again. I was going to have to sit down soon. "But I'm afraid it was my fault. I was trying to find your house, and you know, you're a little off the beaten path, so I was driving very slowly. It's no wonder you hit me."

"You were trying to find my house?"

He nodded. "Remember? I asked about seeing it? As a . . . study, sort of? I've sent you a few notes through Melissa, but . . ."

"Something tells me she might have . . . forgotten to tell me," I said, glancing back at the station wagon, where Melissa was pretending to ignore us.

"I thought it might be something like that," Mr. Barnes agreed.

I handed him my insurance card. "Here. Just write down the information. I'm sure they'll pay for the repair."

He took a moment to assess the damage again. "What repair?" He handed me the card back. "There's not enough damage to bother. A little rubbing compound and it'll look just like new. Probably better—it'll be the first time I've washed the bumper in years."

"Are you sure?" If I could just see *his* insurance card, I could finally find out his first name. "I don't want you to have to drive around with a dent just because it's my first accident."

"I'm certain," he said. "But if I could get that tour of the house . . ."

Oh man, not now! Not while my face—I mean, the *house*—looked like this. "I'd love to show you the house, honestly, I would. But Melissa and I are meeting her grandmother for dinner, and we just don't have the time. Can we maybe set up a time?" I'd apologize to my mother later for using her as a fictional excuse. If I told her about this at all.

"Not a problem," he answered. "But I'm going to hold you to that tour. And listen, Melissa is a terrific student. She's really smart, and she really cares. Those don't often go together."

I never know what to say when someone compliments Melissa. I mean, *I* think she's wonderful, but I'm her mom.

Thinking she's great is sort of reflexive. "Thank you," I said. "It's nice when someone notices."

"It's part of my job," he said. "But yes, I noticed. You and her father must be very proud." What do you know—he was looking at my hand and noting the absence of a ring!

"Her father lives in Los Angeles," I said. "We're divorced."

"Well, then," he said. He took a deep breath. "Maybe we can settle this situation over dinner."

Hey, if he was asking me out when I looked like this, he'd be bowled over if I showed up to dinner disguised as a human female. "I'd like that," I managed to croak out.

"Great. How's Friday night?"

We exchanged phone numbers and agreed on a place and time, and I was about to head back to the station wagon when I couldn't avoid the issue anymore. "There's just one thing," I said.

Barnes, walking toward his car, turned back. "What's that?"

"I don't know your first name. Melissa always calls you Mr. Barnes, and I feel that would be awkward on a date, don't you think?"

He smiled again, and the same dimples appeared. Dangerous. "Ned."

Ned? Really? There are still people named Ned?

"Nice to meet you, Ned." I walked back to the Volvo (which, in accordance with its reputation, had suffered not a scratch) and got in on the driver's side.

Melissa, arms folded, was waiting for me. "That took long enough," she said.

"It's grown-up stuff. You wouldn't understand."

She twisted her bottom lip. "You were flirting with him, weren't you?"

Busted. "I had to," I said. "Our insurance card expired last month."

Eye-rolling.

Nineteen

"What do you suppose Ned is short for?" I asked Tony.

Tony was studying the plaster mold he'd made of the crevasse in my hallway wall and concentrating. "Edward. Why?" He and Jeannie had been quiet about it, but since he'd heard there had been threats made against me, one or both of them had been calling or dropping by at least once a day. They were watching us, in a nice way.

My mother, who was more obvious without even knowing there was anything to worry about, was in the kitchen unloading groceries she thought I could use, like paper plates, plastic utensils, plastic cups and other things that were destined to destroy the environment.

I was grateful for her help, but wished she'd stay home.

"But there's no *N* in Edward," I told Tony.

Tony measured the mold for the sixth time, then went back and measured the hole in the wall for the seventh. "Okay, so *Nedarsky*. Why do I care what Ned is short for?"

"Melissa's history teacher is named Ned Barnes," I told

him. From inside the kitchen, I could hear Mom talking to herself. She had done that since I was little. I worried that I'd start soon.

Tony looked up from his measuring. "Uh-oh."

"What? Something wrong with the mold?"

"No, you. Worrying about Melissa's history teacher's name. I'm guessing this Ned isn't some sixty-two-year-old guy with thinning gray hair and liver spots."

I tried not to look him in the eye. "We're going to dinner Friday night," I said.

Paul suddenly appeared through the floor, startling me, but I couldn't say anything with Tony in the room. I gasped a little, and Tony took that as a cute little signal of my interest in Ned. He grinned and said nothing, then walked to the section of wall with the hole in it, and dipped a trowel into the bucket of plaster he'd left on the floor near there.

"With whom are you going to dinner on Friday?" Paul asked. Canadians can be so grammatically correct.

"I don't see why you think a simple friendly dinner with Melissa's history teacher is so significant," I said, ostensibly to Tony.

"You're having dinner with Melissa's history teacher?" Mom, in sneakers so she could, you know, *sneak* up on me, stood at the end of the hall.

"I'll tell you about it later, Mom," I said. "It's not a big deal."

"When you say that," she reminded me, "it's usually a big deal." Then she turned and walked back toward the kitchen.

Paul glowered. "If the repairs to the house are taking up so much time that you might not be able to investigate our deaths, I don't see how you have time for a social life," he interjected. He already felt I wasn't giving the investigation the time it deserved. He got cranky whenever I came back to the house to work, rather than going out on some mission he'd devised.

"So just calm down," I added.

"I am calm," Tony said as he spread plaster on the wooden studs in the wall that he'd exposed when we (okay, he) measured for the mold's dimensions. "I want this to be wet when we put it in," he said. "We can't screw it to the studs the way you would with wallboard; it would break."

"You are a genius," I reminded him.

"We'll see." Tony finished spreading the wet plaster, and motioned me to the right side of the mold, which was resting on two sawhorses a few feet from the wall. "Get over there, and lift when I say."

So I did. "I mean, it's really *not* a big deal," I said, returning to the topic of my date. "We had a minor fender bender, and he offered to buy me dinner to discuss it." Okay, so I fudged it a bit, but I had to wipe that smirk off Tony's face and the frown off Paul's.

"You're insured, right?" Mom called from the kitchen.

"Unpack!" I shouted.

I had no better luck in this room—Tony's smirk just got bigger, and Paul's frown didn't budge. "Uh-huh," Tony said. He walked to the left side of the mold, took hold of it and nodded for me to do the same. "Gently," he said.

We gingerly lifted the mold, about three feet square, and moved slowly to the wall. "Now, just *rest* it on the studs," Tony said. "Don't try to force it. It'll be a little bit smaller than the hole; we can fill it in later." We maneuvered the mold into its space. It seemed to fit almost perfectly into the hole, but I was convinced that if I let go, it would fall and shatter.

"Hang on," Tony said. He took a length of two-by-four he'd left on the floor and propped it up against the mold to steady it. "Okay. Let go."

I did, and the patchwork piece did not move. We stood and admired it for a long moment. "I told you," I said. "You're a genius."

"We'll see," said Tony.

"Stop saying that."

We stood and stared at it for some time, hardly believing there was something approximating a whole wall where there hadn't been before. Tony, convinced the patch was steady, removed the two-by-four, and the patch held. We both exhaled.

"So tell me about this history teacher," Tony said.

"Yes, Alison," Mom called in. "Let's hear."

And that was when Maxie appeared, walking directly through the section of wall where we'd just placed the mold. "Ooh, look who's here," she said, *whooshing* into the room with more gusto than she should have.

The mold began to wobble and, before either Tony or I could reach it, had cracked on both sides where it met the studs and collapsed onto the floor, where it crashed into a ridiculous number of pieces. And some dust. A lot of dust.

"Oops," Maxie said. "My bad."

My jaw moved up and down a few times. No sound came out. Tony sighed and nodded, as if he'd expected this to happen.

"I guess we'll have to think of something else," he said.

Twenty

When Terry Wright had failed to call back and give me the Prestons' new address, I tried googling them and came up with nothing. But then I remembered what a great friend Bridget Bostero had said she was to the couple, and I figured that since the mayor and I were now tight buddies, I could call and get the information from her.

"Oh, I'm sure they'll be delighted to hear from you," Bridget told me on the phone, although I couldn't think of a reason why they would be. I didn't ask.

"Thanks for the help," I told her.

"I checked on that thing you asked me about," the mayor volunteered. What thing?

"Oh, that wasn't necessary," I told her, although, for all I knew, it might have been vital.

"I love helping," said my public servant. "Chief Daniels assures me that the investigation into those two deaths at your house is ongoing, just as I told you."

She had told me nothing of the sort. "The investigation is ongoing?" I repeated.

"Mm-hmm. The chief says the case is still open. But I can't give you any more details, you know, because the case is . . . open."

Right. "Well, thank you, Mayor," I said.

"Not at all," she said. "And let me know if you're interested in that hair coloring we discussed."

Madeline Preston was a gracious hostess. She had put out a plate of cookies, which appeared to be home baked, and a pot of coffee, which she assured me was decaffeinated because, "I wasn't sure, and when you're not sure, it's better to go without." I couldn't argue with that. I could have used the caffeine, though. After I'd kicked Tony and Mom out of the house and cleaned up the broken plaster and the dust myself, Paul had once again gotten after me about the investigation, without so much as an apology from him or Maxie about the damage done to my wall-repair plans. Ghosts, it should be noted, can be infuriating.

"We were surprised to hear from you," Madeline said.

Her husband, David, walked in and immediately picked up a chocolate chip cookie before I could introduce myself. When he held out his hand to shake, I got a smear of chocolate on my thumb.

"A pleasure," he mumbled through a bite.

Before either of them could start asking questions, I sailed right in. "I've been wondering about why you sold the house," I said. The two of them sat staring at me for a few seconds, and I realized I hadn't phrased my opening in the form of a question. "So, why *did* you sell the house?" I asked.

"The children had all grown up and moved away," Madeline said politely, but her expression clearly said,

Why did this nosy person drive all this way—(it was actually only a twenty-minute drive from Harbor Haven to Eatontown, but I was projecting)—*to ask why we've moved out of the house she bought?* "The place was just too big and too quiet. And David was tired of all the maintenance the house required."

"Are we starting this again?" her husband said. "I dug up the well for you; I must have dug fifty other holes in that backyard in the last two years. What else did you want?"

I was going to interject, but Madeline just went on. "It wasn't just the *gardening*," she told me. "It was the painting, and the cracks in the walls, and the kitchen. You know how old houses are."

"I'm finding out," I agreed.

"It's different when you're not in your thirties anymore." David tried to defend himself. "I'm not a young man, and all that digging . . ."

"Oh, enough, David." Madeline scowled. "Poor Alison will think we didn't like the house."

Poor Alison?

"I understand," I said, although the opposite was true. "I'm just getting used to the burdens of homeownership. I'm sure it got difficult for you after all those years." *That's right, Alison, butter them up by calling them old. Nice work.*

"We didn't even know the house had been sold again," Madeline said. "We sold it to a young woman on her own named Maxie." She smiled, indicating she thought Maxie was a cute name.

"Yes, I was wondering—I heard that Adam Morris had wanted to buy the house. I hope you don't mind my asking, but why didn't you sell it to him?"

It was David who spoke up, with a grumpy look on his face. "Morris came in a month after we'd sold it. We could have made a lot more." He looked distraught over that last part, and consoled himself with another cookie.

"Well, I'm sure you heard about what happened to the woman who bought it from you," I answered, half hoping Madeline would rise to the bait and confess.

"No, what happened?" she said, looking concerned.

Swell. I told her about Maxie's death, and Madeline looked positively stricken.

"David," Madeline said, "that's just awful. Can you believe that poor girl killed herself in the house?" She said *the house* in a way that obviously referred only to one house, the one she clearly still thought of as "home."

"That's awful," David agreed through a bite of oatmeal raisin. If his voice had any more inflection, it would have had inflection.

"I'm not sure she did," I said. "It's possible something else happened."

"You think it was an accident?" Madeline asked.

"No."

Madeline's eyes took on an expression of absolute clarity, and registered *FEAR* in bright neon letters that could probably be seen from space.

"You think she was killed?" she asked.

"I really can't say," I answered. *Because you would think I was nuts.*

Madeline shot a glance toward her husband, who was eyeing the rest of the cookies and did not return it. Suffice it to say that she didn't appear pleased, neither with my answer nor with David's cookie fetish.

It was my cue to go on. "I was just asking because I'm doing some renovations now, and I've found a few things that were, I dunno, odd, I guess." *Like dead people who still hang out in the house.*

"Odd?" Madeline asked as David threw caution to the wind and dove on a peanut butter–chocolate chip. "Odd in what way?"

Luckily, Paul had coached me on what to say here. "I get the feeling there have been other renovations on the house, and I'm trying to pinpoint when they were made."

David was chewing his cookie, so after replying, he had to repeat himself: "Of course there were renovations. The house is more than a hundred years old."

"For example," I went on, trying not to look at his mouth while he spoke and ate, "the kitchen was obviously redone, but I can't tell when. Did you do the upgrade?" You learn words like *upgrade* when you're researching how to open a guesthouse.

"Yes," Madeline said proudly. As if the kitchen I'd just gutted had been a legitimate source of pride. "We did the entire room from the ceiling down in the seventies, sometime. New cabinets, new countertop and new appliances. I think we even did the floor in there, didn't we, David?"

David made a noise, but I think it was more related to digestion than renovation.

"If I might be so bold," Madeline said, "I'd like to ask *you* a question, Alison."

"Sure."

"We heard from the real estate agent, Terry Wright, and she mentioned something about you finding some old documents in a kitchen drawer."

I could feel my face flush. "I'm sorry about that, Madeline," I said. "I have to admit, I misled Terry because I wanted to come meet you myself; I didn't want her just answering my questions for me."

Madeline's face took on an intensity that hadn't been there before—she was interrogating me, rather than having a conversation. "So you didn't find any documents?"

I felt like she was standing over me, but she was still seated on the couch. "No, nothing," I stammered, almost adding *Your Honor,* but catching myself at the last second. "Should I have found something?"

Madeline's eyes closed off communication with me. "Of course not," she said.

There wasn't time to get in another question—and Paul had wanted me to ask who they'd bought the house from themselves, and what kind of condition it had been in then. It was clear that the house was the center of the matter, the reason he and Maxie had been murdered and why I was getting threatening e-mails. So I was ready to jump in on that line of questioning.

I would have, too, except that the phone rang.

Now, I've seen people who are startled by a noise in the room, even one as familiar as a phone ringing. I've seen people who are alarmed at any sudden noise, no matter its source. I've even seen people who would rather screen all their calls than answer a ringing telephone, especially when entertaining company in the house.

But Madeline wasn't startled, surprised or worried about my opinion of her as a hostess. She was absolutely frightened beyond all reason.

"Don't answer it!" she yelled at David when he turned his head in the direction of the phone. *"Don't you dare answer that phone!"*

David stood up, and Madeline's pale complexion went absolutely white. "No, David, *please*," she pleaded. "It's *them*!"

"Just calm down, Maddie," he said. "You don't know who's calling."

"What's wrong?" I asked Madeline, ignoring her husband entirely. "Who's calling that has you so—"

"It's nothing," David jumped in. Great. Before, I couldn't get him to open his mouth, and now he was answering questions that weren't directed at him. I shot him an unkind look, but he went on. "Madeline believes someone is stalking her." He practically guffawed.

The phone kept ringing. Did these people not *own* an answering device?

"They *are*," Madeline moaned. She turned to me, her momentary ally. "People have been threatening us—

threatening *me*. And if you want to know the truth, *that's* why we sold the house. Because of *that*!"

"Maddie!" David shook his head in disbelief that she'd told me something they had clearly held in confidence. "We haven't gotten one of those calls since we moved. Calm down."

Finally, the ringing stopped, and in the next room I could hear David's voice on an answering machine say, "It's David and Madeline. Please leave a message after the beep."

Madeline's eyes widened to the size of hubcaps in the second between David's message and the tone indicating the caller should speak. She drew in her breath.

And the caller said, clearly, "This is Monica's Tailor Shop. Your pants are ready. We're open until five." And hung up.

Madeline Preston deflated in front of my eyes. She seemed to become smaller, flatter and weaker in the time it would take most people to blink. And then she did the weirdest thing I could have imagined she'd do.

She smiled at me.

"So, dear," Madeline said. "Was there anything else you wanted to ask?"

Twenty-one

A kitchen is like a jigsaw puzzle.

No, it's not.

A kitchen is like a house of cards: You pull out one wrong piece and the whole thing collapses.

No, that's not it, either.

A kitchen, when all is said and done, is like a kitchen. But it has so many functions, so many stations, so many moving parts and systems that it's not like any other room in a house.

The sad truth is: A kitchen is a pain in the ass.

And in the interest of full disclosure, I hadn't done much work in the kitchen since the day I'd been conked on the head by a maliciously dropped bucket of wall compound. That had led to me seeing ghosts; if anything else were to go wrong in there, I might start seeing vampires or werewolves, and I honestly didn't think I could handle that.

The two ghosts I *could* see watched me fasten new doors on the refinished cabinets (and even Maxie had agreed they looked wonderful—all right, she hadn't made any disparaging comments, which to Maxie is the same thing as saying they looked wonderful). The next step would be to hang the cabinets back up on the "new" (meaning with cracks filled and freshly painted) walls, but that would require other people to help, and would necessitate getting on a ladder, something I was not yet ready to do in Maxie's presence.

"So the Prestons said that they'd gotten some threatening phone calls, and then she asked if you wanted a cookie?" Paul was all business, as usual. Why did that bother me?

"Not exactly, but the change was just about that abrupt, and then she pretty much shooed me out of the house. What do you suppose it was all about?" I was nearly done with the doors, and then I would have to decide what problem to tackle next.

"Well, from what you've told me, it seems they were as much under siege as you and Maxie have been. Interesting, though, that the Prestons were contacted by phone and not e-mail." Paul stroked his chin in thought.

"Madeline told me they don't have a computer at home, so I guess that would account for the phone calls," I told him. "David said they're not getting calls anymore, but I don't know if I believe him. This one wasn't threatening, though—it was about pants."

"What's *really* confusing is why the Prestons are still alive and we're not." Paul seemed to be speaking to Maxie.

"I don't see the point," she replied. "Even if you figure this out, we'll still be dead."

"Obviously, you seemed to be more of an obstacle to the killer's plans," Paul told Maxie.

I finished the last door and stood back to admire my work. Not bad at all, if I had to say so myself.

"Why would Maxie be more of an obstacle than the Prestons?" I asked Paul.

"I'm formulating an opinion," Paul said. "I think whoever is behind the threats is after something, and Maxie was closer to finding it, or getting it, or doing it, than the Prestons were."

I put the good Phillips-head screwdriver (the one with the wooden handle, which I'd inherited from my grandfather) back in my toolbox and thought about that. "Terry Wright practically salivated when I suggested that I'd found some old papers in a kitchen drawer, and so did Madeline Preston," I said. "You think whoever is behind this is looking for something like that?"

"I don't know," he answered. "I don't have enough facts yet. Alison—"

I didn't like where I thought he was going. "I don't want to question anyone else, Paul," I whined. "Can't I take the rest of the case off?"

He grinned, and I had learned by now that was when I should be most afraid.

"You don't have to question anyone, Alison," he said. "Just do a little breaking and entering."

"Why couldn't I just call Terry up and ask her whatever it is that Paul wants to know?" I said—quietly—into my cell phone.

"Paul says that if Terry finds something missing, she won't be able to prove you took it," Melissa said. She was relaying the messages back and forth from the house. I don't know how she managed to get Jeannie out of the room (it was Tony's bowling night, and Jeannie was babysitting), but my daughter can be really sneaky when necessary. "He says you're safer this way."

"You're just doing this to me because I have a date with your history teacher tomorrow night," I suggested.

"Paul says to think about the task, not your date," Melissa said, icicles forming on her voice.

"I'll bet it wasn't Paul saying that," I muttered.

I hadn't planned on telling Melissa about this particular part of my escapades. A quick B and E isn't exactly fabulous role-model material. But we'd determined through trial and error that Paul's and Maxie's voices didn't carry over telephone lines, so my fear of being alone in this endeavor, without Paul's help every step of the way, won out over maternal responsibility. My character, tested, came up flawed—as usual.

I was standing at the back door to Terry Wright's office, a converted home on Breaker Street with six parking spaces in the back. Paul had given me instructions on how to get through a security system's keypad. I was sure I was screwing it up and that the cops would be coming within sixty seconds.

"And tell the judge that Grandma can't raise you if I'm in jail," I added. "It has to be Tony and Jeannie."

"You don't say stuff like that to a nine-year-old," my nine-year-old scolded me. "I could have nightmares. And Paul says you should just get to work. Tell me everything you're doing in detail. And hurry it up. Jeannie's going to come back with ice cream in a couple of minutes."

"Ice cream! Who said you could have . . ."

"You *said* I should get her out of the room."

I sighed. I was being outmaneuvered by a fourth grader and the sad part was, this was the norm, not the exception. I began working at the keypad, and no, I'm not going to tell you how I did it—that would be encouraging others to commit a crime. I'm not even really admitting *I* did it. It's hypothetical, like that O. J. Simpson book. *If I Broke into Terry Wright's Office*, by Alison Kerby.

Suffice it to say that after a few eternities, a good deal of tense hissing and passed-along instructions from Paul, the following things happened:

1. I got the door open without tripping an alarm;

2. Jeannie came back into the room (Melissa had been lucky that the ice cream had been hard as a rock, and had taken longer to serve);

3. Melissa hung up the phone (the better to stuff herself with Rocky Road, which would undoubtedly lead to her getting sick just about the time I got home), so I was on my own;

4. I was free to "explore" Terry's office.

The idea was this: Terry had answered vaguely when I'd asked her about the house and its history. She'd acted suspiciously when I'd mentioned the fictitious documents I had not, in fact, found in a kitchen drawer. There had been an equally odd reaction by Madeline Preston regarding the same fake documents. So it was possible that Terry had concealed some truth about a document that *could* be hidden in the house.

Paul had led me to his conclusion by invoking that rarest of elements, common sense.

"You don't know yet who was responsible for the e-mail messages to you, do you?" Paul had asked. "Well, consider this: The library card they used was obtained using your public accommodations license, right?"

"That's what Detective McElone said," I'd admitted.

"Who has ever had that license in their hands besides you?" Paul asked.

"Nobody. Except . . ."

Paul's eyes had widened in encouragement. "Who?"

"Terry Wright. She picked up the license the day of the closing on the house and brought it to me."

"So Terry could easily be the one sending you threatening messages." Paul smiled.

"It doesn't make sense. First of all, why would she want

me out of the house? She just sold it to me! And how could she get a library card in my name? Everybody in town must know Terry."

"She could have said she was picking it up for you, just like the license. Or, in a town of eight thousand people, maybe the librarians don't actually know *everybody*. But the *why* is the really intriguing question."

"Intriguing to you, maybe. Frightening to me."

"Okay, what about this: What kind of a document would a real estate agent find so intriguing about a house?" Paul had asked rhetorically. "The kind of thing that would be worth killing two innocent people over? Especially in a house that had been sought feverishly by a real estate developer? That would have to be a real estate document. Like perhaps the title to the house. If there's something hinky about that, it could be the very thing we've been searching for."

"Hinky?" I'd said.

He hadn't answered, and now here I was, searching Terry Wright's office for a copy of the title to my own house.

There had to be something wrong with that, but the logic behind everything that had happened since I'd gotten hit on the head was so twisted that there was no chance I'd ever be able to sort it all out. Better to follow orders blindly.

I didn't turn on the lights. Instead, I took the Maglite out of my pocket and turned it on, as I'd been advised. It helped me to focus on something other than the office's kitten-based décor (now with added cartoon vampires and cat ghosts for Halloween). In two weeks, it would be turkeys dressed as Puritans and after that . . . it was frightening to imagine what Terry might do for Christmas.

The target tonight was any locked file cabinet (since the open ones probably didn't have the *good* stuff). I was somewhat pressed for time, what with being on the premises without, shall we say, the protection of the legal system.

I found three such cabinets at the far end of the office,

thankfully away from the picture window. And having done extensive work with locks in my previous employment life (one of the departments I'd worked in at House-Center involved cutting keys for people and selling locks, and I had done some work with locks at the lumberyard, despite it having nothing to do with my actual job), I could pick through the absurdly rudimentary locks on the files in no time flat—well, no more than ten minutes. Fine. You try it sometime. At least I got them open.

Most of the files were of absolutely no interest to me or, by extension, Paul and Maxie. In fact, the only one that held the slightest bit of promise was—not surprisingly—the one marked with my address, "123 Seafront Avenue."

The plan was that I'd take everything in the file, which seemed massive to me, and copy it to bring back for Paul to peruse at his leisure, of which he had a great deal. But just as I was heading for the copy machine, located in a small room just outside the main office, I heard the exact sound I hadn't wanted to hear.

Someone pressing buttons on the keypad just outside the front door.

I thanked Paul silently for telling me not to turn on the lights, and literally dove into the copy room, where I stayed on the floor, trying to remember any prayers from my misspent youth. The best I could come up with was, "I pledge allegiance to the flag of the United States of America," so I recited that silently as the front door opened wide as Kerin Murphy, blazered and on the job, walked in, juggling a briefcase, an open file, a cup of coffee and the cell phone into which she was talking.

"I'm telling you, they'll come down another six thousand," she was saying. "If we hold out, we can get the property for less than four."

I did my very best to stop breathing temporarily, in the hope that I could avoid anyone making me do so permanently. If Kerin hit the main light switch, there was no chance at all she'd miss spotting me. And for all I knew, she was a homicidal maniac (obviously *somebody* around here was). That was a terrifying thought—the woman was so *thorough* at everything she did.

Kerin struggled with her various loads and stumbled to a desk, where she dumped the briefcase and the file. She held on to the coffee and continued to keep the cell phone in place by craning her neck into a wholly unnatural position.

Then she walked to another desk in the corner of the room, which I could see clearly from my position (and which made me twice as nervous, because that meant she could see me clearly if she chose to look in my direction). That desk, the largest in the room, sat under a photograph of Terry Wright shaking hands with an official-looking man in a business suit. They looked quite pleased with themselves.

"No, Neil," Kerin continued. "I've got the figures right here." And she reached for a light switch.

I racked my brain for a plausible explanation of my position and my presence. Believe me, your brain can go through myriad scenarios in a split second when you're lying on the floor wondering if your last words to your daughter had been about not eating too much ice cream.

But the light switch illuminated only the desk lamp, a Pixar-style Anglepoise bent-necked model, and that actually worked in my favor. Kerin could see what was on her desk, but if she looked in my direction, the lamp would block her view.

"It was at four two seven, but that was six months ago, and the property is still on the market," Kerin went on. "In this market, they'll be thrilled with any price that covers their expenses, believe me."

Now my concern became how long I would have to lie on this threadbare carpet, which smelled of dog. If I could just stay still, and if Kerin would just find the paper she was looking for so she could leave . . .

But Kerin didn't seem to be concerned with anything on her own desk. It was the one that I could only assume belonged to Terry that occupied her time. She started to go through the unlocked drawers. That seemed odd—wouldn't Terry object to an employee searching her desk?

"I've got it right here, Neil," she said, without actually holding a specific document. She opened the top drawer and reached in. "Wait. I'll make a copy for you."

Uh-oh.

But she didn't head for the copy machine, which I considered a major plus. She did pull what appeared to be an address book or daily planner out of the desk and smiled triumphantly.

"You *have* a copy?" Kerin said into her phone. "You make me schlep out here in the middle of the night and you already *have* a copy? What are you doing to me, Neil, seriously?"

She tucked the book under her arm and turned off the desk light, still grinning that strange smile of accomplishment.

"Okay, then. Go ahead and make the offer to your client and call me in the morning, okay? Good night, Neil. Yes, I adore you, too."

Kerin walked back to her own desk and slipped the address book (or whatever) into her briefcase. Then she pushed a button on her cell phone, and almost immediately began talking. "It's me. I've got it. But what do I say when she misses it? Yes, she will. No, I can't come now. I *can't*. I'll drop it off there tomorrow. Now, about the house on Seafront."

What?

She opened the door and redid her balancing act, pushing buttons on the security system to set the alarm again. Swell. Now I'd have to figure out how to get out without setting off sirens from here to the police station.

"I think I have an idea," Kerin said. "All you have to do is . . ."

And she was out the door, which she closed behind her.

After I heard her car pull away, I stood up and peered out the front window. I wasn't happy about being in the office anymore (not that I ever had been happy about it). I looked at the file in my hand. It was thick. And I really wasn't in the mood to stand at the copy machine for an hour, feeling exposed and on edge the whole time.

Still, it made more sense than stealing the file and being exposed to burglary charges, even if I could get out of the office without setting off the alarm. So I trudged back into the copy area and, this time, with all the window shades down, felt confident enough to turn on the light.

And that was when I saw Terry Wright lying on the floor in the back of the room. There was a cup in her hand, and a coffee stain on the rug next to it. Her eyes were wide-open.

She was quite dead.

Twenty-two

"So you broke into Ms. Wright's office and found her dead on the floor of her copy room, is that it?" Detective Anita McElone shook her head and started walking back and forth behind her desk, which didn't take long. It wasn't a large room. "That's about as shaky an explanation as I've ever heard."

"I *told* you," I said. "The office was open when I went in to see the file of my own property, and I must have gotten locked in while I was examining it." It was my first time coming up with such an excuse; I was sure I'd get better at it. "I didn't even know Terry was there until I went in to copy my file. And that's the truth."

McElone stopped pacing and gave me a look that contained as much pity as irritation. She couldn't believe what a complete idiot I was. "It probably is," she said. "I don't think even you are stupid enough to go into her office, kill her, and then call the police to come get you."

"Was it murder?"

"Like I would tell you."

"So, can I leave now?" I picked up my canvas bag from the floor, but the glare I was getting from the detective indicated I'd gone a trifle too far. I put the bag down.

"So far, I've been pretty lenient in the way I've treated you," McElone said slowly, with great gravitas, indicating she was trying very hard not to draw her service weapon and kill me. "But I can't abide breaking and entering, I can't just dismiss you as a suspect and I can't let you off just because you think you're witty."

"Lenient?" I asked. "You hijacked my computer for almost a week, you called me in because you thought I was sending threatening e-mails to myself and now you accuse me of—something—and you think you've been lenient?"

"Nice try," she countered. "But the fact is, you were the only person in the room with a dead woman, and you appear to have broken into her office. That's a serious problem, and I have to tell you in all candor that if I were you, I'd call a lawyer."

"I wasn't the only person in the—" Whoa. "Are you arresting me? Are you telling me my rights?" I asked.

"What did you mean, you weren't the only person there? Who else was there?"

"Depends. Should I call my lawyer?"

McElone curled her lips, irritated. "Fine. I'm not charging you. Yet. Who else was there?"

I told her about Kerin Murphy's visit and the address book she'd seemingly pilfered from Terry's desk. "Does that mean anything? I mean, Terry was clearly already dead before either of us showed up."

McElone didn't get the chance to answer. As she jotted down some notes, her phone rang and she picked it up, spoke quietly enough that I couldn't make out the words and very quickly hung up. "Get going," she said, standing.

"What do you mean, 'Get going?'" I asked. "A second ago you were sending me up the river, and now I can go? What happened?"

"I'll tell you what happened," McElone said, betraying nothing with her tone. "The desk sergeant told me the initial report is that Ms. Wright died of a heart attack."

Twenty-three

"I've never had to bail you out of jail before," my mother said.

"You're not bailing me out of jail," I told her. Again. "You're giving me a ride home until I can go get my car tomorrow."

"Do they think you killed that woman?" Mom asked. She sounded more intrigued than worried.

I'd left the Volvo a couple of blocks from Terry's office, and when the police had come and decided to take me back to the station, I had left it there. Then the cops had asked me where it was parked so they could search it, and they'd impounded it until the next morning. When I'd called Jeannie (with my one phone call, which McElone told me could be two phone calls) to let her know I'd be a lot later than planned, she'd offered Tony as a ride home. But I'd called Mom. Don't ask me why.

Mom drives a Dodge Viper, which she calls her "midlife

crisis car." If this is her midlife, she's going to live to be about a hundred and forty, but okay. We were therefore tooling along looking like we were out to cruise the boardwalk, when in fact she was painfully obeying the speed limit.

"She had a heart attack, Mom. I didn't kill anybody," I said. I left out the part about breaking and entering. I was too tired.

"Of course you didn't," she responded. "You're a good girl."

"Thank you." Maybe that would put an end to the—

She plowed ahead. "So, what were you doing in the office when you found the dead woman?"

"I was just copying some real estate files about the house, that's all."

"You've been acting strange lately," she said.

"I'm not acting. I really am strange," I quipped.

"Oh, you are not," Mom said, slowing down to some sub-ten speed to make a right turn. "Now, what's been going on?"

"Nothing's going on, Mom."

"Of course not." She was pouting.

"Honestly."

No response. For a very long moment.

"I have a date tomorrow night." Maybe I could change the subject.

"I know, Ally." And then she was silent again. For another long moment.

"What do you think Melissa should dress as for Halloween?"

No answer. If I couldn't interest her with her grand-daughter, I was toast.

"Okay, so two people were murdered in my house before I bought it, and I want to find out what happened."

Mom smiled.

"There, now. Was that so hard?"

* * *

Paul was eager to see the copies I hadn't made, Maxie was nowhere to be seen and Jeannie was anxious when I got home. Melissa was supposed to be in bed, but I believed she was upstairs in her room, waiting for the moment she heard the door close and Jeannie's car leave the driveway.

Mom, of course, insisted on coming inside, which made the scene that much more chaotic. Especially since Jeannie had no intention of leaving just yet.

"Okay, you have a *date* and I have to hear about it from *Melissa*?" she growled before I had both feet inside the house. Then she noticed Mom. "Oh. Hi, Mrs. Kerby."

"Call me Loretta," my mother reminded her. "You're a grown-up now."

"Loretta," Jeannie said dutifully, then turned to me. "He's a teacher? Is he cute?" she asked.

"In a minute, Jeannie." I sighed. "It's been a long night."

I sat down on the floor, letting Mom have one of the folding chairs. It was the first time in my life I would have actually killed for a Barcalounger. Paul, hovering near the ceiling, asked, "Where are the files?"

"Your date," Jeannie continued. "Spill the beans, Alison."

"The *files*," Paul insisted. "What did you do with them?"

"I was at Terry Wright's office," I told Jeannie (and Paul). "Terry's dead."

Paul stopped in mid-gesture. I saw Maxie stick her head in from the ceiling, then withdraw it.

Jeannie stared. "But . . . but you said you were going to a PTSO meeting."

"She's dead?" Melissa stood at the bottom of the stairs in her nightdress, eyes wide. I guessed she couldn't bear the wait any longer and had come down.

After the inevitable brouhaha over Melissa's arrival (Mom hugging her, Jeannie scolding her for getting up, me just sitting and waiting), I explained that I had discovered Terry's body at the office, but I left out a few choice details, like the fact that I had broken into the office, that I'd hid from Kerin Murphy and that I had been, at least briefly, a suspect in Terry's death.

"Turned out she had a heart attack," I finished up. Jeannie looked stunned.

"That's so sad," Melissa said.

"So you didn't get the files?" Paul asked. I wasn't sure whether all ghosts were so single-minded, but he certainly had the capacity.

"I know, honey," I said, pulling Melissa onto my lap and holding her close. "It's very sad."

"I can't *believe* you didn't get the files," Paul muttered. I glared at him for a second.

Mom's eyelids fluttered and she frowned for a moment, then she looked at me. "So what's the plan of action?"

Everybody, alive and otherwise, looked at me.

"Plan of action?" I asked. "I'm going to bed. I'm exhausted."

Cries of protest came from every section of the room. I stood up and headed for the stairs.

"But what about your date?" Jeannie asked.

"I'll call you tomorrow. Thanks for the ride, Mom."

My mother looked disappointed, but walked to the front door with Jeannie after Melissa delivered the hugs for which she is so deservedly famous. I reached out my arm after they left, and my daughter walked over and let me lean on her.

"You didn't get . . . ?" Paul started.

"Good night," I said, and went upstairs. Paul did not come up through the floor to continue the conversation, and I went to sleep.

Twenty-four

"So I hear you broke into Terry Wright's office and killed her last night," Phyllis Coates said.

She'd called early this morning to flesh out her story, and offered to drive Melissa to school and me to my car when I mentioned my lack of wheels. An exclusive interview for the *Chronicle* was the price of such service, despite the fact that no other media outlet had called. We'd dropped Melissa off, and were now on our way to my Volvo.

"I *did not*," I insisted.

Phyllis laughed. "Calm down, honey. I don't really think you killed Terry—it was a heart attack. At least that's what my friend in the ME's office says is the official cause of death until the full report comes back. But you *were* there, weren't you?"

I looked away. "I thought so," Phyllis crowed.

"You don't miss a trick, do you?"

"In my business, you can't," she answered. "Newspapers— real ones, dailies—are having enough trouble surviving.

I've got to give people the most local stuff, things they can't even get online, except when I put it there. So I know everyone and everything that goes on in this town."

"You're very good," I told her honestly.

"Thanks. So tell me what you saw."

I told her the story (leaving out Kerin Murphy) on the condition that she not mention my name when writing about it, since I could be incriminating myself in print. After I'd gotten through with the tale, we'd reached the police pound where my Volvo was parked.

"I've heard them all, and that's a new one," Phyllis told me.

"Stick with me, kid," I said. "I'll make you a star." I got out of the car but didn't close the door. "Thanks for the ride, Phyllis."

"Thanks for the story, Alison. I'll let you know when I hear anything from my friend in the ME's office about Terry. I'll know before the cops do."

I shook my head with respect. "That's some friend you have," I told her.

She gave me a significant look. "Viva Viagra," she said.

"You didn't get the files," Paul reminded me later.

"The police took them. What did you want me to do?"

I was expanding the space in one of the guest bedrooms by making one of the closets smaller (people staying for a week don't need as much storage space as full-time residents), so I was wearing goggles and was, at the moment, mostly covered in dust, but I had framed out the new closet almost completely. I could hang the drywall now and fill in the nail holes with compound and taping later. It's grueling, tedious work, but it's not difficult, just time-consuming.

"You saw Kerin Murphy taking something from Terry Wright's desk that it's a safe bet to say was not authorized," he went on. The wheels in his head, although transparent, were always turning. "Tell me again what she did while she was there."

"She talked to somebody named Neil about a real estate deal, then she went into Terry's desk and pulled out an address book or something, and then she hung up and called someone else and said something about the property on Seafront—this house."

"Are you sure?" Paul asked.

"Have you looked outside recently? Everybody else on the block sold out to Adam Morris. This is the only house a real estate agent would have cared about."

Paul stood back—his right arm actually disappeared into the wall—and thought. "Are you sure it was an address book?" he asked.

"It looked like one," I said. "But no, I didn't really get a close look."

"The first thing they teach you in detective school is not to make assumptions," Paul told me. "Describe it to me."

"It was a black book with one of those plastic covers and a spiral binding," I told him. "Not big enough for a file book. I thought it looked like an address book."

"Could it have been an appointment book? A calendar?" Paul had a way of asking questions like he already knew the answers.

"I guess so," I said. "Why?"

"Because that's the kind of thing that could be most damaging. If someone's name is listed on a schedule to meet Terry Wright around the time she died, it could be important to get that item out of the office before the police arrived."

It took me a moment to absorb all that. "You think Kerin Murphy killed Terry?"

"I think it's more likely she was covering up for someone else, even if she didn't know that was what she was doing. But we can't rule her out as a suspect."

"Do you really think Kerin could get herself involved in a murder?" I asked.

"I have no idea. I've only seen her once."

"What about Maxie? Did she know Kerin . . . before?"

Paul shook his head. "I asked, and she said she didn't."

"So, how do we find out what kind of book it was?" I asked Paul. I should've known, though, that Paul would have a plan, because he always did, and I rarely enjoyed hearing them.

"I don't know how I let you talk me into this one," I said out loud as I tailed Kerin Murphy. My cell phone, open, rested on the passenger seat of the Volvo.

I didn't get an answer, and I didn't expect one.

Paul had made sure I'd called the house phone, which was finally working since Verizon had visited the week before, and then I answered it myself. I'd put it on speakerphone and then left, leaving my cell phone on and plugged into the charger in the Volvo.

He couldn't answer me (the ghosts' voices didn't make it through telephones), but he could hear what I said. I felt like I was talking to myself, which was only about the seventeenth weirdest thing I'd done today. And it was just two in the afternoon.

"She's not going to be home, you know," I'd said to the phone. Paul's plan—to trail Kerin Murphy and see where she took the book—seemed to have more holes than a Swiss cheese factory. "She probably dropped the stupid book off with someone last night."

Imaginary Paul in my head said, "She said she couldn't do that. She said on the phone that she'd have to meet with the other person today."

I hate it when the imaginary people in my head are right.

It's very hard to follow someone in a small town,

especially if they know you and your car. Paul had instructed me to stay at least two cars behind Kerin, but there weren't always two cars available, so I did the best I could. I didn't think she'd seen me, but then, this was my first such endeavor, and I had no idea how you made that determination.

Twice I was tempted to pull over and pretend to park, but there were no parking meters—and therefore no parking—in this area of Harbor Haven. So on I drove, feeling more each second like I was driving a shocking pink Hummer with fireworks shooting out of its roof.

I felt especially lucky when Kerin, who had left her house with a briefcase that might or might not have contained the item in question, pulled into a lot next to Oceanside Park. I waited until she was out of her car and walking away before I parked the Volvo in a space as far from Kerin's as I could get.

I had a sudden rush of anxiety when a police car drove by, but then I reminded myself that I wasn't actually doing anything illegal. Still, feeling like I might need to make a quick getaway, I stayed in the car and left the engine running. I observed Kerin walking into the park and toward the playground. She wasn't carrying her briefcase.

But in her hand was the book.

I watched as Kerin sat down on a bench near the playground equipment, all of which had been carefully selected and designed so as not to be at all dangerous (and therefore not at all fun). The only other occupants of the area were a toddler in a little pink jacket—all the bigger kids were in school or preschool—and her mother, who was so devoted to her daughter that she didn't even look in Kerin's direction. I watched as Kerin waited for ten interminable minutes.

Finally, from three blocks away on the other side of the park, another woman walked over. She was blonde and slim, but from this distance I couldn't make out her face. I relayed all this to Paul, whose imaginary voice chided me for not taking the binoculars like he'd told me to, mostly because the only ones I owned were from Melissa's toy chest, a remnant of her *Spy Kids* period.

The two women didn't stay together long, however; in fact, Kerin stood up and walked away almost as soon as the woman sat down on the bench. She seemed in a hurry to get back to her car.

But she left the appointment book on the bench, and the blonde woman picked it up.

I was trying very hard to decide whether to follow Kerin or the blonde, and had decided Paul would want me to follow the blonde because she had the book, so I didn't notice that Kerin had headed, not for her car, but for mine. I almost jumped through the roof when she appeared in my window.

"Alison!" she enthused. "Are you ready for next Thursday?"

What the hell was she talking about? "Next Thursday?" I stammered.

"*Halloween!*" Oh yeah.

It occurred to me that Kerin, whose boss had been dead for only about a day (and who had obviously had some shady goings-on, um, going on), had bigger things than trick-or-treating to worry about, but then, her bringing up the subject reminded me that, no, I *hadn't* gotten Melissa's costume together. The woman was like a giant Jiminy Cricket.

"Almost," I lied. The blonde had gotten up and walked back the way she came. Another thirty seconds and I'd have no chance to catch her. "I was just on my way, Kerin. Nice seeing . . ."

"Wait a second," Kerin said. She gestured toward my passenger's side door. "Let's talk."

What excuse could I use? Sick child? Nah, she'd find out I was lying. Sick mother? I didn't want to send bad luck

Mom's way, and besides, she'd have to be *really* sick to require my presence, and if that were true, what the heck was I doing at Oceanside Park?

"Sure," I said, and unlocked the passenger side door. It didn't matter; the blonde woman was gone by now, anyway.

Kerin sat down opposite me and smiled amiably. "So," she said. "Why were you hiding in the real estate office the night of Terry's death?"

Whoa! Didn't see *that* coming!

"I have no idea what you're—" I began.

"Alison." The smile faded just a bit, then quickly returned. To anyone watching, it would look like we were chatting pleasantly about Halloween costumes. "Let's not play games. I know you were there. Your file was open on the desk when I got there. The police took you in for questioning. Don't you think I heard about it?"

"Okay, I *was* there," I admitted. "But I was just looking through the file on my house. I didn't see anyone else, and I didn't even know Terry was there until after you left."

For a second—and *just* for a second—Kerin's eyes widened. "You saw me there?"

I guessed, I wasn't supposed to say that. "Um . . . yeah, just for a minute."

"Did you say anything about me to the police?" Her face was positively vibrating with urgency. No, really. If you've never seen a vibrating face, you'll have to trust me on this.

"No," I lied, since in fact I *had* told Detective McElone about Kerin. Why hadn't the police talked to Kerin yet?

The smile became wider, but not warmer. "Listen to me, Alison. We can help each other. If you don't tell anyone you saw me there, I won't tell anyone you were there, either. And we can both breathe easier. How does that sound?"

It was a lot of work to keep my eyes from spinning in their sockets. "Um . . . sounds good. Yes. Let's do that," I said.

Kerin opened the door. "I'm so glad we had this chance to talk," she said.

And then she left. And Paul had heard the whole thing through my cell phone, which had been lying on the floor at her feet the whole time.

Twenty-five

Paul had indeed overheard my conversation with Kerin earlier today, and reamed me out royally for not having brought binoculars or shaking Kerin fast enough to follow the young blonde woman. But he'd agreed with me that our list of suspects (now including Kerin Murphy, Adam Morris, possibly the Prestons and everyone on the planning board) was expanding. That didn't make me feel better.

I had therefore decided to instead concentrate on having a nice evening out with a very attractive man and, for once, I could actually do that.

"So I hear you have ghosts in your house." Ned Barnes, dimple, tousled hair and all, sat across the table and studied my expression with mischief in his eyes.

"I beg your pardon?" I sputtered.

"Ghosts. It's the talk of the school."

Ned had been frustrated in his desire to see my house. His Acura had, ironically, broken down (not the fault of our minor fender bender), and I'd had to pick him up in the Volvo. So he had complained, but good-naturedly.

We'd chosen the restaurant—a Greek place imaginatively named the Parthenon—because it was located a few towns over in Point Pleasant and decidedly not in Harbor Haven. Ned was a teacher in the local elementary school and I . . . well, I appeared to be the talk of the town. Or at least the fourth grade.

"I can explain that," I told Ned.

Ned waved a hand. "Not at all necessary," he said. "Nine-year-old girls say all sorts of interesting things. Melissa's moving into a new house and her dad's not around. She's probably trying to spice things up a bit. I think it's very creative, actually."

"I'm glad you understand." Dodged *that* bullet!

Ned smiled. "She told a few of her friends this ghost story, and they told a few and, well, now it's . . ."

"The talk of the school? Let's make a rule: While we're out on a date—this is a date, isn't it?"

Ned nodded emphatically—oh yes, this was a date, all right.

"When we're out on a date, no talk about Melissa. It's like shop talk for you, and a little un-romantic for me, frankly."

He smiled. "You're absolutely right, Alison. So tell me about you. You grew up in this area?"

I nodded. "I grew up in Harbor Haven, spent a couple of years at two different colleges, dropped out, worked at HouseCenter, got married, moved up to Bayonne with my husband, had . . ."

"Don't say her name," he teased. "It's a rule."

"*Right*. So we moved back down here, first to a little house in Red Bank. My ex paid for Melissa to go to school in Harbor Haven because I knew the schools were good."

Ned tilted his head. "Thank you."

"You're welcome. But then The Swi . . . Steven and I

decided to divorce, and I remembered that I hadn't always wanted to work at HouseCenter or in a lumberyard. I wanted to open a guesthouse in Harbor Haven. So I started looking for the right house, and we ended up . . . well, you know where we live now."

"I think it'll make a great guesthouse," Ned said after the waiter took our order for souvlaki and pastitsio. "I'd still love to come by and see it."

"I'd love to show you around," I heard myself say. Boy, he seemed eager. I mean, I'm not bad-looking by any means, but I don't usually inspire men to pursue me quite so fervently.

"As long as the ghosts don't object," he said with a twinkle—yes, an actual twinkle!—in his eye.

"So tell me about yourself," I said, shifting gears with the ease of a twelve-year-old tractor-trailer with rusted gears.

"I don't have a very interesting story," Ned told me. "I grew up in Seattle."

"Right away, that's interesting to a Jersey girl," I said.

"Well, for me, it was cold and rainy," he answered. "And I got out of there as quickly as I could, when I was eighteen."

"You escaped to the tropical climate of New Jersey?"

Our waiter appeared at that moment with our appetizers, which consisted mostly of breaded and baked cheese, and olives (because it was a Greek restaurant and you have to have olives).

"New Jersey wasn't my initial destination," Ned told me when the coast was once again clear. "Actually, it was Peru."

"Peru!" Heads turned at other tables. Oops.

"Yes, you might have heard of it. It's in South America. Go south and make a right at Brazil."

I pursed my lips to indicate that his drollness had found its mark. "Okay," I practically whispered. "But why Peru?"

"I was fascinated with the history of the Incas, and I wanted to see it for myself. But I spent all my money getting there, and didn't have a nuevo sol or a college degree to my name. So I picked up work in construction and in a copper mine."

"It's a good thing you don't have an interesting story," I told him.

Ned mimicked my "droll" face. "Long story short, I got lonely for America, and American history, so I saved up my wages and found my way back here."

"To Harbor Haven?"

"Eventually. First I went to college and got degrees in history and education, and then I taught up in Poughkeepsie, New York, for a while. But when the history teacher job opened up in Harbor Haven, I jumped at it."

"Why?"

"For an American history nut like me, there are few better places," Ned said. "The Revolutionary War is all over New Jersey, and that's my favorite period to explore. So I'm very, very happy to be here."

Another period of silence accompanied the arrival of our dinners, which I for one was already far too stuffed to consider. I took a few bites to be polite—okay, I ate half of it, but it was really delicious.

"I wasn't aware the shore areas had much in the way of Revolutionary history," I said. "I thought it was all further north and west, in Morristown and in Trenton where Washington crossed the Delaware." Sure, I know a little New Jersey history. But not that much—I was an English major at Drew and a business major at Monmouth University before I dropped out altogether.

"Not at all," Ned told me through bites of his lamb. "There was a constant watch on the shore, even if just to try to spot ships heading for the ports of New York or Newark. And Washington himself spent a lot of time on the shore. He actually loved it here."

"Big George was a shore bunny?"

Ned laughed, and was even suave enough that he managed not to have souvlaki come out his nose. "I wouldn't have put it that way, but yes. Washington became very enamored of the Jersey Shore, and apparently had his eye on some property here."

"Here?"

"Well, in Harbor Haven, although that wasn't the name of the town then." Ned nodded. "But in the summer of 1778, Washington spent a good deal of time attacking the British in Freehold, not far from here."

"I know where Freehold is, Ned. Bruce Springsteen is from Freehold. It's the closest thing New Jersey has to Mecca."

"Well, during that time, the story goes that Washington found exactly the parcel of land he was looking for in what became Harbor Haven."

"No kidding! Which parcel was it?"

"Yours," Ned said.

Twenty-six

Ned didn't know much more than that, but promised to "research it with a friend of mine at Princeton." We hadn't discussed anyone else more than two hundred years old again that evening, and over Ned's protests, I drove him home after dinner rather than back to my house.

I told him I did that because I was tired, but the fact was, I was hoping that postponing the tour would force us to have another date, and the strategy worked—he asked me out again for Tuesday night. Then I dropped him off and, dammit, he didn't insist I come inside his place, either.

Nothing's perfect.

"This is beginning to make sense." Paul spoke very slowly the next afternoon. He was kneeling—hovering, really—next to the radiator cover in the dining room, while I finished detailing the paint on the molding around the ceiling. I'd been reserving the ladder-related activities for whenever Maxie wasn't around, and I knew she and Melissa were upstairs watching episodes of *Gilmore Girls* on Hulu.

"It is?" I'd learned in the past two days that George Washington was among the people who had once had designs on my house; that my real estate agent, Terry Wright, was dead from what seemed to be a really coincidental heart attack; and that Kerin Murphy had taken something from Terry's office and given it to a mysterious woman. I still didn't know anything about either of my original dilemmas: who had killed Maxie and Paul, and who was leaving me threatening e-mails. "How is what making sense?"

I interrupted the conversation to take a cell phone call from Jeannie, who wanted to know every possible detail about my date with Ned. I told her I was in the middle of a repair—because I was *always* in the middle of a repair—and that I'd call her back. Which I intended to do, in a couple of days.

When I hung up, Paul was engaged in trying to move a quarter, which I'd left on the radiator cover at his request. He had told me it took intense concentration for him to move physical objects (unlike Maxie, who seemed able to move objects with little to no difficulty; your classic bratty poltergeist), and he wanted to become more proficient at it. So his answer came after a long pause, and in gasps.

"The part about . . . George Washington . . . doesn't make any sense yet," he began. "But it does point to the idea that this property is more valuable than you or Maxie might have expected, and *that* could be a motive for murder. It's obvious."

"To you, maybe." I wanted to paint a narrow mauve stripe under the white molding on the ceiling, and I had put up blue painter's masking tape at very careful one-inch parallels to the molding in order to achieve it. I was using a thin brush to get the color where I wanted it and nowhere else.

"Simple." Paul flicked at the quarter, but his finger went through the wooden radiator cover and disappeared. "Damn." The hand came back out. "Someone wants to get their . . . hands on this house, possibly for a reason that has historical . . . implications. . . ." He bit his lower lip and stopped talking. Then, instead of stabbing at the quarter, he moved his finger slowly toward it. "They tried to scare . . . Maxie out, but she wouldn't go, and so the next . . . tactic was more violent, and I was . . . careless so I . . . paid the price, as well."

It was the first time I'd heard him refer to himself so casually in the past tense, and the moment sent a shiver up my spine.

I decided to lighten the moment. "So tell me," I asked, changing the subject. "What made you become a private eye?"

"Private eye?" the dead man asked me. "I was an independent investigator."

"Okay, so why? A nice boy like you. You couldn't be an accountant, like your brother Irving?"

"Ma," he said, playing along with the joke, "you always liked Irving better than me. You got him a new bike, and I had to keep the tricycle until I got my driver's license."

His finger made contact with the quarter, and it moved about two inches across the surface of the radiator box. Paul smiled and exhaled. "There."

"Nice work," I said. "If I ever need a quarter moved, I know the guy to call. Now, come on: why an 'independent investigator'?"

"I started off as a consultant with the Royal Canadian Mounted Police in Toronto," Paul said, once again working on the quarter, this time attempting to pick it up with his thumb and forefinger. "I worked on some profiling—my background was in psychology—and I helped make some arrests. But I wanted to come to America, and I made my way down through New York State until I got here. I talked to the state police about what I'd been doing for the RCMP, but they had no use for it, and I was tired of wandering. I met this sergeant at the state police who suggested getting an investigator's license, and since it was the only thing I was ever good at, I figured I'd go ahead. Worked for a year at an agency in Camden, and then I moved here to begin on my own. And just when I was getting started . . ." He stopped, sighed, and then looked at me. "Right now, let's concentrate on figuring out who's after you, and how to keep you alive."

"Could it be Kerin Murphy?" I asked. "I'd really like it to be Kerin Murphy."

"Why?"

"I already don't like her."

"Well, she certainly is involved in *something* . . ." he said. He made another grab at the quarter and missed.

"It's better when you move more slowly," I told him, pointing at the quarter with my paintbrush. "When you grab at it, you always go through."

Paul looked at me a moment, then looked at his hand, as if that was going to tell him something, and nodded. I guess it *did* tell him something. He turned his attention again to the quarter.

"Terry Wright might have been the person sending the e-mails to you and Maxie and making threatening phone calls to the Prestons," he said, moving his hand very slowly toward the coin.

I needed to move the ladder. "Oh please," I said. "Terry sold us the property—why would she want us gone? Plus, she was as threatening as a piece of angel food cake."

"Kerin Murphy, or someone she knew, was threatened enough to steal Terry's address book, or appointment calendar." Paul had a point. Paul always had a damn point, and it always made things more complicated for me. He stared intently at the quarter. "I'll have to ask some other ghosts about the interaction with objects," he said to himself.

"You can talk to other ghosts besides Maxie?" I asked. "How can you do that if you can't leave the property?"

Paul stopped and considered. "It's hard to explain," he

said. "Occasionally, other people who have died are sort of . . . available to us. It's not just thought projection, but it's less than talking. You can sort of send out questions, and you get answers, but you don't always know where they're coming from."

"Sounds like Facebook," I said. "Wait a minute." I paused, brush in mid-air. "Doesn't that mean you can just find and *ask* Terry what happened to her? Will she be back at the real estate office?"

"No, everybody's circumstances seem to be unique to them," Paul said, not looking at me. "Not all ghosts are tied to one place, and not all people who die appear as ghosts. Terry Wright seems to be one of those; I would know if she was available to talk to. Some ghosts can move around and some can't. In the same way that Maxie can move things easily, but it's much more difficult for me. I don't know why—maybe I'll know more when I've been dead longer."

"So how do we proceed from here?" I asked. "Any other dead detectives you can ask on the Ghosternet?"

"No." Paul looked annoyed, but he pushed on. "So . . . to make a plan, we need to operate on a theory. And the only one we have now is that Kerin and someone she's working with *are* the people trying to scare everybody out of this house. So we assume it's because they want this house or something in it. Maybe the best way to get them to stop trying to scare you out of the house is to convince them . . ." His hand moved down, into the radiator cover, and then came up through its top, and when it did, the quarter came up with it. He held it aloft. "Aha!"

"Convince them of what?"

Paul beamed, looking at the quarter, which he moved from one hand to the next, very slowly. "Convince them that whatever it is they want, you have it."

Twenty-seven

"I didn't think I'd hear from you again," Adam Morris said. He walked from the door, where he'd let me in, to his desk, and gestured that I should sit in the low-slung leather chair in front of it. Indeed, I hadn't expected him to be in his office on a Saturday—I'd expected to get voice mail—but there he was, plotting to take over the world, or at least part of the Jersey Shore.

I chose the stiffer, but less-cruel-to-animals, fabric-covered seat a few feet away. I pulled it to the desk and sat down. This was the first stop on Paul's prescribed tour-o-suspects (which meant my reinterviewing everyone, in person this time, including the planning board), so I'd have to pace myself. No sense showing any hostility yet.

Adam's assistant, Bianca, (no doubt thrilled to be working on the weekend) was the usual woman in her early-to-mid-twenties with the kind of lovely face that looked like you could have seen it on a dozen other lovely women the same day. Adam had shown a less-than-genial side of himself when he hollered at her through the door that he wasn't taking any visitors without appointments, and then, just like last time over the phone, had changed his mind when he heard I was here to discuss 123 Seafront. My name wouldn't open any doors in this town, but my address apparently would.

His office was attractive in an institutional way. There wasn't anything the least bit personal in it—no photographs of family on the desk, no pictures or diplomas on the walls. A few paintings, mostly of buildings Adam had developed.

Adam himself was equally attractive, and equally impersonal. He was a handsome, dark-haired man whose face I would be at a loss to describe ten minutes after I left.

"Well, I said I'd be thinking about your offer on my house," I told him. "And I'm here to give you my decision. Are you still interested in buying it?"

"Possibly." Adam Morris was nothing if not a keen negotiator. "It would depend on the price."

"Well, I'm sorry, but I'm not interested in selling at any price," I said, and waited for the eruption.

There was none.

Paul had been emphatic in his advice that I not "play games" with Adam, that I stick to the script Paul had worked out, but seriously, what fun is there in doing something if you know how every part of it will go before you start? Especially if you can irritate a man you instinctively don't like? The rules were already going by the wayside.

"I'm sorry to hear it," Adam answered, showing not one second of disappointment or anger. "I would have liked to include that property in the development, but I guess we'll have to work around it."

"The development would continue anyway, even without my house?"

Adam nodded. "Oh yes, absolutely," he said. "We'd always planned on continuing the project either way. It just would have been easier, and more aesthetically pleasing, to include that piece of property. Too bad we can't."

Visions of condos surrounding my quaint little guest-house—condos whose owners would probably rent them out during the summer months as vacation homes—once again filled my head. I could actually hear my income projections hit the ground and keep tunneling. I pictured Melissa and myself living in a homemade tent on Seafoam Avenue next to a sign reading, "Will See Ghosts for Food." I could picture all the happy vacationers going by with boo-gie boards and beach umbrellas toward their rented new-construction condos, while Melissa and I were bundled up in unseasonable overcoats, scarves and hats with earflaps.

"Are you all right?" he asked. I must have seemed like I was going to pass out. But only because I was.

"I don't know. "What . . . how much . . . where is the land you've already acquired?" I asked.

Adam stood up and walked to a floor-to-ceiling wood cabinet. Then he opened the doors and reached in for a tube. He walked back to the desk, watching my face the whole time.

"This is a plan of the development," he said, pulling a rolled-up map from the tube. "Normally, I'd show this to you on a screen, but I wasn't set up for a presentation when my assistant said you were here." In fact, I'd heard him yell something quite rude to poor Bianca about how she'd better get the A/V system working or she'd be looking for work soon.

"Sorry for the intrusion," I said.

"Not at all." It was a reflexive reaction; no matter what Adam Morris thought of my busting into his office, he'd be civil about it. You can't trust people like that. "Now, here's the section where the townhomes will be built."

He pointed to an area on the map where the Atlantic Ocean met Harbor Haven. In other words, where I lived. "There will be two hundred and eighty-seven units built within two years after we break ground this coming March. That's phase one."

I noticed a large open area just a little south of the map's center. "Is that my property?" I asked.

"That's right!" Adam said, sounding as proud as a parent whose child had just recited the alphabet for the first time. He reached up and dropped a transparent plastic overlay on the map. "And this is what we had planned it would look like with your land included in the project."

I looked. On my land, which currently held the old Victorian and a tremendous backyard on its two acres, Adam Morris's master plan had envisioned six new buildings. "What are those?" I asked. "A clubhouse or something for the condos?"

"No, that's phase two," Adam answered, doing everything but puffing out his chest with pride. "Those are six single-family luxury dwellings, including marble floors in the foyers, twenty-foot ceilings in the entrance halls, wet bars in the family rooms, exercise rooms and home theaters."

My stomach was starting to move around involuntarily. "And just out of curiosity, what would the price of each of those . . . dwellings be when they're finished?"

Adam's face became serious, as he was about to discuss a matter of sad tidings, indeed. "Well, you understand that the real estate market here in New Jersey has suffered in recent times, just like the rest of the country." The man spoke in press releases. It must have been exhausting to have to think like that.

"I understand," I said. "How much?"

"Probably about two-seven."

Wow—the market *had* been hit pretty hard if shorefront property like that was going for such prices. "Two hundred seven thousand?" I asked, just to clarify.

He laughed. "No, Alison—two million, seven hundred thousand dollars."

I don't remember the next few seconds. I imagine I blinked a number of times; I'm prone to blinking uncontrollably when I have to process information that insane. "Two-point-seven million dollars?" I said. "For one-sixth of my property?"

"That's right," Adam answered. "But I'll tell you what—if we settle for a price on your property now, we might just be able to let you have one of those homes at our cost. And with what we're willing to pay for what you own now, you could just about live in it for free. What do you say, Alison?"

It was dizzying—it was almost even attractive. The idea of a brand-new, state-of-the-art (albeit cookie-cutter McMansion) luxury house, in exchange for the toil and marketing nightmare that a guesthouse surrounded by new-construction town houses was going to be—that was pretty enticing. Not having to make mortgage payments. Saving for college. Getting a job back at the HouseCenter and still making ends meet without the headaches of running a full-time business.

Not worrying about the hole in the plaster wall.

Adam Morris must have taken my hesitation for a sign of possible interest, because he added, "Perhaps we could discuss it over dinner." He smiled very pleasantly. Smooth.

But Paul had told me to make Adam think I had something he wanted, and I was going to see it through, damn it. "I really can't, Adam," I said. And then I did my best to smile a cat-post-canary-dinner smile. "I'm afraid I've discovered something more valuable in the house as it is."

Adam Morris's head swiveled with a velocity usually reserved for Italian sports cars. "Really!" he said. "And what is that?"

"I'm not at liberty to tell you," I told him, leaving out the truth, which was that I had no idea what I was talking about. "But suffice it to say, I'm not in a position to sell the property until I can realize the value of my find-ing. And I expect that value to be quite high." Bluff of the century.

His eyes narrowed to slits, but the smooth nature of his voice never wavered. And he smiled his sharky smile as convincingly as he could.

"Isn't that good for you," Adam said.

I left his office grinning like the winner of the Power-ball lottery. And as soon as I cleared the doors from Adam Morris's suites, I made a beeline for the ladies' room, went inside and threw up.

I had barely managed to get myself into presentable shape (and into my Volvo station wagon) and make it home before I came under siege from an unexpected front.

My mother swept into the house without having men-tioned she'd be visiting. "It's coming together so well!" she said. "You're a genius."

"Thanks, Mom. Why are you here?" It wasn't supposed to come out that fast, but Maxie was changing clothes—literally, different clothing would appear and then be replaced by something else—in the room and otherwise trying to distract me as I polished the brass stair rail.

"Do I need a reason to see what my little girl has been up to?" my mother asked. Maxie actually guffawed. It was not a pretty sight.

I love my mother, but Loretta Kerby has always been able to embarrass me more easily and more deeply than any other person on the planet. I make a daily vow not to do that to Melissa, one I regularly break. But at least I'm aware of it.

"Her *little girl*," Maxie crooned. "Oh, that's *wonderful*."

"I'm not a little girl anymore, Mom," I said, and to prove it, I put my mask back on and returned to the brass polish. You can't be too careful.

"No matter how old you get, you'll always be my little girl," she answered. This time I couldn't blame her; I had left that door far too wide-open for her not to walk through. "But I'm actually here to deliver a package that came to my house addressed to you."

"A package?" I hadn't lived in my mother's house for more than twelve years. Who would send me a package there? "Why are you getting packages for me?"

"I don't know," she answered. "But it has your name on it."

Mom reached into her backpack and pulled out a small box covered in brown paper, like it had been wrapped in a paper grocery bag.

It was, indeed, addressed to me, in care of my mother.

Maxie changed from a pair of ripped jeans, thigh-high boots and a t-shirt that read "AC/DC" into a black leather jacket over black tights and a top with black-and-white horizontal stripes. She looked like a French biker mime.

I took off my rubber gloves and Mom handed me the package. I regarded it carefully—it was very light and, as far as I could tell, not ticking. But there was, of course, no return address on the package.

There wasn't any postage on it, either. It had been hand delivered to her mailbox.

I took a box cutter from the side pocket on my tool belt and slowly cut the tape on one side of the box. Then I raised the flap on the paper wrapping and looked inside. The box was from a local jeweler, Mason Gems.

"Is there something you want to tell me?" Mom asked hopefully. "The teacher?"

I gave her a snide look and tore the rest of the paper off. The box did not appear to be new; it was worn at the corners and the embossed *Mason* on the top flap was almost invisible. I shook it a little, and nothing happened.

The only thing left to do was open it.

The box contained a small, velvet-covered ring case,

which probably got Mom's heart pounding. She hadn't ever approved of The Swine, and was now letting that hang over me without so much as an "I told you so." The woman was much more devious than most people would ever imagine.

I opened the ring box. Inside was nothing more than a small piece of paper, about the size of a Post-it note. I unfolded it.

Printed in a nondescript font were the words, "We'll be in touch."

But the real message was clear: "We know where your mother lives."

I must have paled in a hurry, because Mom grabbed my forearm and said, "Ally, are you all right?"

Maxie, now in a teal jumpsuit, had not been able to see the message on the paper. "Ally!" she shouted. "Oh, that's great! This day keeps getting better and better!"

Mom looked at my face, and hers took on a stern expression. "Alison, you tell me right now what's going on."

And then she pivoted, pointed at Maxie and said, "And *you* mind your manners."

Twenty-eight

It took a few minutes of hysteria before I could get the yelling under control. But eventually, I calmed down. It just took some adjusting.

"So, how long have you been able to see . . ." I pointed at Maxie. "Her?" I asked my mother, trying very hard to breathe normally and failing.

"Just her, or all the ghosts?" Mom's innocent expression was so perfect that Dakota Fanning herself would've been proud.

Maxie's hand went to her mouth. She was laughing.

"*All* the ghosts?" I repeated, because coming up with words of my very own seemed as difficult as . . . something really difficult. See what I mean?

"Yes," Mom answered. "I've seen the poor dears for as long as I can remember. I still talk to your aunt Cecilia every now and again." My father's sister had died in the back of a 1964 Corvair ten years before I was born. She had not, according to family folklore, been wearing a seat belt. Or underwear. "She's still just eighteen years old, can you believe it?"

"You . . . Why? How?" One-syllable words were becoming my specialty.

"Well, I don't know," my mother said. "I suppose it's just an inborn talent, you know, like being able to roll your tongue into a circle." And she did just that, to show what she meant. Out of the corner of my eye, I saw Maxie trying, too. She couldn't do it. Mom looked at me. "You mean you can only see the two here?" she asked.

My head was starting to hurt again. I was having bucket flashbacks. "They're the only ones I've seen," I confirmed.

"So far," Maxie interjected. Thanks, Maxie.

"Don't feel bad, Alison," Mom said. "I'm sure you'll see more. There aren't that many of the poor dears around the Jersey Shore. I'm told there are more in places like Chicago, but those are mostly gangsters."

"But you never told me," I said. I was already sitting on the floor, but lying down was starting to look like a really good option. Maxie hovered about halfway between the floor and ceiling. Mom had the lawn chair. That Barcalounger was starting to sound even more attractive.

Mom closed her eyes and raised her eyebrows in an expression that said, "What do you want from me?" "When you were a little girl, I looked for signs that you could see them, too," she said. "But you couldn't, so I didn't want to scare you. And after you got older, well, there didn't seem to be a point to letting you know. Why make you feel bad?"

"You've been here before," I said. "You've stood in this very room, when Maxie and Paul were here, and you didn't so much as blink."

Mom pursed her lips. "Well, of course not. I've had a lifetime of practicing just acting natural when anyone else was around. When Melissa first told me what she was seeing, she didn't really understand it, but we agreed it was best not to say anything to you. You know how you are when things are just a little off, Ally. But now you've gotten the ability, too! I *knew* you could do it—you're so smart!" She beamed in Maxie's direction. "Isn't she amazing?" my mother asked.

"That's not the word I'd use," Maxie answered, hovering up out of my arm's reach.

But I was just now comprehending what Mom had just told me. "Melissa!" I said. "You knew Melissa could see ghosts, and you didn't say anything to me?"

Mom looked a little contrite, like a little girl who'd been caught in a white lie. "Well, now, Melissa and I ran into a lovely Civil War veteran when Melissa was just a tiny girl, and I realized she'd inherited the gift. But we both knew you wouldn't understand."

"I'm her mother!"

"And if she'd told you then that she could see and talk to ghosts . . ."

I admitted it: "I'd have taken her to a team of therapists."

"And if I'd told you I could, too?"

"I'd have taken *me* to a team of therapists."

"Exactly," Mom agreed, gleeful at my brilliance in picking up her meaning. "So Melissa came to me, and I told her I could see them, too, and what a special thing it could be for us. I thought it had skipped a generation—you know, my mother couldn't see spirits sitting right next to her on the subway—but now you've developed the ability, too. Isn't that wonderful?"

"It only happened because your close buddy here dropped a bucket of compound on my head," I told Mom.

Mom took on a stern expression. "Was that you, Maxine? That was very wrong of you, you know. You could have hurt Alison very seriously."

Maxie, to my amazement, dropped her head in what

appeared to be genuine remorse. "I'm sorry, Mrs. Kerby," she intoned.

But Mom had bigger fish to fry. She turned to face me. "Now, you tell me exactly what's going on and why someone is sending you strange notes in ring cases to my house."

So I told her everything—how Paul had asked me to find out who killed him and Maxie ("My goodness!" was my mother's reaction); why I'd agreed to do so after getting the first threatening e-mail ("Oh, no!"); how I'd broken into Terry Wright's office and found her body ("Alison, didn't I bring you up better than that?"); and why I suspected Adam Morris might be involved ("Son of a bitch."). You don't mess with my mother's daughter and expect Loretta to remain ladylike.

"So you think this is someone's way of threatening you through me?" Mom asked when I'd concluded.

"That's right."

Mom smiled a tight, malicious smile. "They don't know who they're dealing with, do they?" she said.

I looked at my mother with a different kind of respect than I'd ever had for her before—a fearful kind. "No, ma'am," I said.

She rubbed her hands together. No, seriously. "We need to mobilize," she said. "Alison, where is the other ghost— the young man—right now?"

I looked at Maxie. "I'll find out," she said, and vanished into the kitchen wall. I was awed at Mom's ability to command obedience from the otherwise uncontrollable.

Once Maxie vanished, Mom's tone turned confidential. "She's a nice girl, but you can't depend on her," she told me, gesturing in Maxie's previous direction. "But the young man, he's very dependable. And I *was* wondering why you never answered when he spoke to you; it makes sense now. If only you'd known him when he was alive."

I decided to redirect the conversation before it got even

weirder. "The thing we have to do above all else," I told Mom, "is to make sure Melissa is always safe."

"You bet," she answered. And her look told me she'd already thought of that.

Maxie appeared through the floor, dragging Paul behind her. "He was in the basement," she dutifully reported to Mom.

"I'm tired of looking at the other rooms," he said. "Hello, Mrs. Kerby. You know, you really should have said something to us before."

"That would have been impolite to Alison. Paul, is it? Well, listen up," Mom said. "You've gotten my Alison into a very difficult situation, so you bear some responsibility here. You're going to be in charge of security."

Paul looked as if he'd been hit in the face unexpectedly—his eyes bulged and his lips retreated into his mouth. "Security?" he asked.

Maxie cocked an eyebrow. "He didn't do such a hot job for me," she said.

"Nonetheless, he has the experience and he has the time to devise strategy," Mom went on, savoring her role as company commander. "Maxine . . ."

I did my best to giggle. "Maxine," I said.

Maxie glared.

"Max*ine*," Mom went on, choosing to ignore my juvenile disposition, "you're going to be watching Melissa when Alison can't be here. But also . . ."

"Wait a second!" I protested. "I'm the mother here—that's *my* daughter you're talking about. *I'll* decide who watches her. And it's not going to be *Maxine*!"

"Don't be petty, Alison," my mother admonished.

"I'm not being petty," I said, dropping my tone to a normal conversational level. "Suppose there's an emergency. What's Maxie going to do? She can't call nine-one-one."

Mom put a finger to her lips. "That's a good point," she said.

Maxie's eyebrows dropped to a V shape "Cell phone," she said, and held out her hand. I didn't move, but Mom handed over her own ancient model.

Maxie opened it, and mimed pushing buttons. "Nine-one-one," she said.

"Yeah, and what are you going to do when they answer?" I said. "Even if the police dispatcher has the gift, they'll hear nothing."

"It doesn't matter," Maxie said. "They send someone out whether they hear you or not."

Paul, envious, shook his head. "You handle objects so easily," he said to Maxie. "I'm still trying to pick up coins."

"What else do I have to do?" Maxie said pointedly. "You're always working on our 'case.'"

"Very well, then," said Mom, getting us back on task. "So Maxine will be watching Melissa when necessary. But she'll also be doing research."

Maxie looked like something suddenly smelled bad. "Research?"

Mom nodded. "Yes. We need to know about the ownership of this house since it was built, not just from before you, Maxine. It would be good if we knew when Adam Morris began buying up properties around here, to the day. And that would be available to anyone with access to the Internet." Mom grinned. "Seeing as you're so good at pushing buttons already."

"I always did bad on research projects at school," Maxie protested.

"Here's your chance to improve," Mom said, in a modified version of an adage I'd heard from her all my life: "Keep expanding your horizons, and you'll do well."

"What's the point of improving?" Maxie whimpered. "I'm dead."

"Oh sure, you can complain about the bad break you've gotten, or you can rise above it," my mother told her. "You can moan and groan about your circumstances, or you can find new ways to be useful and happy. So you're going to contribute, Maxine, and do you know why?"

"Because you'll drive her crazy until she does," I offered, ever the pupil with her hand raised high.

"Exactly," Mom said.

"Okay," Maxie agreed with a certain tone of inevitability.

Paul smiled and looked in Mom's direction. "But security—and by that I assume you mean concentrating on keeping Alison and Melissa safe from whoever is behind our deaths—isn't all I'm good for, Mrs. Kerby," he said. "I've been directing the investigation through Alison, giving her assignments and overseeing her progress."

"And how's that been going so far?" Mom asked.

"Actually, fairly well. We don't know how the puzzle fits together yet, but we have a good number of pieces now."

"I don't know . . ." Mom said.

"Mom," I started. "I appreciate your taking charge, but let's keep in mind that this is my problem and Paul is helping me solve it. Paul knows his business. Don't go crazy being General MacArthur here."

Mom smiled broadly. "You're so smart," she said.

Twenty-nine

"Why didn't you tell me that Grandma could see Paul and Maxie, too?" I asked Melissa as she tied her left sneaker the next morning. Ned Barnes was taking the class on a field trip to the Thomas Edison National Historical Park (actually the site of Edison's lab), yes on a Sunday, and we needed to be out the door. Ten minutes ago.

She looked up quickly, worried at being caught and wondering what the punishment was going to be. Salad for lunch every day? Extra leaf raking in the admittedly huge backyard? Or something really awful, like a week without her iPod?

"You're not in trouble," I assured her. "I just want to know why, after it was clear I could see Paul and Maxie, you didn't mention to me that your grandmother and you have been talking to deceased strangers behind my back for years."

Melissa went back to tying her sneaker. "I was four or five before I could figure out what was going on."

"And you never told me?" I said. Yes, I was going to inflict guilt if possible. I'm a mother. It's not so much part of the job as a perk.

"I tried," she answered. "Remember when I told you there was a man who lived in my bedroom closet in the old house?"

"Well, yeah, but all kids think . . ."

"His name was Albert Henderson, and he was a forklift operator for twenty years before his no-good wife ran off with the dentist down the block and Albert drank himself to death."

I considered that. "I thought you had a vivid imagination."

Melissa sent a look my way that spoke encyclopedias. "I was five," she said.

I shut up. For a moment. "Well, what about Grandma? Just recently? You knew I could see the ghosts, and you knew *she* could see the ghosts, but you didn't say anything. How about that?"

"Didn't you teach me that keeping a secret was a sacred trust?"

"Yeah, except when you told half the fourth grade we had ghosts in our house. Now everybody thinks I'm weird."

She stood up. "Everybody already thought you were weird, Mom," my daughter told me. "Marlee Murphy's mom told her to stay away from our house, and I didn't even invite her here." Kerin Murphy strikes again.

We got into the station wagon and I pulled out of the driveway. "The thing is, Liss, I'm going to be trying to get people to come stay at our house starting next spring. And it's going to be bad for business if they think scary ghosts are living there, even if they can't see them."

"But Maxie and Paul aren't scary ghosts." Sometimes, Melissa doesn't converse so much as point out how you're wrong. It's her father's genes that make her do that.

"The people renting rooms don't know that," I said.

"Maybe you should tell them."

I drove toward her school in silence for a while. It's demoralizing to be constantly shown up by a nine-year-old.

Finally I said, "So, what are you going to be for Halloween?" We were only five days away, counting today.

"We're all going together: Me, Wendy, Clarice, Ron and Marlee."

"Marlee Murphy? I thought you didn't like her."

"I don't, but Clarice does. So I think our costumes are going to be a theme thing."

Melissa and her friends had been talking about going trick-or-treating as a group, and now they were going to be dressing as various characters in a story. "Harry Potter?" I guessed.

"I think *Star Trek*."

"Are you Uhura?"

"Spock." It figured.

"What do you need for the costume?" I asked.

Melissa put on a show of thinking about it, although I was sure she had it all worked out in her head. "A blue t-shirt, black pants, black hair dye . . ."

"You're not dying your hair. I'll find a wig."

She rolled her eyes in my direction. "Black sneakers and pointy ears."

"It's all easy except the ears," I said. "That's going to take a little thought. I'll see what I can come up with. Maybe construction paper or felt."

"I was thinking we could get some fake ears at the Halloween store," Melissa said, ending all debate.

When we finally reached the John F. Kennedy Elementary School, I felt lucky to have survived the trip with a shred of self-esteem intact. Melissa got out of the car without giving me a kiss like she would have at home (can't be seen by the peers, you know) and hefted her little backpack onto her little shoulders. Having kids makes you want to cry at odd moments. But I'm a champ at controlling it.

"Bye, Mom." And she was off. I wondered if she'd be that nonchalant when it was time to leave for college. Probably. But I'd be bawling my eyes out.

"You're picturing her leaving for college." Ned Barnes was leaning in my driver's side window. "I know the look."

"Busted," I said. "But she was a baby only ten minutes ago."

"That's how it works. I've only been teaching here three years, and some of the kids I used to teach are already taller than me."

"You're a history teacher," I reminded him, because clearly he thought he was a philosopher. "You're supposed to understand the march of time."

"Speaking of history," he said, "I've been doing a little research into your house and George Washington's interest in your property."

That brought me out of my melancholic reverie. "Ooh, tell me!" I said.

"Uh-uh."

"Whaddaya mean, uh-uh?" I asked.

Ned smiled a smile that made me warm in a number of interesting places. "I'll tell you over dinner tonight."

"Tonight? I thought we were going out Tuesday night."

"We are," Ned said, "but this information can't wait. Besides, my car's back, and I want to see what you've been doing with that house."

It was a tough choice: sanding floors versus dinner with a very cute guy who could tell me mysterious things about the house I lived in. I'd have to think that one over.

"Sounds good," I said.

We decided to meet at the house so Ned could finally see it, and then he headed into the school and I pointed my station wagon in the direction of said enormous-drain-on-my-bank-account-that-everybody-seemed-interested-in-but-appeared-to-be-decreasing-in-value-by-the-minute. It was an interesting, if frustrating, contradiction.

I spent some of the morning preparing the floors for sanding and putting up plastic sheeting in the dining room, since I'd be doing that floor first. Maxie watched with mild interest for a while, complaining that she'd prefer a darker stain than the one I was preparing to use, then left to do the research Mom had assigned to her, grumbling all the way.

Paul appeared up through the floor almost immediately after Maxie left. I think they might have been getting on each other's nerves after so much time cooped up together; they rarely showed up in the same room at the same time anymore.

"Maxie's been researching Adam Morris on the Internet," he said as soon as his head was all the way into the room.

"Good morning to you, too," I responded. "What has she found out?"

"We don't know why he didn't buy the house from the Prestons," Paul said. He was showing an atypical lack of charm this morning. "Maxie says he made an offer to her right after she moved in, but she was adamant, and he didn't bother again. With the Prestons, we only know what David Preston said, and he's not a trustworthy witness."

"So what's our plan from here?" I asked.

"I don't know." That was *it*?

"What's bugging your deceased butt this morning?" I asked Paul, but he just scowled and remained silent. Fine.

"Nothing," he said after a very long pause.

"You sound like Melissa."

"No, I don't." Wow, he was going to be a lot of fun today. But I'd learned by now that Paul abhorred silence, and if I waited long enough, he'd eventually say whatever it was on his mind.

"All right," he finally spit out. "I don't think you should see this Barnes fellow anymore."

I spent a good long moment blinking. It didn't do any good, but I couldn't think of any other reaction to that outburst. "I'm sorry?" I asked.

"I don't think he's trustworthy," Paul continued. "He seems to be interested in you only because you own this house, and we know that whoever is threatening you has an unusual fixation on this house."

That was even more preposterous. "You're saying you think *Ned* is the person behind the threats? You think *he* killed you and Maxie? Did either of you even know him when you were alive?"

Paul turned his head away. "No," he said. "But I don't trust his motives."

Suddenly it dawned on me, and I grinned without meaning to. "You're jealous," I told him.

"I am not." But Paul still wouldn't look me in the eye.

"You *are*—you're jealous of Ned. You don't want me to be interested in him because . . . It's flattering, really, Paul, but you have to understand, I have my daughter to think about. It's important that the only men I date are the ones with a pulse."

"Mark my words," Paul said, and then he vanished without a sound.

Mark *what* words?

Thirty

Melissa refused to come downstairs when Ned arrived to take the tour of the house and pick me up for our date. She was of the opinion that her mother dating her history teacher was, and I'm quoting now, "creepy."

But while she was upstairs, no doubt playing the Game of Death with her designated babysitter (and preparing to be dropped off at Tony and Jeannie's since, despite what my mother thought, I felt that leaving my nine-year-old daughter in a house that appeared completely devoid of supervision would be at best suspicious and at worst illegal), Ned was drinking in the house with his eyes and, from all indications, finding it astonishing.

I was amazed he wasn't dead on his feet after shepherding twenty-two fourth graders through Edison's lab, but history seemed to invigorate Ned. When I was in school, it had usually had the opposite effect on me.

"This place is marvelous!" he gushed. "There's so much history here."

Sure, history, but what about all *I'd* done? "It's only been here a hundred years. There are houses in this county that go back to before the Revolution, you know."

"Oh, I know," Ned answered, moving from the living room to the dining room. "But this one has so much character."

From upstairs I could hear Maxie complaining to Melissa that a person *always* got to go twice when they rolled doubles, something that I could be sure wasn't true in whatever game they were playing. "Yeah," I muttered to myself. "It has a whole cast of characters. Are you ready to go?"

Ned stopped in his tracks. "Go? But I haven't seen the whole house yet."

"Well, you've seen the whole downstairs, and the upstairs wouldn't interest you," I told him. "I'm modernizing up there, adding a powder room."

He grinned a knowing grin. "I'm not giving you enough credit for all the incredible work you've done here." He held out his arm, gesturing for me to come closer. "Alison. It's beautiful, and I think you have done truly amazing things in this house."

Okay, so then I *did* walk over and let him put his arm around my shoulders. "A girl shouldn't have to fish so hard for compliments, Ned," I admonished him.

"It won't happen again," he promised. And then he leaned over and kissed me.

I'm not going to say it changed my life, or that kissing Ned was an experience so intense that it defied description. That said: The man could kiss. Seriously.

But then I heard footsteps on the stairs, and broke off the lip-lock in fear that Melissa would catch us and proclaim the sight "gross." I turned to see her just starting down toward us. She hadn't witnessed the horrible offense.

"Hi, Mr. Barnes," she singsonged, as little kids will do when prompted to be civil no matter what or they'll never get another piece of chocolate cake. For example.

"Hi, Melissa," Ned answered, smiling something other than the plastic, unconvincing smile teachers paste on their faces when seeing a student outside class.

From the look on her face, I could see it was best to get out of here as quickly as possible.

"Are we ready to go?" I asked.

"If you're sure I can't see the upstairs . . ." Ned began.

"Maybe next time," I said, before I realized the implications of what I'd said.

I'd been thinking more about getting him the hell out of the house before Maxie cast her technically not-present eyes upon him. I had threatened to "walk off the case" if either Paul or Maxie dared show up when Ned was around, but I didn't trust Maxie under any circumstances. "When it's done," I continued. "I don't want to show off a work in progress."

Melissa glanced around the living room, with its partially sanded floors, half-detailed walls and access to a lovely hallway with a hole in it, and I could tell she was about to mention that the room we were in fit the "work in progress" category. But she thought better of it. Besides, if I let Ned come upstairs, she'd have to hang around with her teacher for a longer period of time.

"Okay," Ned agreed, and gestured Melissa and me toward the front door. I locked up when we got outside, and we all piled into Ned's Acura. Ned accidentally annoyed Liss by asking about her Halloween costume, which I hadn't helped assemble yet, so she scowled and was silent all the way to Jeannie and Tony's house.

Jeannie clearly approved of Ned with her eyes, while Tony took me to the side. I thought it would be his usual warning about what guys really want (Tony apparently thought that A. I was fifteen years old, and B. he was my father), but he had another purpose in mind.

"I think I've got an idea for the hole in the wall," he started, absolutely giddy with anticipation. "We do another mold, like the first one, but with predrilled holes for screws to attach it directly to the studs when we install it. Then, once it dries, all you have to do is smooth out the seams and cover the screw holes. Good as new."

"It sounds great!" I gushed. "When can we try it?"

"Give me a couple of days to work out the kinks."

I hugged him. "You know I love you," I told Tony.

Ned came around the corner at that moment and smiled. "Should I be worried?" he asked.

"Depends," I told him. "Can you plaster?"

"I don't know," Ned answered. "I've never plasted." I groaned, and Ned reminded me we had reservations at a restaurant. "We have a lot to talk about," he added.

Ned and I drove toward Manahawkin, where the restaurant he had chosen was located (I had not been consulted, which was just as well, since my idea of an elegant night out is to take the paper wrappings all the way off the sub sandwich and use a real plate underneath it). "So," he began. "George Washington."

"Father of our country, first president, first in the hearts of his countrymen, could not tell a lie, defeated Cornwallis and had wooden teeth," I said. "How am I doing?"

"Almost as well as my fourth graders," Ned answered. "But at least you knew about Cornwallis."

"Flatterer."

"May I go on?" I gestured that he should continue, and mimed locking my mouth shut. That always impressed the guys.

"In the summer of 1778, Washington went ahead and sent a letter to his wife, Martha, about finding some property in the area. And there were documents drawn up that would indicate he was interested in purchasing the parcel of land that included the lot where your house sits today. Maps from the time, which I looked up at the New Jersey State Museum in Trenton, confirm most of this, and the rest I got from a friend at Princeton."

I gestured toward my mouth, and Ned waved a hand to indicate it was all right if I spoke. "Cool," I said, and then mimed a zipper reclosing my mouth. It's good to have some variety in your comedy arsenal.

"But here's where it gets interesting," Ned said while executing a hairpin right turn that normally would have made me throw up, but which he handled smoothly. The man could drive and he could kiss. Two good things, one better than the other. "I've been looking into the purchase, and there's no existing record of the sale ever going through, except one. In the records dating back to when this was part of Monmouth County, there is a record of the transaction from Mr. Junius R. Smith to General George Washington, a parcel of land that included sixty acres on the shore, two of which are now yours."

"So why is that so unusual?" I asked, having forgotten my miming.

"Because the records from the time indicate a deed was drawn up and signed by all parties involved. Story was, the deed was written on your property and then lost for decades. It was found when they were taking down a barn, and eventually ended up in the house someplace. No one since has been able to find that deed in over a century, dating almost precisely to the beginning of construction on your house." Ned smoothly pulled into a parking space in front of a restaurant called Barnacles. Oh no. I hadn't told him I detest all seafood. I felt a cold sweat start behind my neck.

"Well, that doesn't matter, does it?" I asked to cover up my anxiety. "It's not like George is going to drop by and demand his land back, is it?" Of course, given the people currently "living" in my house, anything was possible, but the general had managed to stay away so far, I was pretty sure.

"You're not getting the picture," Ned said as he walked around the car and put his arm around my shoulder, leading me toward my fishy downfall. *Most of these places have steak and salads on the menu, don't they?* "The document was signed by all the parties to the transaction."

"So?"

"So, do you have any idea how much an original document hand-signed by George Washington would be worth today?" Ned's eyes almost glowed. I couldn't tell if it was the historical find that excited him, or his having an arm around my shoulder.

"Quite a bit, I'm guessing, but my house wasn't built until more than a hundred years after the president died," I said. "What's this got to do with me?"

He opened the door of the restaurant for me, and the smell of fish hit me full in the face. This was going to be a tough evening. "Alison. The deed disappeared just as your house was being built. A search made by a local historian sixty years ago turned up nothing, but local rumor has it that the people who built your house inherited the deed and hid it somewhere while the place was being constructed."

"You mean there's an original George Washington in my house?" I asked.

"I cannot tell a lie," Ned answered.

Thirty-one

The rest of the evening had been a contest between my inability to eat any seafood and the fact that Ned was a truly charming companion who kept giving me electric jolts whenever he looked at me the right way.

He'd laughed, initially, when I told him I didn't eat fish, but once he realized I was serious, he immediately offered to go to a different restaurant. I looked at the menu and saw a good number of selections I'd be happy with, so we sat down anyway.

Ned scolded me for not having mentioned my dislike for seafood ("How can you live near the ocean and not eat fish?"), but we got past our dietary differences quickly and had a lovely evening.

Except.

That man couldn't stop talking about history. Even when we'd get off topic for a moment, his enthusiasm for the American Revolution and George Washington— apparently a hero of Ned's—was a little disconcerting.

By dessert, I felt like I'd actually had dinner with George, and wondered what had happened to that Ned guy who'd picked me up for a date. That deed, supposedly stashed away in my house somewhere, was a real source of fascination for him.

"Do you think that's what this is all about?" I asked Paul the next afternoon. "Somebody's after an old deed signed by George Washington?"

There wasn't anything Paul liked better than being consulted about what he had begun referring to as "The Case." He got to show off his private-eye expertise without fear of argument, since he knew I didn't have a clue how one went about investigating anything.

He stroked his chin and paced a little, although his feet weren't exactly touching the floor. And then he looked at me and said, "It's certainly possible. I'm not sure how much such a document would be worth, but I'm sure it's quite valuable."

"Ned said similar documents signed by Washington have gone at auction for almost half a million dollars," I told him.

"That's motive enough for murder, I'd think," he said.

Maxie, literally poking her head in from the library (I was quite proud that I'd managed to install all those the floor-to-ceiling bookshelves in a single day), asked, "You know why they killed us?" So she *did* care after all.

I let Paul tell her about the deed and its possible value, and then I asked Maxie if she'd seen anything like that around the house.

"I saw some old papers in a closet when I moved in, but that's all," she said. "They were all about the furnace and the roof on the porch, things like that. I scanned them and threw the originals away. They had to be thirty years old."

"But not two hundred and thirty years old," Paul said, mostly to himself.

"No."

"So then," Paul went on, his face brightening, "where would you put a document like that in this house if you wanted to hide it?"

"Why would they want to hide it?" I asked. "This house was built more than a hundred years ago, but way more than a hundred years after Washington signed the lease. Why not sell it then, or donate it to a museum or something?"

"Maybe they thought it would continue to appreciate in value if they waited long enough. But that's speculation. It's a good question," Paul admitted.

"You think any question you can't answer is a good one," Maxie retorted. "Like why we're dead."

Paul chose to let this taunt go by; he seemed much less grumpy today than he had been the day before. "Can you find out what the name of the original owner of this house might be, and the exact date of its construction?"

There was a long pause, and then Maxie said, "You mean *me*?"

"Of course, I mean you. You're in charge of research."

She made a noise with her lips that I won't try to describe. "No way, private dick. *This* one never got my laptop back from the cops, and that thing she calls a computer takes, like, an hour just to boot up."

I pointed a knowing glance in Maxie's direction. "I'll tell my mother on you," I said quietly.

Maxie actually made a huffing-and-puffing noise, muttered something about not having to put up with this crap, and vanished back into the library, from whence she had come. My mother's disapproval was becoming a very valuable weapon.

"Now, you," Paul said, turning his attention to me. "You have more interviews to do."

Before I could protest once again that I didn't see the investigation going anywhere, my cell phone rang, and the incoming number was one I didn't recognize. I took in a deep breath, and opened it.

"It's Phyllis Coates," the voice said before I could ask. "I'm at the *Chronicle* office, and you need to come down here before the police come looking for you."

That was a lot of information to get in the first two sentences of a phone call. "Why would the police come looking for me?" I asked.

"I just got a call from my friend in the coroner's office," Phyllis said. "Turns out Terry Wright *was* murdered."

Thirty-two

Phyllis brought me a cup of coffee in a mug that read, "New York's Hometown Paper," as the cell phone in my jeans pocket vibrated for the fifth time in the last half hour. The caller ID confirmed it—the police were looking for me.

"Originally, they thought she died of natural causes," Phyllis said. "But the preliminary report from the ME showed a trace of pilocarpine eye drops, something someone with glaucoma might have in the house. Put enough of it in a drink, a glass of wine or something, and it's deadly."

"She had a cup of coffee in her hand," I said. My mind hadn't really wrapped itself around this idea yet.

"That would mask it well enough, I'd think. What about the two people who died in your house?"

I snapped to attention. "Paul Harrison and Maxie Malone? You think the same person killed them?"

"I don't know what I think yet. I'm asking what you think."

Wait a minute . . . "Is this conversation on the record?"

Phyllis smirked just a little; I'd figured her out. "You tell me what you know, and I'll tell you what I know," she offered.

"I'll tell you everything I know: nothing."

"I'll bet you know more than you think," she said.

"Anything's possible. Okay. I saw Terry on the floor and the coffee spilled on the rug. She looked like she was asleep, only with her eyes open. It was weird."

"Who would want her dead?"

"I really didn't know her. That's it. Now, what do *you* know?"

"Not so fast. If you weren't the last person to see her alive, who was?"

"How the hell would I know?" I asked. "All I know is that I'm the first person who saw her dead, and if Kerin Murphy hadn't come in and scared me . . ."

Wait. Kerin Murphy!

Suddenly Phyllis was all attention. "Kerin Murphy was there?" It figured she'd know Kerin; Phyllis knows *everybody* in Harbor Haven.

"Yeah, but Terry was already dead."

"But it's something to follow up on," Phyllis said, already making a note on one of the myriad pieces of scrap paper on her desk. "Why didn't you tell me before that she was there?"

"I thought she'd get mad," I told her. "You can't let Kerin know I said she was there."

Phyllis waved a hand. "Your name will never be mentioned."

"That's it, Flash. I've told you what I know. Now what do *you* know?"

Reporters get into their field to share information, and I could tell Phyllis had been dying to answer the question. "First of all, regarding Harrison and Malone, turns out that death wasn't brought on by the Ambien in their systems.

In fact, according to the new ME report, it seems that the Ambien was injected into them after they were dead, probably to distract the doctor from looking for what else was there."

My brain was starting to hurt. "Then why didn't the cops start a murder investigation right away?"

Phyllis smiled and nodded; yes, she'd anticipated that question. "Because the needle marks were hidden behind their heads, which a normal autopsy might not reveal—they couldn't very well inject themselves in a spot where they couldn't reach. The ME didn't catch them the first time, and didn't go back and look at all the pictures and slides they'd taken until I started asking questions. You don't find poisons unless you look for them. Besides, like I said, Westmoreland wasn't the most industrious of detectives. McElone's trying harder. She's been here less than a year; she's trying to make a name for herself."

"Poison," I said, my (okay, Paul's) suspicions confirmed.

"That's right. Something called"—she referred to notes on her desk—"acetone. Common in a number of products, like paint, automobile coatings, nail polish remover and some inks. But put it into drinks in the right dosage and you end up with two dead people."

"Wow," I said. "Is it strange that the killer used two different kinds of poison?"

She shrugged. "I don't know. Maybe he couldn't get his hands on the same stuff again. But now we've got to concern ourselves with your problem."

My . . . oh yeah! "Do the police really think I killed Terry?" I asked.

"Probably not," she said. "But McElone isn't going to cut you any breaks."

I rolled my eyes. "Is she the detective on the case?"

Phyllis nodded. "It's a small town. We're not flush with detectives. But what you really have to concern yourself with is receiving threats from someone who may have killed three people already."

"I'll try to remember not to eat anything I haven't cooked myself," I said, more thinking aloud than talking to Phyllis. But who was I kidding—I never cooked.

"You need a plan of action," she said, bringing me back to the conversation. "What are you going to do?"

I exhaled. Putting this off wasn't going to do me any good. There were probably police cars outside my house right now. Melissa couldn't come home to that. If I hurried, maybe the questioning could be done by the time I had to go get her, or Mom could pick her up.

"I'll answer the phone the next time it vibrates," I said.

"Good plan." Phyllis nodded in approval. "Go see Anita McElone. And give me a call when you get out."

"In five to ten years," I said. "Will you wait for me?"

"Faithfully," Phyllis agreed.

Thirty-three

"You really are a bonehead," Detective Anita McElone said after the uniformed officer ushered me into the interrogation room, which was barely big enough for the two of us. "The police are looking for you, and you duck the calls. Who do you think you are—Bonnie Parker?"

I gave her my best weary look. "You thought I broke into her office. . . ."

"You *did* break into her office," McElone insisted. "And you found her body. But now, the evidence points to a murder, and you are the last person we can put in a room with the victim."

"Oh, come off it, Detective," I said. "You don't think for one second that I killed Terry Wright, any more than you thought I was sending myself threatening e-mails. So what am I doing here?" McElone struck me as someone who was trying hard to be accepted in a new job, and I respected that. But if she was trying to gain respect by making me a sacrificial lamb, my respect was a little less, um, respectful.

It was McElone's turn to look weary. She hung her head for a moment, as if she couldn't bear to deal with an idiot like me for one more second. "First of all, I have not yet formed an opinion about whether you killed Ms. Wright. Until I know that you didn't, you're a suspect. But you are here," she said very slowly, "because you are somehow connected to these two cases. You are here because you bought a house which two people died in a year ago." She pointed a finger to the sky. "You are here because those people *and* the one whose body you 'found' appear to have been poisoned." Another finger went up.

"You don't think . . ."

"Don't interrupt me. You're here because you made a complaint about someone sending you threatening messages, which you claimed were similar to ones sent to the woman who was poisoned in the house you now own." McElone was counting my criminal connections on her hand, and she was up to three.

"What do you mean, 'claimed'?"

She ignored me, but smiled in a malevolent fashion. A fourth finger went up. "You're here because the real estate agent involved in the sale of that house was found lying dead in the office you broke into." McElone put her hands down on her desk and used them to push herself up to a standing position. "Don't you think that's enough?"

I stuck out my lips a little. "Not really," I said.

"Well, I do." McElone actually looked like she wanted to put her feet up on her desk, but settled for threading her fingers behind her head and leaning back in her chair. "You see, even if I *don't* think that you killed Ms. Wright—and I'm not saying I don't—I still want to know how you're involved in everything that's been going on around her, because maybe that would lead to an arrest."

"Of me?"

"Only if the gods are truly smiling upon me." She grinned.

"I can only tell you what I know," I said. "I saw the original e-mails. I've *gotten* e-mails. I was worried, and all *I* wanted was to find out about the history of my house."

McElone's face perked up.

"I went to Terry's office to find out about the transaction before mine, the one in which she sold the house to Maxine Malone, because I thought something about it might have led to the threatening e-mails to Maxie and to me." I didn't wait for her to answer. "The only other thing I can tell you is that, just before I discovered Terry's body, I saw Kerin Murphy in the office, but she works there."

"Yes, and she took something out of the desk," McElone reminded me.

I decided to also tell the detective about the young blonde woman in Oceanside Park whom I saw Kerin give the book to, and McElone's eyes got wide and angry. "What were you doing running around following people?"

"I was curious," I said. "But I couldn't see the blonde well enough to identify her."

"Trust me: The last person to see Ms. Wright alive was *not* your blonde woman."

We stayed there for another hour, McElone asking me the same questions and me giving the same answers, me asking her questions and she giving me *no* answers. She finally threw up her hands and let me go with the warning that "I'll find out what's going on, and if you're involved, you'll get no special treatment from me."

Which I actually found sort of reassuring.

I picked Melissa up from school just in time and drove back to the house. Melissa couldn't understand why I was being so quiet, but she respected my feelings, mostly because she knew that not doing so was going to get her into an area where she didn't want to go.

But she wouldn't leave the room when Paul insisted on hearing about my interview with McElone, not even when Maxie offered to watch the second season of *Friends* with her on the laptop. Melissa wasn't budging.

"What do you think you're going to say that will be so bad for me?" she asked. "I already know Ms. Wright is dead. Somebody killed her, didn't they? Like they killed you two." She pointed at Paul and Maxie.

Paul nodded. "Probably, Melissa," he said.

"So I already know that." Not a glimmer of fear in my daughter's eyes. Mine, on the other hand, were filling with tears. "So go ahead and have your talk. You're not going to get rid of me." If she hadn't had that squeaky little voice, she would have been truly intimidating. She sat down on the kitchen floor and adopted her "just try to move me" face. The one she'd put on the night The Swine left for California.

Paul looked at me, shaking his head just a little. "The women in your family are really something," he said, and I'm not sure it was meant to be complimentary.

"My great-grandmother pulled a plow," I said.

"We need to take some action," Paul went on, hand to his chin as it usually was when he was thinking. "We can't just wait for things to happen anymore."

"Sure," I told him sarcastically. "Let's pi—Let's get them angry. What have *you* got to lose?"

Paul, as had become his custom, went on as if I hadn't spoken. "If we rattle the cage a little bit, something's bound to happen that we can work with."

"Something already *has* happened," I reminded him. "Terry's dead."

"And since McElone held on to the evidence, you never got a good look at that file you were . . . borrowing," Paul reminded me. "That might have told us why Maxie's estate sold the house to you and not to Adam Morris."

I stole a glance at Maxie, who was pretending not to

listen but was looking at me out of the corner of her eye. "Who would have represented your estate, Maxie?"

She scowled. "Probably my mother," she said.

"Well, that makes things simple." Paul brightened up.

"Oh no," Maxie said. "Absolutely not."

"I'll let you pick out the colors for the upstairs bathrooms," I offered.

She considered, then shook her head. "No. It's not worth it."

"And you can choose the border paper in the kitchen."

"Border paper!" Maxie was appalled. "What is this, nineteen seventy-seven? You have to go for decorative tile backsplashes in the kitchen. Have a little fun."

I played it coy. "I don't know . . ."

But Maxie caught on right away. "This is blackmail," she said.

Melissa's head had been toggling back and forth between Maxie and me. She was watching the tennis match with supreme interest.

"You can say what you want, but I have the working body," I told Maxie. "It'll be border paper."

"Fine! Go ahead! Call my mother. But you have to do *exactly* what I say in the bathrooms and the kitchen!"

Maxie didn't stick around for a response. She knew I'd agree.

Melissa looked up at me. "Nice work, Mom," she said.

Thirty-four

Maxie's mother, who told me to call her "Kitty," couldn't have been older than fifty. She must have had Maxie when she was very young.

But today, placing a hot cup of coffee in front of me in her kitchen, Kitty Malone looked at least ten years older. The strain of losing her only daughter had clearly taken a very heavy toll.

That surprised me, since Maxie had insisted that her mother had considered her a disappointment, a failure as a child and a woman. But that certainly wasn't the tale Kitty was telling me today, and I was starting to believe her.

"Maxie was the funniest little girl," she said, her eyes staring dreamily off into the past. "She asked me one time why there was the color white. She thought it was a waste of space where there could be other colors." Kitty chuckled a little to herself. I'm not sure if she was aware of my presence in the room right then.

"That's lovely," I said, in spite of myself. I had told Kitty

I knew Maxie from a time when we both worked at an establishment called the Club Sandwich, a business about which Maxie would tell me nothing other than it "wasn't a place you'd go to look for a hero." She probably was laughing hysterically to herself back at the house. "That's not the Maxie I knew, but at the same time, it is."

Kitty smiled. "I'm glad you two were friends," she said, and I saw no need to contradict her. "And now you're living in that house." The way she said "that house," I could tell she wasn't crazy about the place.

"Yes," I said. "It's not really a coincidence. Maxie had told me about the place, and when I saw it, I thought it really fit the plans I had for a guesthouse in the area." I'd been very carefully coached—after Paul had somehow convinced a reluctant Maxie to help—to cover any and all possible topics of conversation. "I don't want to be insensitive, and I hope you don't mind my asking, but would you like to come and see what I've done with it?"

"No," Kitty said immediately. "I don't want to see it. Maxie and I had a . . . falling-out over that house. I thought she was getting in over her head, and she wanted to borrow money for a down payment that, frankly, I didn't have. We only spoke a few times in the months after she bought it, and things were never the same again. So no, I don't want to see it, thank you."

"Of course," I answered. "You inherited the house from Maxie. I saw your name on the documents I had to sign when I closed on the house."

"Yes, and I wanted to get rid of it as soon as I possibly could. Do you have any children, Ms. Kerby?"

"I have a daughter named Melissa. She's nine."

"Then I don't think I have to say any more," Kitty answered. "I didn't want to own that house for one second longer than I had to, and so I guess you got a pretty good deal."

I had, in fact.

"I told that Realtor to sell the place for what was left on the mortgage and the real estate costs," Kitty went on. "I paid off the debt and made sure I didn't clear a dime of the blood money from my daughter."

"I appreciate the gesture. But I don't understand," I said to Kitty. "If you wanted to get rid of the house as soon as you could, wasn't there someone else who wanted to buy it before I made an offer?"

Kitty came back to the present, and scowled. "You mean that developer guy?" she said, in a tone that indicated she was not Adam Morris's biggest fan. "I knew about his plans for the house, and Maxie had told me how hard she was fighting to keep him from bulldozing the place. I couldn't let that jerk touch a blade of grass on the lawn. Maxie wouldn't have wanted it, and it was Maxie's house. End of story."

"You really loved her," I said, about 80 percent unaware it was coming out of my mouth.

Kitty turned sharply toward me and gave me a stare that could peel the paint off a wall. "Of course I loved her," she said. "She was my daughter. But the part that gets me, that really gets me now . . ."

"Did you not get to tell her you loved her?" That was what happened all the time in the movies.

"Don't be ridiculous," Kitty said. "I told her I loved her all the time. She knew it." That wasn't the impression Maxie had given me, but okay. Kitty's voice caught for a moment. "The thing is, I not only loved her, I *liked* her, too. So I miss her that much more."

I wanted to tell Maxie about my visit with her mother, but she didn't make herself visible when I returned to the house. After debriefing me, Paul retreated to whatever Neverland he inhabited during what I'd come to think of as his off-hours, so I was in the middle of retiling the downstairs bathroom when Mayor Bridget Bostero brought David and Madeline Preston by "to see the lovely job you've been doing on their old house."

"We had just come by to see Bridget on a social visit, and she suggested we take a look," Madeline told me. "She said we'd be impressed." I would have been flattered, except I knew that Mayor Bostero had never set foot in the house as long as I'd owned it.

"Well, thank you," I said in what I'm sure was an unconvincing tone. "I didn't realize you'd been monitoring my progress, Mayor Bostero." I invited them inside, and they stood awkwardly in the foyer.

Bridget Bostero tossed her hair back to achieve a windswept effect (once a beautician, always a beautician). "I'm interested in *every* new business that comes to Harbor Haven, Alison," she said. "I'm sure I mentioned that when we had our lunch together." My goodness—was Bridget trying to impress the Prestons with how well she knew *me*?

I wiped my brow. Tiling isn't incredibly hard, but you can still work up a sweat in a confined space with only a tiny window for ventilation. I think some grout might have been wiped onto my forehead from my index finger. "Well, I'm glad for the distraction and the compliment," I said. I thought that was quite diplomatic, if I have to say so myself.

"You're tiling," David Preston said, no doubt noticing the smudge. "Are you doing the upstairs baths or the downstairs?"

"Downstairs, today," I answered. "The upstairs ones are already done, if you'd like to see." I didn't mention the additional one I'd added, which I'd finally farmed out to Tony's crew, because I wanted to see the Prestons' reaction when they saw it.

"Yeah," David said. The man's wit knew no bounds.

I took them upstairs and showed off the work I'd done. Even though I didn't think for one second that they were actually here to see the fruits of my labor—though I couldn't for the life of me figure out what they *were* here to see—I was proud of what I'd accomplished, and more than a little vain about showing it off.

The past few weeks had been devoted to the renovations I'd needed to make, but now, things were coming together. The new thermostat on the boiler had done the trick, and the heating system was now working. The new doors were on the kitchen cabinets, which were up on the walls. Painting, sanding and otherwise repairing of the walls had been achieved (with one notable exception). All I had left to do was refinish the floor in the dining room, and then the furniture could be delivered, various window treatments hung and area rugs put down, and I'd be able to take pictures of the house to put into a brochure and use for online advertising. People would be planning their next summer vacations soon, many before Thanksgiving. I was just about going to be ready.

In the new powder room, which I'd just finished painting that morning, the first reaction came from Bridget Bostero.

"This wasn't here before, was it?" she asked.

Wait a minute—how would she know that if she hasn't been here before?

"No," David Preston jumped in before I could. "We had a larger bedroom here."

"It's all within the code," I assured the mayor. "I've got the building permits."

She assured me showing her the paperwork wasn't necessary, but the look in her eye indicated she'd check the minute she got back to Town Hall, and I silently thanked the gods that I'd hired Tony's crew, because I probably wouldn't have bothered with permits but, being professionals, they had.

Madeline was consistently overpraising my work, which

led me to believe (especially given how tightly her jaw clenched as she spoke) that she hated everything I'd done to the fond memories she had of her home, and was plotting my demise even as she smiled at me.

I did notice, however, that all three of them were peeking into corners and examining walls that had seen no repairs at all, aside from fresh coats of paint. But it wasn't until we got back downstairs and into the main hallway that I started to suspect what might have been the catalyst for this uninvited visit.

"You'll have to overlook the one thing I haven't been able to fix yet," I said. We reached the wall with the large, now perfectly rectangular hole in the wall, where inside studs were exposed and plaster was still flaking just a little more every day.

You'd have thought I was unveiling the *Mona Lisa*. The three visitors flocked around the hole in the wall and stared at it, seemingly mesmerized by its incredible allure.

It was, I have to admit, a little spooky. Especially when Paul emerged through the wall behind me and asked, "What's all this, then?"

I started just a little, and David Preston looked at me. "What's the matter?" he asked.

"Just not happy about everybody looking at my most glaring failure," I answered.

"I don't think it's a failure," Bridget offered. "It gives the room character." I was quickly confirming my initial impression that Mayor Bostero was an idiot.

Madeline Preston's head was almost all the way inside the hole. "My goodness," she said, her voice muffled. "How will you fix this one, dear?"

For a second, I thought she was asking her husband, and that was strange enough. It was even more discomfiting when I realized she was addressing me. "We're working on a few ideas," I said. "Maybe a patch."

"A patch?" David asked. "What's the point of a patch? This is plaster. And the wall is curved. It'll never patch right." A great wit *and* an eternal optimist. All the good ones truly are taken.

"He's right, dear," Madeline said to me, again initiating an uncomfortable level of affection. "We had problems with these walls for years. You should save yourself the trouble and take them all down."

Take my walls down? *All* of them? Was she on drugs?

I didn't get a chance to ponder that further, or to inform my "guests" that I had no intention of doing anything so destructive, because there was knocking at the front door. Seemed my location was more popular than I realized— good news for my business plan.

Detective Anita McElone stood on my doorstep, straight and tall as always, looking just a little like Wonder Woman in less flamboyant clothing.

McElone looked at me, then at the group behind me, then back at me, and said in a loud, clear voice, "Alison Kerby, you are under arrest for the murder of Teresa L. Wright. You have the right to remain silent . . ."

I didn't listen to the rest of my rights, since the handcuffing and being walked to the police car at the curb distracted me. But I did see to it that the door was locked after McElone ushered the mayor and the Prestons out.

Thirty-five

If you've never sat handcuffed in the backseat of a police detective's car, let me tell you, you haven't missed a thing. Combining the view of the back of McElone's head and the weight of the handcuffs (metal ones—she hadn't used those plastic zip strips that seem to be all the rage on *COPS*—but at least they were in front of me and not behind my back), the trip had all the allure of . . . well, a ride to jail.

"This is ridiculous," I told McElone, who didn't answer. "What led you to this wacko conclusion?"

Again, no response. She didn't even turn her head.

"You can hear me, right?" I asked. You never can be sure. But the detective made not a sound, and didn't even seem to be watching me in the rearview mirror. How did she know I wasn't going to open the door and flee?

"Look, Detective," I said. "Maybe we've gotten off on the wrong foot. I'm just a single mom trying to make a living. I realize I've said some snarky things to you, and maybe I was out of line. But this is really going way over the top, don't you think?"

Nothing.

Fine, be that way. Here I'm trying to reach out and be a human being, and she doesn't want to know about it. Reach out a hand to some people, and all they do is cut you off at the wrist.

"You know, I was just trying to be friendly, Detective. But if you're too cold and robotic to see where I'm coming from, then fine, arrest me. I didn't kill anybody; I'm trying to stay out of the killer's way myself. And as a public employee, someone whose salary we taxpayers subsidize without complaint, you should realize . . ."

McElone sighed loudly, and pulled over to the side of the road. She stopped the car.

"What the hell is this all about?" I asked.

She got up, opened the car door and got out of the car. Then she reached over and opened the door in the back, the one on the driver's side.

The one where I was sitting.

"Hey, look, if that taxpayer crack was insulting, you have to remember I'm under a certain amount of stress here."

Without uttering a word, McElone, her face a portrait of irritation, reached for me. I gasped.

Especially when she unlocked my handcuffs and motioned me out of the car.

Rubbing my wrists (more because I had seen it in the movies than out of any actual discomfort), I stayed in my seat and stammered, "Um, Detective, I don't want to seem rude or anything, but you have a good twenty pounds on me, and you're probably trained in, you know, martial arts or subduing perpetrators and things like that. I'm not really interested in fighting you. . . ."

"Oh for goodness's sake, get out of the car," McElone said.

So I got out of the car.

"You got a cell phone?" she asked.

Baffled, I nodded that I did.

"Do you have someone you can call for a ride?" McElone continued.

What sort of trick was this? "My mother," I offered. Always lead with a mother when you're going for sympathy. "Why?"

"Because I'm leaving you here. Call your mother and get a ride. Go anywhere but back to that house, okay? Don't go home for at least a few hours."

I narrowed my eyes in the honest belief that I wasn't seeing what I was seeing or hearing what I was hearing. I would have narrowed my ears, too, but there are limits to being human. "What are you talking about?" I asked.

"I'm releasing you. We have insufficient evidence. Go away. Get your daughter from school. Take her out for a pizza. But don't go back to your house for a while. Tomorrow would be even better." McElone closed the car door behind me and turned toward the front.

"What are you *talking* about?" I repeated. "A minute and a half ago I was Public Enemy Number One and now you're dropping me off on the side of the road? How do you know I'm not a sociopathic killer planning her next strike even as we speak?"

"Let me get this straight," McElone responded. "You *want* to be arrested?" She had a point. "Get yourself a ride and get out of here."

"Why?" I asked.

"Why do I need a reason?" she asked, settling into the front seat of her unmarked police car. "I'm the police. Scram." And she started the car up and drove away onto Oceanedge Avenue.

So I called Mom. "How'd you like to take your daughter and granddaughter out for a pizza?" I asked.

"As long as there's no hot peppers," she answered. "You know how they give me heartburn."

I had time before Mom showed up, so I also called Phyllis, who had been asking when she could send a photographer for a feature she wanted to write about the guesthouse. I fudged and told her it would be a while longer before I could get the place into proper shape. I got the feeling Phyllis wasn't so much interested in a feature as she was in getting background on me in case I turned up as another victim. But she was too classy to say so.

While I had her on the phone, I also asked her if she'd ever heard this rumor about a George Washington deed, because Phyllis, being a good editor, knows everything that ever happened in Harbor Haven. "Oh, that old story," Phyllis said. Naturally. "That one's been going around this town pretty much since Washington left. I don't know if there's any truth to it, but if there is, you could be in line for a lot of money."

"If I live to see it. Tell me, how much of the legend is true?"

"Nobody knows; that's why it's a *legend*," Phyllis answered. "As far as I know, nobody's laid eyes on the document for at least a century."

"Did Madeline and Dave Preston know the story?" I asked.

Phyllis snorted her amusement. "*Everybody's* heard that one, kid," she said. "But I don't remember them ever taking much interest, tearing the house apart or anything. They were too busy with the nine kids."

I felt it was unnecessary to tell her I had a team of ghosts examining every square inch of the place even as we spoke.

"Did you know anybody who was especially interested in the story? Someone who'd ask around about it? Anything like that?" Maybe that would point toward someone desperate enough to kill two people over a two-hundred-year-old piece of paper.

"As a matter of fact, there was someone," Phyllis said after a minute. "He was *very* interested in the rumors, but it was before you bought the place."

Finally, a clue! Paul would be thrilled. "Who?" I asked.

"The history teacher, Ned Barnes," she answered. "Do you know him?"

"A little bit," I said.

"So she arrested you, drove you two and a half miles, then let you go?" Mom's brow was furrowed. She was thinking hard.

We'd ended up at Dinner in a Pizza, a Harbor Haven pizzeria with what it considered a "novel" gimmick: Each pie was modeled around a traditional multicourse dinner. We'd gotten the chicken-salad-bread combo, which isn't as odd as you'd think, but couldn't hold a candle to good old pepperoni, in at least this one diner's humble opinion. "I can't explain it," I told Mom.

Melissa had been listening carefully, but hadn't said much, which I attributed to confusion over having cucumber slices and chicken on an otherwise normal slice of pizza. But she started chewing on her bottom lip—something she calls "scratching" it—a sure sign that she was thinking deeply.

"Aren't police officers supposed to protect people?" she asked. It's so cute what they teach fourth graders.

"Well, yes," I answered. "That is part of the job. But sometimes when an officer is trying a little too hard . . ."

"How was Detective McElone protecting you by arresting you?" Melissa asked.

"Well, she wasn't," I said. "If she thought I was a criminal, then she'd be protecting *other* people by arresting me."

Mom swallowed a bite of her slice (having removed the

cucumbers and carrots, which she said "don't happen in
nature on a pizza") and broke in. "I don't think so," she
said. "I think maybe Melissa's right: The detective *was* trying to protect you."

"By putting me in handcuffs and shoving me into the
back of a police car?" I asked. "Since when are you on *her*
side?"

Mom pointed at me with the business end of her pizza
slice. "She wanted you out of that house for a few hours.
Suppose she thought something dangerous was going to
happen there—like a bomb."

It took keeping every muscle in my face perfectly still
not to roll my eyes. "A bomb?" I asked, my voice dropping
to James Earl Jones territory.

"A bomb," Mom repeated. "Or maybe someone coming
to search the house for this George Washington thing. Suppose she believes the killer is planning a return visit, and
she wants to stake out the scene of the crime."

"You have been watching *way* too much *CSI*," I told my
mother. "Stake out the scene of the crime? Who are you,
David Caruso? McElone doesn't like me, and she wants me
to be guilty of something, but she must have gotten cold
feet and realized she doesn't have enough evidence to hold
me, so she let me go."

"Then why did she tell you to stay away from the house?"
Melissa asked. I was being double-teamed by my mother
and daughter. We middle-generation children always have
it the worst.

"If she was trying to protect us so much, how come
she arrested me but not the Prestons or the mayor?" I
asked. "Wouldn't they be in just as much danger at the
house?"

Melissa chewed thoughtfully, which isn't easy for a
nine-year-old. "Well, didn't you say they left the same time
as you?" she asked.

"That's it," I told my mother and my daughter. "The two of you are splitting the bill. And I'm having dessert."

"I don't have any money," Melissa protested. "I'm a kid."

"Don't worry," her grandmother told her. "Your mom's just joking." She was wrong, of course, but it made Melissa feel better.

"We don't need to stake out our own house," I said to Mom. "Paul and Maxie are already in there. They'll tell us anything that goes on."

And yet, here we all were, sitting in the Volvo wagon (Mom considered her 2006 Dodge Viper "too sporty" to be a stakeout vehicle). We were parked on the hill overlooking my colossal investment that would soon be surrounded by luxury condos and gain a reputation as the house where the crazy ghost-seeing lady lived with her equally insane daughter. It was possible I didn't have the right attitude for the guesthouse business.

"But if the crooks run out past the sidewalk, they won't be able to chase them," Mom said. "We're here as backup."

Melissa nestled in the backseat. "I'm getting cold," she said. "Can't we turn the heat on?"

"If we turn the engine on, we'll be tipping off the bad guys," Mom said. "Don't you have a blanket or something back there?"

"I dunno. I'll look in the way back." Melissa turned around and started rummaging through the controlled chaos that is the cargo area of my station wagon. "I have to get up for school tomorrow, you know."

"If the house isn't under attack in a little while, we'll go inside, sweetie," I said.

"What'll happen to Maxie and Paul if a bomb goes off in there?" Mom asked.

"They're already dead," I reminded her. "The proper question is: What happens to *me* if a bomb goes off. . . . Will you get off this bomb thing, already?"

"I found a drop cloth," Melissa said. "Can I use that as a blanket?"

"No," I said. "It's full of paint and compound."

"But I'm *cold*!"

"How's the Dr. Spock costume coming, baby?" my mother said to distract Melissa.

"*Mr.* Spock, Grandma," she responded. "And it's okay. I've got everything but the ears. Do you know how to make pointed ears, Grandma?"

"Not really," Mom admitted. "Alison, do you . . ."

I shushed her when I saw something in the living room window. A light! "Somebody's in there," I whispered, as if the intruder would hear me if I spoke at a normal volume a hundred feet away.

"I think we should go down and see who it is," Mom said.

"You're not going anywhere," I told her. "You are staying here with your granddaughter and letting me go take a look. If you don't hear from me in ten minutes, call the police." I was an idiot, but a brave idiot; you have to give yourself points for something like that.

Mom didn't argue with me, and Melissa, although she looked scared, did not protest about staying behind. I'd hoped at least one of them would try to talk me out of it. I opened the car door.

Ding! Ding! Ding! Ding! Ding! Din . . .

I'd forgotten the key was still in the ignition, and the car was reminding me to take it out before I locked the door. Thanks a ton, car. But there was no visible movement in the front window, so I closed the car door and started walking—very, very slowly—toward the house.

Okay, I'll admit it: One of the reasons I was walking so slowly was that I was hoping the light would leave the house entirely, it would turn out to have been a hallucination induced by pizza with cucumber on it and I'd be able to turn back and forget the whole thing.

But it didn't matter, because as I approached the house from the right side—so I'd be able to see through the dining room window—the light started zinging around inside. Just my luck; cucumber on pizza is probably even good for you.

I don't want to say I crept up to the window, but *tiptoed* sounds so wimpy. However I got there, I was on my toes, peering in my own dining room window, and wondering exactly what it was I'd do if I *did* discover someone trying to blow up my house.

I pondered that for a minute or two and, having come up with no answer at all, decided to stumble ahead and see what happened. I didn't want to go into the house unarmed, but the only tools available were the ones already in the house, and they weren't doing me a ton of good just now.

All I had on me was a three-inch putty knife, the kind I used to spread drywall compound on small holes or cracks. Well, it was better than nothing. A little better.

I could have climbed in through the window (if I'd had a box to stand on), but there were certain issues of pride and dignity at stake: This was *my* house. Let the burglars come in through the windows. I'm walking through the front door.

I unlocked the door and opened it as quietly as possible, but the sound from the hinges sounded to me like the Squeak That Ate Cleveland. Once inside, I decided against turning on the lights, not wanting to give the intruder(s) a better shot at me. I knew there wasn't much in the house to trip over, and there was a little moonlight coming in through the window in the front room.

It's at a time like this that every creaky floorboard seeks out a foot to spread out under. There are advantages to houses that are less than a hundred years old, and one of them is the quiet floors and doors. I'd have to remember that the next time I weighed new construction versus quaint.

I couldn't have felt more conspicuous if I'd strapped on some cymbals, a bass drum and a kazoo and barreled across the living room as a one-woman band.

But I had an advantage over the intruder—I knew where I'd left my toolbox. If I could reach it before he/she/they knew I was there, I could arm myself with a screwdriver, a hammer or maybe a heavy wrench.

Hey, someone was in my house who hadn't been invited. And I was getting good and tired of this game.

I inched toward the toolbox, which I knew was just under the side window in the dining room, and I probably would have made it there, too. But then I heard a loud chorus of "Everybody's Got Something to Hide Except Me and My Monkey."

My ringtone. I'd forgotten to turn my cell phone off.

I checked the incoming number—it was my mother. Which left me with a dilemma: Answer and give away my position, or don't answer, have her think I'd been killed, and see Mom come charging down the hill.

There wasn't time to decide, however, because from behind me, a voice said, "Don't move." A man's voice. An oddly familiar man's voice. I was only a couple of feet from that great big wrench. . . .

But then I felt a strange warm rush through my body, not unlike a breeze. And I thought this was an awfully odd time (and about ten years too soon) to start getting hot flashes. Until Paul's voice, very quietly in my ear, whispered, "It's okay. I'm here." I didn't know whether that was a good thing or not. I considered telling him to get Maxie, who could at least pick up objects to throw.

And then the overhead lights came on.

Standing in the kitchen doorway, holding a hammer

like a weapon, Tony stood as tense as a tiger and twice as unable to speak. He just seemed to breathe in and out and stare at me.

"What are you doing here?" he finally managed.

"Shouldn't I be asking *you* that? This is my house." The phone continued to ring. I opened it, said, "I'm okay, it's just Tony," and closed it. I looked at Tony again. "Would you please put that hammer down?" I asked.

Paul hovered to one side, a hand on his hip, looking confused. Which made him as much like the rest of us as he'd ever be again.

Tony stared at me, then looked at the hammer, then turned back to stare at me. He shook his head and we both started laughing.

"What the hell is going on here?" I asked him when we both had exhausted ourselves and sat on the floor. "Why are you here, and how come you had the lights turned off?"

"I had the new plaster mold to try on the wall," Tony explained, and pointed toward the hallway where the hole in the wall seemed just as large as ever. "We were just going to bring it in."

"Who's 'we'?" I asked, and then I realized. "Come on out, Jeannie," I called.

The basement door opened, but instead of my best friend, Ned Barnes walked in. "Who's Jeannie?" he asked. He looked over at Tony. "The lights worked fine, no sparks," he said.

I stood up and Tony followed suit. "So, tell me again how come the lights were out?" I asked him. I noticed Paul, above the fireplace in the living room about fifteen feet away. He was watching Ned with what appeared to be concern—or distrust—on his face. "I don't feel very *secure*," I said in Paul's direction.

Tony shook his head. "I know you're squeamish about electricity, so I figured I'd check your service. I was surprised you had circuit breakers, and not fuses, in a house this old. We tripped a circuit breaker to see how the service rebooted."

"I had the electrical service replaced two weeks ago," I told Tony, "the same time the super-sized water heater was installed, so it's a brand-new . . . Hang on, what the hell are we talking about? *Why* are you two here together?"

"I was driving by and thought I'd get the rest of my house tour, and I found Tony outside," Ned told me.

I looked over at Paul without saying anything to confirm. Paul shrugged a shoulder.

"Wait a minute," I said. "Where did either of you park? I'd have recognized Tony's truck, and Ned, I never forget a car I hit."

"We both parked around back," Tony explained, shaking his head to emphasize how obvious that should have been to me. "It's easier to unload the truck backed up against the kitchen door than to walk a heavy piece of plaster up the front stairs."

Oh.

"From the outside, it looked like there were burglars," I said, looking meaningfully at Paul. "*Someone* would have seen something."

Paul scowled. "It's dark for ghosts, too," he said. "I've been meaning to ask you to leave a light on at night."

I exhaled audibly. "All right, where's this slab of plaster I've been hearing so much about?"

"In the truck," Tony answered. "I'll get it."

"*We'll* get it," Ned chimed in. "I'll bet it's heavy."

"All right, boys," I told them. "Everybody gets to show off his muscles. Let's go."

We started toward the kitchen door with Ned and Tony (mostly Tony) leading the way. But behind me, quietly, I heard Paul gasp. "Alison!"

I stopped and turned back, and I saw what had made Paul stare. I gasped, too.

On the near kitchen wall, directly across from the back door, was a one-dollar bill. And written on it in thick black marker was: "YOU HAVE THREE DAYS."

The dollar was affixed to the wall with a very sharp-looking knife. Which had been plunged right through the middle of George Washington's face.

Thirty-six

"Yep, that looks like a definite threat to me." Detective Anita McElone, who apparently handled every police call in Harbor Haven, studied the dollar-bill manifesto with what appeared to be a combination of interest and admiration on her face. "Somebody stuck that to your wall real hard, too. Very strong, I'd say, someone who could do real damage." McElone had a point, and so did the knife that cleaved the message to my wall.

"Don't try to make me feel better, Detective," I said. "Give it to me straight."

I'd called the police after consulting with Tony and Ned, who had given up on retrieving the plaster patch when they heard my yelps, and somewhat one-sidedly with Paul and Maxie. But after letting Mom and Melissa back into the house, it was decided that the police had to be alerted.

For the record, I was outvoted six (two dead) to one.

I hadn't felt it was worth calling the police because I found the message was clear: Somebody wanted that George

Washington deed in three days, or I was going to suffer the same fate as the previous residents of my house. Otherwise, why stick a dollar bill to my wall with a nasty message?

Maxie and Paul were both watching, Maxie half exposed through the overhead cabinets I'd only recently reinstalled, and Paul pretending to sit on a radiator across the room, never taking his eyes off Detective McElone.

"You sure this isn't just someone trying to get the early inside track on that 'first dollar you earned here' sweepstakes?" she asked me.

"You're a riot, Detective," I said. "Are you taking this act on the road?"

"I was just trying to lighten the mood," McElone said.

"Like when you arrested me just for the sport of leaving me on the road by myself?"

McElone, surprised, gave me a sharp look,. "You haven't figured that one out?" she asked. "Wow, you really aren't that bright after all, are you?"

Paul leaned forward.

"No," I told the detective. "Why don't you enlighten me?"

McElone shook her head. "I think you can get it on your own," she said. "Now, *this* one." She pointed to the impaled dollar bill. "This one is a little trickier. You have three days for what?"

"Apparently, I have three days to find a deed that George Washington signed for this property in the seventeen hundreds and, presumably, to give it to whoever stabbed my wall," I told her. "You hadn't figured that one out? I guess *you're* really not all that bright, are you?"

Strangely, McElone did not accept that as an answer, so I told her about Ned's research into the Washington deed and why it now seemed someone thought I had it, or that I could get it, and that it was in some way rightfully theirs.

She didn't interrupt me once during this recitation, but when it was over, the detective looked me over and said, "I should bring you in on suspicion of possession."

"But I don't have the deed."

"I wasn't talking about the deed. That's the shakiest reasoning I've ever heard."

She took another photograph of the object stuck so nastily to my freshly painted wall, and then reached up with her gloved hand and pulled it out carefully, trying very hard not to exert too much force on the knife handle. Once out of the wall, the whole objet d'art was dropped into a plastic evidence bag.

"What do you think?" I asked her.

"I think you're hiding something," McElone said. "But I can't figure out what."

I glanced at the ghosts, but said, "What do you think about the knife in my wall?"

"I'd take the timetable seriously, at least," she answered after a moment's reflection. "Someone is clearly upset with you over something and wants to make sure you're aware of it."

"I'm aware of it," I assured her.

"I have no doubt. I'm not a hundred percent sure I believe that whole cockamamie story about George Washington, though."

"The knife was put through a one-dollar bill," I pointed out.

"Yeah, because usually when you're doing something like that, you like to use a fifty," McElone retorted. "They hold up so much better under the magic marker."

"You don't think it's significant that the knife was put right through Washington's face?"

She made an *eh* face and said, "Not when the treasury prints over sixteen million of those suckers every single day. Now, for the time being, I wonder if there isn't someplace you can find to stay for the next three days."

"Why? That's the second time you've told me to stay out of my own house."

"Yeah, and look how well you listened the first time."

I'd been hoping she wouldn't bring that up. "Isn't it enough that someone is threatening you?"

Paul shook his head *no*.

"The threat doesn't say they're coming to get me *in the house*," I reasoned lamely. "They could come after me at my mother's, or at my friends', or when I'm picking Melissa up from school." Then I remembered a detail I'd forgotten to tell Paul, and figured McElone might as well hear it, too. "By the way, Mayor Bostero said something strange when she was here. She made a comment about the upstairs powder room."

"She didn't like the wallpaper?" McElone asked. "Hardly criminal."

"It would be criminal to *put* wallpaper up there," Maxie muttered.

"That's not the point," I said. "She commented on how it wasn't there earlier, but she's never been inside here before. How could she know that?"

"Just because she hasn't been here since *you* owned the house doesn't mean that she's never been here at all," Mc-Elone answered. "She could have visited when Malone or the Prestons owned the place, or she could have come over to look at it with the Realtor, Terry Wright. You're reaching." But Paul looked impressed, and stroked his jawline in thought, while Maxie shook her head to indicate that the mayor hadn't come over when she'd owned the place.

"Even if she dropped by to visit her pals the Prestons, would she have gone up to their bedroom?" I asked.

"I still think you should leave for a few days," McElone went on, ignoring me. "I want to put an officer in here to act as bait, and I can't do that if you're here."

"That's crazy," I said, echoing what Paul was telling me. "There's no point in having someone here if the bad guys are trailing me somewhere else."

"All right, I'll say it," McElone grunted, looking more embarrassed than annoyed. "This house creeps me out."

I felt my lips withdraw into my mouth, and I bit down on them. I think I was trying to suppress a laugh, but it's also possible I was just stunned. "*What*?" I finally croaked out.

"You heard me," the detective said. "I get a weird vibe off of this place, and I've heard stories around town about ghosts."

Involuntarily, I turned my head to look at Paul. Maxie, who had turned on her side and was floating like Cleopatra on a barge, spat out a laugh, and I think McElone shuddered when it happened. "Did you hear that?" she asked.

"Hear what?" I felt like such a jerk, but what was I going to do—introduce everyone around? *Oh, and here are my two friends: They're dead, and you can't see them.* That would have gone over big.

"I thought I heard a laugh, from far away," McElone said. Her eyes looked around the room, as if she were waiting for skeletons to stampede her or for the walls to start dripping blood.

"Must be somebody's television," I attempted.

McElone shook her head. "Not that laugh," she said.

"Okay, so let me get this straight—you're creeped out by the house, so *I* should stay away?"

Anita McElone grimaced and looked away. "Fine," she said. "Don't leave. But I'm not coming here again unless your body is found and they need me to say, 'I told you so,' as they cart you away."

Maxie reached her hand out and the lapel on McElone's jacket flapped. All the color drained from the detective's face and she inhaled quickly.

"You can reach me at the station," she said, and was out the door before I could reply.

I turned toward Maxie and put my hands on my hips.

"Oh, like you wouldn't have done it if you could," Maxie said.

She had me there.

Thirty-seven

Once again, my team of "experts" felt that I should high-tail it out of the house and go hide somewhere. Tony and Jeannie offered their home, but I declined. My mother suggested Melissa and I stay with her for the duration, but I wasn't about to stop work on the house now, and staying with Mom would only make me suicidal, which would defeat the original purpose.

I thought about asking Ned, but it would have been odd to get a guy you've only been out with twice involved in such a conversation, and besides, he'd probably want to come stay in the house with us, if only to experience its historical legacy up close for a longer period of time. It's disconcerting to date a man more interested in your house's architecture than your own.

Only Melissa agreed we should stay in the house, on the flimsy reasoning that "Maxie and Paul won't let anything happen to us." Melissa seemed somewhat oblivious to the fact that our two roommates were deceased, but I welcomed her agreement with my decision. We stayed.

The next afternoon, Maxie took off for points unknown (but obviously nearby—maybe the attic), and Paul watched me put finishing touches on the paint job in the kitchen.

"Were you a *good* private investigator?" I asked Paul as he watched from the stove (where he was seated).

"I only had my license for about six months before . . . this happened," he replied after a moment. "I never really got a chance to find out."

"So that's why you're so intent on finding out who did this," I speculated out loud.

Paul smiled his enigmatic smile, the one that made him look like a more muscular Clive Owen. "Well, that's part of it," he answered. "But the fact is, getting killed is sort of a large offense. It tends to bring out the vengeful side of a guy."

I nodded. "McElone seemed to think I should know why she let me go right after she arrested me. You're the detective. What's your theory?"

He seemed to be grateful for the change of subject. "Think about it, Alison," he said. "What was going on when she arrested you?"

I stopped detailing and stood on the ladder, thinking. "Mayor Bridget Bostero—whom I've decided is an idiot, by the way—and the Prestons had invited themselves in for a tour, and they were trying to humiliate me by spending most of their time looking at the great big hole in my hallway wall."

"And that's when the doorbell rang?"

I nodded. "Yes. I was trying to figure out what was so fascinating about the break in the plaster when McElone showed up and carted me off."

"So," Paul said, leading me as any good teacher would, "when you opened the door, what did Detective McElone see?"

"Me, standing there with a smear of something on my

forehead, and a group of people mocking my one failure amid a sea of jobs done well."

Paul grinned with one half of his mouth and shook his head. "You have some serious self-esteem issues, you know that? Think of it from the detective's point of view. What did she expect to see when the door opened?"

"Me, I guess."

"And what did she see instead?"

I pursed my lips. "Me, with everyone else behind me, looking into a hole in the wall."

"Good. Now, I was there too, so I have my own perspective. But I'll ask you what *you* saw. From that first second when you opened the door until she said you were under arrest, did Detective McElone's expression change?"

Her expression? "I don't know. It was forever ago."

"It was yesterday."

"Fine. Yeah, I guess her expression changed. She looked mad."

"And that's when she decided to arrest you."

"You don't think she came here to do that?" I asked.

"It's not what I think; it's what *you saw*," Paul said. He could be annoying that way.

I stopped, more to make a show of thinking than to think. But dammit, it worked. "She saw the mayor and the Prestons behind me. And she didn't expect to see them. So she arrested me on the spot. Why?"

"Why do you think?" Paul was smiling in the way a good teacher smiles at a pupil who's figuring out multiplication for the first time. I felt like an idiot.

"She wanted to get me out of the house. She wanted to get me away from them." That was the only way it made sense, but it *didn't* make sense. Why would Detective McElone care if Mayor Bostero and the Prestons were in the house? Why not just tell me whatever she wanted to tell me and leave? "Do you think she considers them, or at least one of them, suspects in your killing?" I asked Paul.

He grinned. "By George," he said with an exaggerated British accent. "I think she's got it." He picked a spoon up off the table and put it in his mouth, pretending it was a pipe.

I went back to painting, but I'll admit I was pleased at the compliment. "You're doing much better at picking things up," I said, referring to the spoon.

"Thank you, but Maxie is still miles ahead of me."

"Yeah, but at least you're nicer to me than she is," I said.

Paul shook his head. "Maxie's jealous of you. You have everything she wanted. And I can tell you from experience: Being dead is a very difficult thing to adjust to. I think we're both still adjusting."

I got back up on the ladder to reach behind the sink. "What do you mean, I have everything she wanted?"

"Well, the house of course, but mostly Melissa."

I turned my head too quickly, and almost made a mark on the wall where I didn't want one. I caught myself just in time. "Maxie wants Melissa?"

"That's not what I mean. I think she always wanted to have a child, thought she'd have had plenty of time for that, and look what happened. And she does truly adore your daughter," Paul said.

"So, great. If the killer gets me, we can all haunt the house together and raise Liss like the dead parents every child wishes for."

"We need to mobilize about that," Paul said. "You only have two days left."

"The warning said three."

"That was yesterday." A ray of sunshine, this ghost.

"Swell. What are we going to do?" I had been trying hard not to think about my deadline, and the way that word sounded so much more literal than it ever had before.

"Well, the good thing about having a time limit is we can assume nothing will happen today or tomorrow. So first thing, Maxie and I need to step up the search for this Washington document. We can move about more easily and look into places you can't. If all else fails, it wouldn't be a bad idea to have the actual item in your possession when the time comes." Paul was in full private investigator mode now.

"What should I be doing?" Hey, he was the professional. More than me, anyway.

"Redouble your efforts. Detective work is about perseverance. Start with Phyllis; see if she knows anything new. And get back on the trail of that book Kerin Murphy took from Terry Wright's office."

I got down off the ladder and stood in the center of the room. The room was truly looking wonderful—understated, homey without being hokey, and subtle without being invisible. "I hate it when Maxie's right," I said.

From under the floor, without the sign of a physical presence, came the last voice I wanted to hear at that moment. "The feeling's mutual," Maxie said.

Thirty-eight

Phyllis Coates had her New Balance shoes up on her desk when I walked in for a cup of coffee and an exchange of information. Since I had no information Phyllis hadn't heard, the exchange was somewhat one-sided.

Melissa, now insistent on being at every meeting with Phyllis (the two had bonded over hot chocolate), listened to what I said, even the part about the dollar knifed to my wall, without comment. But she had a pencil behind her ear, like Phyllis, and was examining the way the editor sat back in her chair.

Phyllis's "friend" at the medical examiner's office had called again, apparently. "They reexamined the tissue samples they took at the time, and I hear the coroner is going to issue a report on the two 'suicides' tomorrow. They figured out how the poison was administered."

"Really!" Paul would be transparent with envy when he found out I'd hear first. "How did they do it?"

"Judging by the contents of their stomachs and the way the poison—the acetone—had circulated through their systems, the best guess is it had been taken in a glass or two of red wine each. Probably about forty-five minutes to an hour before they died."

It took a moment for that to sink in. But Melissa is quicker than I am. "So whoever did it was probably at Café Linguine when Paul and Maxie went there after the planning board meeting," she said.

"You get the blue ribbon, kid," Phyllis said. "So the killer has to be someone who was at the restaurant, and probably at the meeting before that, too."

Melissa beamed at the compliment. She sipped her hot chocolate (which, unlike Phyllis's, was not spiked with rum) and grinned.

"Phyllis," I said carefully, "Mayor Bostero owns part of Café Linguine. She even might have been at the bar or in the kitchen that night."

"I know, honey," Phyllis said. "But the interviews the cops had with the bartender and the waitstaff didn't mention her doing anything except sitting at the table with the planning board and ordering shrimp."

"I'm going to have to tell Paul," I said to myself.

"What was that?" Phyllis asked, confused.

I caught myself. "I said, 'If that don't beat all,' " I told her.

"Uh-huh," she said.

I tore Melissa away after three cups of cocoa and as many trips to the bathroom and, thanking Phyllis, headed out on our most serious errand of the day. Halloween House of Horrors, a specialty store that had set up shop temporarily on Route 35, was packed to the gills, which wasn't surprising, seeing as how Halloween was all of a day and a half away. Melissa, in an uncharacteristically fatalistic mood, was dragging her feet next to me, and not crazy about taking my hand.

"People will see us," she whined. "I'm not a baby."

"You're *my* baby," I told her, which I'm sure was exactly what she wanted to hear. "And I'm not letting you get swept up in a human tide and taken from me forever."

"I have a cell phone," she pointed out in her best "my mom's an idiot" voice. Honestly, it was a miracle I could dress myself without her help in the morning, I was so stupid.

"I'm holding your hand. Deal with it."

Melissa put on a grump face and said nothing, but didn't try to yank her hand out of mine, which I counted as a minor victory. Our mission for the day: Find a pair of pointed ears, preferably not already attached to another person. If my daughter wanted to be a blue-shirted, bowl-hair-cutted, eyebrow-raising (she wanted me to shave them halfway to make them more pointed, but *that* wasn't going to happen) male Vulcan for Halloween, so it would be. Everything was in place but those freakin' ears.

The sales desk was packed seven deep, so asking for help from someone behind the counter was a lost cause. And since there was no large sign with red twenty-two-inch letters reading "Pointed Ears," I'd have to do some investigative work on my own. If only Paul were here.

"Why don't you want to be a ghost for Halloween?" I asked my daughter. "That's easy."

She looked at me with pity. "Ghosts look just like everybody else," she said. Oh yeah, I'd forgotten. She was actually friends with ghosts. The whole sheet-over-the-head thing would probably be considered a form of discrimination, or an unbearable stereotype, to my fair-minded daughter.

We hadn't walked very far down the aisle (which seemed to be filled with fake bloody body parts, and try saying *that* three times fast) when I heard a voice from behind me. "Alison! Alison Kerby!"

I turned, and there stood Kerin Murphy. I looked down at Melissa, who was considering a rubber hand with a rubber knife through it and rubber blood gushing from the rubber wound. It was charming, and only seventeen ninety-five. Obviously, my daughter wasn't going to be much help.

Kerin was wearing the most casual of high-end clothes, not exactly a jogging suit but something that clearly could be used during exercise, yet had cost as much as my television. She had no doubt just arrived on her way home from the fitness center at Buckingham Palace.

"Kerin!" I said. "So you were late thinking about Halloween too, huh?" At least I could wallow in the idea that someone else was as negligent a parent as I was.

"Oh no." Kerin waved a hand at that notion. She dropped no hint that we'd both been in the room with Terry Wright's corpse. "I'm here dropping off my oldest. Syndee is working here part-time as part of a work-study program at the middle school." No doubt Syndee was also volunteering at a homeless shelter on weekends and staying up nights knitting nuclear bomb shields for the Middle East. "What about you?"

"We're just putting the finishing touches on a costume we're donating to a shelter for gifted children," I said. Melissa's face shot up toward mine with an absolutely appalled expression on it. "Then we're going to Staples to pick up an *appointment book*." Melissa knew better than to say anything, but her face was asking if I'd lost my mind.

"Well, maybe I can get Syndee to help you," Kerin offered. She didn't so much as blink.

"Oh no, we're just fine."

Melissa started scanning the crowd, no doubt looking for a better mother she could adopt.

"Good," Kerin said, and for a golden moment, I thought she was going to walk away, but she stopped and spoke to me in a confidential tone. "Oh, by the way, Alison," she hissed. "I know your secret."

It occurred to me to say that I knew hers, too, but I played it safe. "Really? You'd better not tell me, or it won't be a secret anymore."

"I know about the ghosts," Kerin went on, oblivious to my incredibly witty remark.

I froze. Maybe she meant something other than what I thought. "Ghosts?" I said.

"Sure. The girls have been talking about it for weeks. I hear you have two ghosts living in your house." Kerin smiled the most annoying smile I'd seen since The Swine had taken the highway to the Golden State.

I reflexively looked down at Melissa, who was suddenly very interested in studying her shoes.

"Girls like to tell stories," I said, staring at my daughter. "You know how it is."

"Of course," Kerin said. Then she looked down at Melissa and said, "Did you make up the ghosts, sweetie?" When I was Melissa's age, I would have decked someone who talked like that to me, but my daughter is much more evolved, and doesn't have the same reach with her left.

"No," Melissa said, staring straight into Kerin's eyes. "Maxie and Paul are real."

Nice covering, Liss.

"That's so adorable!" Kerin gushed. "I wish Marlee had such a vivid imagination."

"It's not imagination," Melissa countered, voice as calm as a mid-May breeze. "They died in our house, and now they can't leave. They're my friends."

Kerin's smile faded a little bit. "But you have some *real* friends, don't you, sweetie?"

"Her name's Melissa," I reminded Kerin. "And yes, she has living, breathing friends as well." What the hell, I thought. My business was doomed from the start, anyway. I might as well shovel dirt on its grave. Seemed appropriate, somehow.

"As well?" Kerin was quick enough to pick up on that.

"Yes. In addition to Paul and Maxie, the ghosts, Melissa also likes to play with living people. So on Thursday, we'll be skipping the SafeOWeen to have some *real* fun. Now if you'll excuse us, we're off to find some pointed ears."

We walked off, and Melissa actually reached out and took my hand.

Thirty-nine

The ears were sold out.

After another two stores with no luck, I followed Maxie's suggestion (to my irritation) and we ended up buying some Silly Putty at a Toys "R" Us in the hopes that we could figure out a way to attach it to Melissa's actual ears and fashion it into the proper configuration. That was the plan, anyway.

But I wasn't thinking about it yet because Halloween was still two nights away. At the moment, I was thinking about how Ned Barnes was a very charming man who was looking at me with a good deal of warmth, a real asset in the late-October chill as we strolled down the boardwalk in Point Pleasant, one town over from Harbor Haven.

"Whose idea was this, anyway?" I asked him, snuggling into my very alluring puffy down vest. Could I dress to entice a guy, or what?

"Yours," Ned answered. "I had suggested a movie. In a nice warm theater."

"Fine. Lord your sanity over me." It was hard to remind myself that Phyllis had mentioned Ned being interested in the Washington deed long before I bought the house.

Before Ned and I left, Paul had informed me that the "very thorough" search he and Maxie (mostly Paul) had made of the house had turned up no documents emblazoned with George Washington's John Hancock. "It's entirely possible the whole story is just a myth," he'd said.

"But then you and Maxie . . ." I hadn't thought before speaking.

"Yes. If we're right about the killer being after the deed, we'd have died for nothing." Paul's face had been so unspeakably sad and angry that I'd left him alone, mostly because he'd asked me to do so.

Now, on the boardwalk, Ned grinned at me, which was altogether unfair, and shook his head. "I'll never claim to be the sanest guy in the room," he said. "I gave up copper mining to teach history to nine-year-olds."

"Yeah, who wouldn't pine for the romantic life of the copper miner?"

He put his arm around me, ostensibly because I looked cold, and I didn't do anything to dissuade him of that notion. Yet while I was reasonably warm in my down vest, I noticed that Ned himself wore nothing but a thin blue denim jacket, which would have set off his eyes if we hadn't been mostly in the dark.

"I've decided not to let you out of my sight until Friday," Ned told me. "This deadline you've been given is not something to take lightly."

I shivered, and not just because it was cold. "I've been trying not to think about it," I admitted. "I've been joking about it, pretending it isn't real. I keep thinking something will happen, and I'll wake up and this will have been an odd dream. I won't have seen . . ." Oops. He didn't know about my boarders.

Ned stopped and looked at me. "You won't have seen what?" he asked.

"*Seemed*," I "corrected" him. "I won't have *seemed* like a hysterical maniac to you."

But Ned wasn't buying: His eyes narrowed, and he grabbed me gently by the upper arms. "Alison, don't play games with this," he said, pleading. I couldn't figure out what he meant. "If you've found that Washington document, you should just give it to these people."

That was what he meant? He thought I was holding on to the deed out of . . . what? Greed? Stubbornness?

"I don't have the deed," I told him, maybe a little too harshly. "I haven't the vaguest idea where it is or if it even exists."

Ned didn't let go of my arms, and his voice got thick. "I'm trying to save your life here, Alison," he said. "Tell me where the deed is, and let's hand it over right now, before another minute goes by."

There was something about his manner—okay, it was *everything* about his manner—that was frightening me. I shoved his hands off my arms. "I *don't have* the deed!" I repeated. "What's gotten into you?"

He covered his tracks well. He put up his hands in a conciliatory gesture and smiled. "I'm sorry," he said quietly. "I'm worried about you. I don't want you to be facing this thing." He held out his hand for me to take. "Forgive me?" he asked.

"Sure," I said, but I didn't take his hand. We walked the rest of the boardwalk in silence, and then Ned drove me home.

I'd left Melissa at the house with Jeannie, and I wasn't in much of a mood to talk when I got back, so it was even worse that Tony had joined her there, and because we'd come back so early, Melissa was still awake. So I had three people wondering what the hell my problem was when I'd just been out to the boardwalk with an attractive man. (Although Melissa was barely hiding her glee that my date with her teacher hadn't gone well.)

Their subtle probing of my mood (Jeannie: "What the hell is your problem?" Tony: "Did he do anything," looking in Melissa's direction, "you know, that I need to talk to him about?" Melissa: "Are you *sure* I can't shave just half of my eyebrows?") didn't last very long, as they could see I didn't feel like talking about it. I changed the subject to the new plaster mold. Luckily, Tony bit.

He immediately got to his feet with enthusiasm. "I still think it'll work," he said. "The screw holes are in line to attach to the studs, and once the seams are dry, you can cover them up so that nobody will ever know they were there."

"Sounds like a plan," I said. "You're a genius, as usual."

"I've got it in the truck," Tony said, sounding as young as a classmate of Melissa's. "You want to try it now?"

And that was how he and I ended up working on the wall at ten that evening.

Tony and I carried the mold—it wasn't all *that* heavy, but it required both of us because it was bulky—into the house and through the kitchen door to the hallway that needed the repair.

I was hoping the two spectral squatters in my house wouldn't notice the noise, or would be out haunting the backyard for a while. The last thing I needed was a replay of Maxie's spectacular *whoosh* through the wall the last time we'd tried to install a piece of wall filler.

No sign of them yet, and we were in place in front of the hole. I held my breath.

"Okay," Tony said. "Let's just rest it on the frame right now and steady it there. Don't let go." So we moved the mold, which had holes drilled into its four corners at well-measured spots, to the wall, and rested its base on the lower end of the hole. I did not take my hands off the left side, and Tony held the right in place with one hand.

"Very carefully," he said, "take my side. I'm going to get the cordless screwdriver and we'll secure this thing to the studs."

"I've got one in the toolbox in the kitchen," I told him, moving over to cover both sides of the mold. I was essentially holding the mold up with my body at that moment.

And naturally, that was when Maxie showed up, sticking her head through the ceiling right above my head. "What is your *problem*?" she demanded. "Why are you hugging the wall?"

Tony hustled back to my side with some drywall screws and the cordless screwdriver. "Okay," he said. "I'm going to work top right first. Move your hand."

"Oh, look who's here," Maxie drawled, and I had to suppress an urge to tell her once again that Tony was not only married, but alive, which made him more than off-limits to her.

I moved my hand, glaring in Maxie's direction whenever Tony wasn't looking as he got the top two screws into place quickly.

"You can breathe a little now," Tony told me. "But don't let go entirely until I get all four in. I can't tighten them all the way, or they'll go through the plaster and straight into the stud."

"That sounds dirty," Maxie commented from above, now with her entire "body" visible near the ceiling. "Of course, everything that guy says sounds dirty." I gritted my teeth at her, and she laughed.

Tony got the other two screws through the plaster mold and, grabbing the studs, told me I could step back. I was reluctant to do so, even though I knew the mold wouldn't fall out now. Sometimes, what your brain knows doesn't match up with what your heart really and truly believes.

I stepped back, and Tony and I admired our (his) handiwork. It was splendid—the hole was completely covered in real plaster, and the gaps around each edge were minimal. I'd be able to fill them with compound, fill in the screw holes, and paint the whole wall after it was sanded down. The patch would be virtually invisible.

"You're a wizard," I told Tony.

"He's not bad at fixing walls, either," Maxie drooled.

I growled a little, way back in my throat. Tony looked over at me and said, "Are you okay?" I nodded.

"Something went down the wrong way," I told him.

"Look at the way those jeans fit," Maxie went on. She descended from the ceiling and started—how can I describe it—*swirling* around Tony, a completely demented grin on her face.

Tony turned toward me with an expression that combined puzzlement with a growing sense of comprehension (yes, I know that sounds contradictory, but it's true). "Alison," he started. "You're starting to scare . . ."

He didn't get the time to finish his sentence, because Maxie, apparently unable to control herself, came to a soft landing directly in front of him, took a deep "breath," and threw her arms around him. She kissed him square on the lips.

Now, if you've never seen a ghost kiss your mentor-slash-best friend's husband (and I'm willing to bet you haven't), rest assured that it is one of the most bizarre sights imaginable. Standing behind them, I could see not only Maxie's back, but through her body to Tony, who looked absolutely astonished.

When she let him go and Tony breathed again, he continued to stare straight ahead, mostly because I was directly in his line of sight. "What the hell was *that*?" he asked when he could.

"What the hell was what?" When in doubt, deny, deny, deny.

"I felt . . . I felt . . ."

"Wait, Tony, don't," I said.

"Somebody . . . something . . . *kissed* me," Tony said. "And you know about it, don't you?"

Jeannie and Melissa, drawn by loud voices, came into the hallway. Jeannie stared at her husband. "Who kissed you?" she demanded.

Melissa, for the first time I'd noticed, looked disapprovingly at Maxie, who seemed not to notice in the euphoria of her moment.

"When I kiss 'em, they stay kissed," Maxie hooted, back on the ceiling again. Then she looked down at Jeannie. "He married *her*?" she chortled.

I looked up with fire in my eyes, and Tony noticed. "You can see her, can't you?" Then he stopped, his eyes widened a little, and he said, "It *was* a her, wasn't it?"

"I don't know what you're talking about," I told him.

"I've been wanting to do that for weeks," Maxie gloated. "Damn, that felt good!"

"It was horrible," Tony said, and Maxie stopped dead (pardon the expression) in what would have been her tracks. "I don't know what it was, but it was like being kissed by a hungry animal."

"That was the *good* part," Maxie protested.

"What the hell is going on?" Jeannie said.

Melissa sighed. "It was Maxie," she told Jeannie.

Tony dropped down into a sitting position. "Oh Lord," he said. "It *was* a guy."

"No, no—Maxie is the girl." The girl who, at the moment, was looking at Tony with a murderous rage in her eyes.

"*What* girl?" Jeannie asked, her eyes narrowing. "Alison, did you kiss Tony?"

"What? No!" I looked at Melissa. "We have to tell Jeannie."

"Tell Jeannie?" Jeannie repeated. "Tell Jeannie *what*?"

Melissa—as always, disturbingly calm under pressure—looked Jeannie in the face. "We have two ghosts in the house," she said very matter-of-factly.

Jeannie looked at her for a moment, then blinked. "Of course you do, Liss," she said.

"No," I told her. "Really. There are two ghosts in this house, and one of them just kissed Tony."

Tony was still searching the ceiling and breathing hard. "They live in the house?" he asked.

"If you call it living."

"Oh, come on," Jeannie said, scanning our faces. "What's the gag?"

"No gag," I said. "Ghosts." I pointed at Maxie, who was scowling at Jeannie and shaking her head.

"I guess he didn't marry her for her mind," Maxie said.

"Oh, cut it out," Jeannie said, and walked out toward the kitchen, shaking her head.

I looked up at Maxie, who huffed and flew up into the ceiling, vanishing from sight.

"Okay." Tony set his jaw. "I'm . . . listening. Now, tell me all about these ghosts."

So I did. Tony listened intently, stopping to ask questions only when I didn't explain something quickly enough for his taste. Occasionally Melissa would add something (like the unfortunate moment she felt it was necessary to mention that Maxie was "really pretty"). When we'd gotten through the whole sordid story, Tony's mouth was more or less puckered, and twisted to the left side of his face.

That meant he was thinking.

"So you think maybe it's one of those 'unfinished business' things? If you find this George Washington thing, they'll be able to move on to Heaven, or something?"

I shrugged. "For all I know, nothing will happen. Or maybe their next stop from here is a body shop in Indianapolis. But either way, I have to find that deed before

Thursday night, or rumor has it I'll be joining Paul and Maxie in haunting this place."

Tony's teeth clenched. "Nothing's going to happen to you," he promised. "I fixed the wall, and I'll fix this. Jeannie and I are on it twenty-four/seven as of right now."

It took a *lot* of convincing, but Tony deemphasized the afterlife angle and emphasized the immediate-danger-to-Alison angle and, ghosts or not, Jeannie agreed we needed guarding. The two of them got sleeping bags out of Tony's truck (he's always prepared) and announced their intention to camp out in the upstairs bedrooms. "We'll be your first guests!" Jeannie said, pretending nobody had mentioned dead people in the room or a specter kissing her husband. She's a trouper. But her eyes were still suspicious.

I was too tired and spent for paranoia, however, so I went upstairs, where I saw no dead people, and went to bed after making sure Melissa did the same.

And when I came downstairs in the morning, the patch on the wall had been smashed in. I looked up at the ceiling and screamed.

"Maaaaaxiiiiiieeee!"

Forty

"It *wasn't me*," Maxie said for the seventeenth time. "Why won't you believe me?"

My eyebrows met in the middle. "What reason have you ever given me to believe you about anything?" I asked the ghost.

Maxie stamped her foot, but she was three feet in the air. "I'm telling the *truth*!"

Melissa rubbed her eyes as she walked into the hallway. "What's going on now?" she asked. Just another day in Spook House.

I exhaled, and looked at Maxie. "Face it. You didn't like the way Tony reacted to your kiss. You got mad, and as soon as we went upstairs, you picked up the mallet"—I pointed to the rubber mallet left lying on the floor next to the once-again-gaping hole—"and you punched in the patch we'd been working on so hard. Just admit it."

Paul, standing in a corner with his arms folded, shook his head. "Not this time, Alison. I saw Maxie when you two left, and she didn't come down here. She was busy upstairs . . ."

Maxie looked at him threateningly. "Don't you dare," she said.

"I have to," Paul answered her. "She was crying," he told me.

If there was one thing I didn't want to do, it was admit that Maxie hadn't done anything wrong. "All right, fine," I said, defiantly. "If Maxie didn't break the wall, who did? How come you guys didn't hear someone smashing in my wall?"

Paul gave Maxie a glance, and she turned her head away from him. "We went outside to get a change of scenery," he said. "We were at the limit of the property in the back, almost an acre away. I didn't see anyone drive up, and we didn't hear anything in the house. Why didn't *you* hear it?"

I didn't answer. Paul looked at the floor. Maxie dropped through it.

"You know, you should give Maxie a break." Paul raised his head and looked me straight in the eye.

I told Melissa to go shower and get ready for school. She protested ("This is going to be the *good* part"), but she went.

I turned toward Paul once Liss had gone. "You want me to be nice to Maxie? After everything she's—"

Paul cut me off. "She's had about as bad a turn as a girl can get. She's *dead*. Is it really that much to ask that you two lighten up on her?" he said.

I couldn't answer that.

Paul shook his head. "There's no time for this bickering now. We need to focus on finding that deed, Alison. That seems to be the only way to save you."

"Tell me something I don't know."

"Let's think about this." Paul closed his eyes. His lips didn't exactly pucker, but they tightened around his teeth. This was deep consideration. "I don't think it's an outrageous assumption that whoever is after this deed is the same person—or people—who killed Maxie and me."

"Agreed," I said. It seemed appropriate at the time.

"So let's consider who that could be." Paul opened his eyes and looked at me. "We've been going about this the wrong way."

"Obviously."

"We've been spending so much time on the house, on the motive, that we've completely ignored opportunity. We can assume, based on the information you got from the newspaper editor, that the poison had to be administered at some point during our dinner at Café Linguine."

"Right. So who was there that night who might have wanted you two out of the way?"

"That's the problem. Almost everyone." Paul wrinkled his forehead. It was adorable. "After the planning board meeting ended, the whole board, the mayor—and even Adam Morris, as I recall—came to the restaurant. Morris or the mayor might have been upset about the vote going against the new construction."

"Was Kerin Murphy there?" I asked hopefully. I was holding out for Kerin being evil.

"I don't remember seeing her there," Paul answered. "But I hadn't seen her then, so it's possible she was."

"That's grasping at straws," I pointed out.

"We haven't got much. The point is, it would have been easy enough for any of them to slip something into our wine."

I gave him a look. "How?" I asked. "I've seen the restaurant. The bar is right near the entrance to the kitchen. The wine comes from the bar to your table, and then the glasses are sitting right in front of the two of you the whole time."

Paul nodded in agreement. "So the poison had to be put in the glasses either at the bar, or on the way from the bar to the table."

"Did you see anyone in that area?" I asked him.

Paul twisted up his mouth again. "I didn't pay close attention to the wine. I wasn't expecting to be poisoned."

I would have patted him on the shoulder, if it had actually been there. "It wasn't your fault. So few of us expect that. Believe me, I'll be watching everything I eat and drink for, essentially, the rest of my life. But if you didn't notice, who might have? Who was your server that night, do you remember?"

Paul's face relaxed; he was happy to have the right answer to a question. "Yes, I remember because he had such an interesting name. Rudolfo."

"I think I'm going back to Café Linguine to talk to Ralphie," I said.

Paul frowned again. "Who's Ralphie?"

I didn't get the chance to answer because my cell phone started creating havoc in my pocket. I dug it out and opened it, noting only that the incoming call screen read, "Out of Area."

"You've found it, haven't you?" a voice said. It was muffled. Either the person on the other end was whispering or holding a cloth over the mouthpiece or both.

"What? Who is this?" I put the cell phone on speaker, and Paul bent over my shoulder to hear. There was the usual feeling of a warm breeze when he leaned a little too close.

"You know who it is," the voice answered. "You have it, and you're going to hand it over."

"I *don't* have it," I said. "I have no idea where—"

The voice didn't have any inflection, and wouldn't rise enough to be identifiable. Not to mention, it cut me off. This was one rude murderer. "You have until midnight tomorrow to deliver it."

"Deliver what *where*?" I asked at Paul's instruction. "And when you say, 'midnight,' do you mean twelve a.m. early Friday or late Thursday?" That last question was all on my own.

"You'll be given instructions at the proper time," the voice said. I still couldn't tell if it was male or female. And the line went dead.

"Well," Paul said, "that wasn't much help at all. Now. Who's Ralphie?"

I called Detective McElone, and she said she'd try to track my cell phone records to see if she could trace the call I'd just received. But she wasn't promising anything, and reminded me that I was still technically a suspect in Terry Wright's murder. The woman had a reassuring manner, to be sure.

Once I'd dropped Melissa at school, I drove to Phyllis's office. She reassured me that the cops didn't have any hard evidence on me, but had little to add. We moved on to other topics, and discussed frequency of advertising once the guesthouse opened (assuming I lived to see it) and I told her I thought the house renovations would be mostly completed by the weekend, although we still wouldn't have any furniture until at least a week later.

At lunchtime, I walked over to Café Linguine and asked for Rudolfo.

"I didn't see anything," Ralphie protested when I started asking him questions about Paul and Maxie on the night they were killed. His skinny little body was all atremble, and his face, just now recovering from the acne that no doubt plagued his high school years, was pinched. "I swear, I didn't see anything. Can I go back to work now?"

"You're sure you remember the night I'm talking about?" I asked him. I felt bad for the kid; I'd taken him out of his lunch shift (which, to be fair, wasn't exactly bustling) and wasn't even ordering a cup of coffee. But the answers to these questions might save my life, so I saw a certain urgency in them.

"I remember. The cops asked me about it then, and they

asked me about again last week," the waiter said. "A bunch of people came in after some board meeting or something. The mayor was here. She and her group were all over there . . ." He pointed at the corner away from the bar, not so close to the exposed ovens and grills that it would be uncomfortably hot. "At a big table. They were all laughing and drinking wine."

"But they'd just had a tremendous argument at the meeting," I protested, trying to prove to Ralphie that he was wrong, and surely *someone* must have been in a separate corner, sulking, licking his or her wounds.

The kid shook his head. "They don't care," he said. "I've seen it a hundred times after meetings. No matter what, they all hang out here afterward and drink and laugh with each other. I guess none of it's personal."

Well, there went the theory that Paul and Maxie had been killed over a political grudge.

The fact was, it was looking more and more likely that my two houseguests had been murdered over the Washington deed, if only because the other motives weren't bearing any fruit in the investigation.

"Who else was here?" I asked Ralphie. If he mentioned a brooding history teacher with a dimple in his chin, I was officially going to spend the rest of the day in a bad mood. On the other hand, if Kerin Murphy was on Ralphie's list, I'd probably buy extra Halloween candy for the celebration of her arrest. You have to have priorities.

"There were lots of people here," he said, lips twisted downward. "I can't remember everybody."

"Do you remember who was hanging out near the bar?" The poison had probably been administered between the bar and the table.

"Just Lisa Pawley." He grinned.

"Who's Lisa Pawley?"

"She was in my junior year chemistry class," Ralphie said, eyes far away. "She's smokin' hot."

I didn't care who was hot, if they weren't hot for the father of our country. "How about this," I asked the kid. "Do you remember whether you got the two glasses of red wine that the people in the table by the window were drinking?" Paul had told me exactly which table he and Maxie had occupied, and I pointed at it for Ralphie.

"Probably. That's my station, so I would've gotten their drinks from the bar."

I rolled my right hand in a *continue* motion, but Ralphie just stared at it, as if it were an especially shiny object and he were an unusually stupid cocker spaniel. "What about the drinks?" I asked finally.

"What about them?" He seemed genuinely puzzled.

"Did anybody touch them? Anyone stop you on the way to the table? Is there any way that those drinks might have been tampered with between the time you picked them up and the time you delivered them to the table?"

"Look, the cops asked me all this at the time, and that lady cop already asked me the same stuff a few days ago," Ralphie said. "I told her: I don't remember anything happening with the drinks, and if they'd gotten spilled or anything, I'd have had to get other ones from the bar."

"I'm not worried about them spilling," I said. "I'm asking if anyone could have put something in the glasses before you got them to the table."

"Like what?"

"Like poison," I answered.

Ralphie's eyes opened to the size of hubcaps. "You think I poisoned their wine?" he asked. "I didn't do *anything*. . . ."

"No, I don't think you poisoned their wine," I assured him. "But I think someone else might have."

"Who?" There was a reason this kid hadn't gone to Harvard after he'd graduated from Harbor Haven High.

"I *don't know*," I told him. "That's what I'm trying to find out."

"Nothing happened to the drinks after I picked them up from the bar," he said. "Honest."

"Could anything have happened *before* you picked them up from the bar?" What the hell; it was worth a shot.

The kid thought for a second or two. "Maybe," he said. "I didn't see Francois—that's the bartender—pour the wine, and I'm pretty sure I had to wait for it until he got glasses from the kitchen. Because I asked him if the glasses were hot from the dishwasher, and if that would mess up the wine, and he told me to go away."

The plot, and my blood, thickened.

"You remember a lot for something that happened a year ago," I told him.

"I just got asked about it a couple of days ago by the cops," he said. "I had time to think."

I nodded. "The glasses for those two people came out of the kitchen, and not from the ones he had behind the bar?" I asked.

"I think that's right," Ralphie said. "Sometimes Francois runs out of glasses and he has to go into the kitchen for the ones right out of the dishwasher."

"Who was in the kitchen?" I asked him, maybe a little too thickly. "Who could have been in the kitchen that night?"

"I don't know; just the chef, Pietro, and his staff, usually." Did they make every employee take on one of these stupid names? "The only other ones who go back there are the owners."

The owners.

"Did the mayor go back there that night?" I asked, trying hard not to gasp for breath. "Did Bridget Bostero make a trip to the kitchen before you brought out those two glasses of wine?"

"No," Ralphie said. "But I think Mr. Morris was back there."

"Mr. Morris?"

"Adam Morris. The developer guy? He's the main owner of the place."

"Did you tell the detective this?" I said when I caught my breath.

Ralphie's head nodded so hard I was afraid it might fall off. "Oh yeah," he said. "She knows everything I'm telling you."

I pulled a twenty out of my purse and handed it to the kid. "Thanks, Ralphie," I told him. "You've been very helpful."

He grinned, pleased with himself like Melissa is when she can help me with a problem, and turned to leave. Then he stopped and turned back toward me.

"How'd you know my name is Ralphie?" he asked.

Forty-one

I was going to call Adam Morris's office to make an appointment, but decided that with less than thirty-six hours left to live, I wasn't bound by the laws of propriety. I barged into his office, barreling past Bianca, his decorative blonde (and no doubt very efficient) secretary. She still looked familiar. But now I remembered why.

Adam Morris, while startled, did not try to throw me out.

Bianca, trying desperately not to be blamed for letting the intruder past the door, asked, "Should I call the police?"

Adam's face contorted. He rolled his eyes with exasperation and hollered, "No, don't call the police! Just get your skinny ass out there and answer the phones!" You've gotta love a guy who knows how to treat his employees.

Bianca blanched and closed the door. I thought I saw her shoot me a look of respect as she left. She probably wasn't used to people barging in on her boss and getting away with it. I nodded back my respect for her, as well (sisterhood and all that), and she seemed pleased. Of course, I could have been projecting.

Morris shifted smoothly into charming mode, and gestured toward the low-slung chair again, but this time I stood in front of his desk.

"It's a charming surprise, Alison, but I have to say it's a little inconvenient for me right now. Can we schedule this for another time?"

"I don't know if I'll have another time, Adam," I said. "Someone is threatening my life, and I'm here to find out if it's you."

Adam appeared more amused than concerned. His smile, if anything, got warmer. He put his palms flat on his desk and leaned over to face me with less distance between us. "Why would I threaten your life?" he asked.

"Because you want my house and what's in it," I answered. I was going out on a limb with that last part, since I had no idea if Adam even knew about the Washington deed, but it was worth a shot, anyway.

"There's something in your house? You mean besides you?" he asked. Okay, so maybe it *wasn't* worth a shot.

"Something worth about half a million dollars," I said, inflating the price for effect.

"Don't sell yourself short," he said, leaning closer.

"Does this sort of line usually work for you?" I asked.

"Actually, it does," Adam said, straightening up.

"I'm talking about an . . . artifact. Something that could be turned into quite a hefty profit."

Adam laughed. "Five hundred thousand?" he asked. "In this state, that'll buy you a medium-sized home in Somerset County. How much did you pay for the Preston place?"

I looked at my shoes for a moment. They were scuffed. I was still in my work clothes.

"That's what I thought," he said. "Now, why don't you tell me why you're *really* here?"

"That *is* why I'm really here," I said, a little deflated.

"Somebody wants me to get out of my house, or they say I'll die."

"And you immediately thought of me? I'm insulted." Adam walked around his desk and stood next to me. "I didn't think I was all that menacing a figure." He seemed genuinely hurt.

"You're not. Or maybe you are. I don't know." I wasn't comfortable with him that close.

Then he leaned in closer. "What do you *really* want here, Alison?" he crooned.

Adam Morris just wasn't going to get off that tactic, but I wasn't buying. "I'm here because two people died in my house before I bought it. They were probably poisoned—on the night the planning board voted against your proposal, and in a restaurant of which you are the principal owner."

I got the desired effect—he backed off. "And you think I poisoned them so I could buy the house?" He laughed. "How'd that work out?"

"I know why you couldn't buy the house after Maxie died," I told him, regaining some of my bravado. "But I'm not sure how angry you were *before* she died. Angry enough to kill her?"

Adam shook his head and walked back behind his desk. If seduction wasn't going to work, the conversation no longer appeared to hold any interest for him. "Believe what you want to believe, Alison," he said. "A couple of people in a restaurant drink some eye drops with their dinner, and I'm supposed to be responsible because I have a financial interest in the building? That's a very long stretch. I'm sorry if someone's threatening you, but it's not me. Now, please stop interrupting my day."

I dropped my head again, did my best to look defeated, and then slunk out of the office, dragging my feet behind me. I dropped a piece of paper on Bianca's desk on my way out.

And the instant I made it outside, I called Detective McElone.

Forty-two

"He said *eye drops*," I told Detective McElone. Again.

"I heard you. I understand the point." She sat back in her chair and didn't move.

I couldn't comprehend her lack of excitement. "You never told Adam Morris that the poison used on Terry Wright was eye drops, did you?" I asked.

McElone shook her head. "You're the only person outside the department I told, and I'm not really sure why I did that," she said.

Still not so much as a blink on her part. "Well, *I* didn't tell him, so that means he knew what killed Terry, and assumed it was the same poison that killed Paul and Maxie. And it wasn't. It was acetone in their wine that killed them."

"I know," McElone said. "But there are so many holes in your logic that I can't begin to tell you."

"Holes? The man slipped up! He said something that only the killer could have known!"

McElone sighed. Having to deal with an amateur like me was a drain on her energy. She held up the ubiquitous finger to begin her count. "One: He said what he said, *if* he said it, to you, a civilian, and another suspect in the case. Two: You didn't have a recorder on at the time, so there's no record of what he said or didn't say, and no proof. Three: *If* he said that, he'd be implicating himself in the murder of Terry Wright, not Maxine Malone or Paul Harrison, and we have no evidence at all of him being involved with Terry Wright. Four—"

I couldn't stand another finger. "Enough. I get it. Are you still looking for the appointment calendar Kerin Murphy took from Terry's office?"

"Remember that badge I asked you for last time?" The one I don't have.

"Detective, Adam Morris might very well be threatening my life. Whether or not I have a badge . . ."

"Mr. Morris has been questioned and will be questioned again. Believe me, I don't sit around all day and wait for you to come in with clues—we've been investigating." McElone stood up in an effort to get me ready to leave. "So please, just go home, stay out of trouble, and let us do our job. Okay?"

"There are times I get the feeling you don't like me, Detective."

"Trust those feelings," she said.

"This isn't getting us anywhere," Paul said.

The strangest council of war ever convened was gathered in my barren front room. Besides Paul and me, Maxie was pouting unconvincingly in one corner, while the more extant members of the brain trust—Tony, Melissa and Mom—were arranged around the room in lawn chairs. Of course, Tony couldn't communicate with Paul or Maxie, but between Melissa, Mom and myself, we worked it out.

Jeannie had outright refused to participate in "this crap about ghosts in the house," and was upstairs, sewing new curtains for Melissa's bedroom.

"I'm waiting for a suggestion," I said. "We're no closer to figuring out who's behind all the threats, and the clock is ticking."

"What should we be doing now?" Tony asked. "I mean, shouldn't we be concentrating on finding that Washington thing?"

"I'm not talking to *him*," Maxie said, and crossed her arms severely over her chest.

"That's a good idea," I told Tony, ignoring Maxie. "Shouldn't the first order of business now be to find the deed? It seems to me it must be outside somewhere."

"Why?" Melissa asked. "Because we didn't find it in the house yet? Maybe it's in the basement or something."

"Or maybe it was discarded or destroyed years ago, and nobody knows it," Mom added. "It's even possible that there never was a deed, so there's no chance we'll find it."

"Wow," Melissa said. "You are harshin' my mellow, Grandma." She'd picked that one up from her friend Wendy.

Let's just say the vibe in the room wasn't exactly buoyant.

"All right." Paul, at least, was trying. "You haven't discovered the deed in all the renovations you've done, so the obvious places are clearly of no use to us."

"And you and Maxie couldn't find it by cruising around the place," I said, just to prove that I wasn't the only incompetent in the room. "I don't suppose George Washington is one of the ghosts you can contact on your Ghosternet, is he?"

"His Ghoster-*what*?" Melissa asked.

"Sometimes, I can get in touch with other . . . displaced spirits," Paul explained. He looked at Maxie, who harrumphed, and I took it that while Paul could communicate with other spirits, Maxie couldn't. Then he turned to me, and with a certain edge, said, "No, President Washington is not on my speed dial. Any other ideas?"

"Do you think it could be hidden in the walls?" Tony asked. He was scared, I could tell. Which scared me.

"In the walls?" I asked.

"Yeah. You said it was probably hidden while this house was being built. The owners knew it would increase in value, let's say, and didn't want anyone to come looking for it. Could they have closed it up inside a wall somewhere?"

I looked at Paul. "Wouldn't you have seen it, flying through walls the way you do?"

"I've told you, Alison: Dark is dark for us, too. And we can't carry solid objects, like flashlights, through walls."

"Why would they do that, anyway?" I asked. "Then the people who hid it would never be able to retrieve the deed."

"Unless they put in a marker, or a secret door to get in," Tony said. "It's possible to put in hinges that nobody can see."

"Was it possible a hundred years ago?"

"Sure," he insisted.

"How would we find them?" I asked.

He raised an eyebrow at me. "The problem is, they're *hidden*."

"This isn't getting us anywhere," Paul said.

I let out a long breath. The fact that finding this object might actually save my life was not making it easier for me to think about where it might be. I put my head down and massaged my temples.

"Might the history teacher know something about where a thing like that could have been hidden back then?" my mother wanted to know. "Why don't you ask him?"

Among the things I'd neglected to tell my mother was that Ned had been acting really strangely about the deed, and I was trying not to bring up the topic when he was around. This didn't seem the time to mention it.

"He doesn't know where it is," I mumbled.

"Suppose you find the deed," Tony said. "How do you get in touch with this person? Have you been given instructions?"

"Good point," Paul answered. "There's no point in threatening violence if there's no mechanism in place to assure you'll get what you're after."

"They said there'd be 'more instructions at the proper time,' whatever that means," I said.

I didn't like the idea of all this talk of violence in front of Melissa, whose eyes were spinning just a little bit. "Don't worry," I said to her quietly. "I'll be fine. It's just talk."

"Oh, I was just thinking about my English quiz," she lied.

"Is it possible to make a fake document?" I asked Paul and Tony. "Does anybody really know what this thing looks like? Suppose we give them something that looks old and has a facsimile of Washington's signature on it. That couldn't be too hard to do. Does Kinko's make phony historical documents?"

"I don't think you want to take that kind of chance," Paul said quietly, and after the translation interval, Tony nodded in agreement.

"Well, I don't know what else to do!" I hadn't intended to shout, but the situation was starting to get to me. "We can try to figure out who killed you two, but the reality is, whoever did it wants the deed, and they want it tomorrow night. We have to find the deed, but I don't know where else to look."

"What about the yard?" Melissa asked. "At school, we buried a time capsule with a notebook and a CD of songs somebody burned and a picture of our class so that people millions of years in the future could dig it up and see what we were like," she explained. "Don't you think they might have done that with the deed?"

And a child shall lead them.

The five grown-up faces in the room, both alive and not so much, all shot up at once (Mom shot up a little slower). That threw Melissa off her game.

"I guess it's a stupid idea," she said.

"You couldn't *have* a stupid idea," her grandmother told her.

"Let's get some shovels," Jeannie said. We all turned to see her in the doorway, finished curtains in hand.

"I thought you didn't believe in ghosts," I said.

"I don't. I think you're all nuts. But somebody really is threatening you, and if it's because of this deed, we need to find it. Now. Where are the shovels?"

"There are some in the shed," I told her. "But where do we look? There's two acres of land out there."

"Didn't the Prestons say they'd done some digging back there?" Paul asked, stroking his chin. "Wasn't David Preston complaining about all the excavation Madeline had made him do?"

He was right. "Maybe the Prestons weren't just gardening," I speculated. "Maybe they were . . ."

"Looking for something," Tony finished.

We were on our way out the back door before anyone could say anything else. Paul took the early lead, since he didn't have to worry about walls or doors or anything.

But he had to wait for us once he was outside, because he wasn't yet able to pick up a shovel and dig.

Tony, however, was taken aback by the amount of dirt flying through the air. Maxie, as usual, was showing off.

An hour later, we assessed the situation. "This isn't getting us anywhere," Paul said.

My backyard was going to need some serious landscaping help. Between Maxie, who had taken the lightest shovel; Tony, who had insisted on the most lethal-looking and heaviest; and I (just a regular shovel), we had made, by my count, seventeen holes in the ground, from just barely beneath the surface of the grass to, in one case, Tony hitting something he thought was a wooden box that turned out to be a vintage glass bottle of Coca-Cola. Melissa, Mom and Jeannie (who always seemed to be looking away when a shovel with no visible human behind it broke ground) had taken over whenever I got tired. Maxie never got tired. Neither did Tony.

"I'm sorry, Mom," Melissa said. She seemed near tears—it had been her idea to dig.

I dropped down to my knees and looked her in the eye. "It's not your fault, Liss. This was a really good idea." I gave her a tight hug, and she relaxed a little in my arms. I stood, and held her hand.

"The problem is, we don't know where to dig," Maxie said. She wiped something resembling sweat from her brow. I had no idea that dead people could overwork.

"No kidding, Captain Obvious," I told her. "How does that help solve the problem?"

"You know, you're mean to me," Maxie said, but she didn't skulk off like she might have under less serious circumstances.

"Sorry," I said, and suddenly, I meant it.

Maxie didn't answer, and then she was gone. She didn't leave; she was just gone. They can do that.

"I *said* I was sorry," I grumbled after her.

"It'll be dark soon," Mom said after a moment. "Where do you want to eat?"

Eat? Isn't that how they got Paul and Maxie? "I think I'm on a diet tonight, Mom," I told her.

She curled her lip. "I'm going to get some subs—from out of town, where nobody knows you. How's that?" And before I could answer, she and Melissa had taken off in Mom's Viper.

Jeannie and Tony went inside to clean up, having insisted they'd spend the night here again. The last of the group, Paul and I, stood out in the backyard as the sun began to set, and I started to feel water on my cheeks. Warm water. When it reached my mouth, it tasted salty.

I hadn't cried since Dad's funeral. Not even when The Swine left. Just when I realized nobody was ever going to call me *baby girl* ever again. But here I was, weeping into my own mouth.

"It's not fair," I whined. "I didn't do anything wrong. I'm just trying to build a life for me and my daughter, and now somebody wants to kill me."

"Welcome to my world," Paul said quietly.

"I hope not," I said. And then I thought about it. "Sorry."

"Don't be. I don't want you to be on this side, either."

I sat down on the grass. "What's it like to be dead, Paul?" I asked. "Should I be scared?"

"You're not going to die, Alison. We'll see to it."

"I will sooner or later. Everybody does."

He thought about it. "It's a lot like being alive," he said finally. "Except you don't really feel things that much."

"You mean you don't care?"

"No. You still have emotions. But you don't feel pain or anything physical. It's like being asleep and dreaming something that's really happening."

That didn't help all that much, with visions of my mother and daughter crying over my open casket (although I have to admit, I looked quite wonderful) barreling their way into my head—after all, there was no guarantee I'd end up like Paul and Maxie; it seemed most people who died didn't. I felt completely overwhelmed, taken up in the current of a river I couldn't fight.

"Paul," I said, "do you think I'll be alive the day after tomorrow?"

"I'll do everything I can to make sure you are," he answered.

"You didn't answer the question," I said.

Paul looked away.

Forty-three

Let's just say it wasn't exactly a restful night.

Mom was sharing a mattress with Melissa, but even on my own, I never really slept at all. Which was too bad, because I was very tired, but not surprising, because I was also—what's the word?—terrified.

The constant threats against my life since I'd first seen Paul and Maxie in the house were finally becoming real to me, and that wasn't a good thing. I had been treating the situation as if it were the work of some harmless crank, and now I was wondering exactly how harmless a crank could be.

I'd very clearly gotten the message that unless the Washington deed showed up in the mail today, I'd be next to follow Paul, Maxie and Terry to the grave.

A thing like that gets you thinking: Is this my last day of life? Is this the last time I'll try to sleep? All those plans I had for the house, for my life, for Melissa—were they all about to be erased entirely?

Was I about to become the third ghost in an already crowded spectral guesthouse?

Things are always worse at night. In the morning, however, I noticed quite clearly that my situation was not improving.

How appropriate that it was Halloween morning.

I finally gave up on sleep entirely, went downstairs, and stained the wood floor in the dining room. One coat of urethane remained and the house would be officially renovated (aside from the mammoth hole in the wall, but I just couldn't deal with that today).

Mom got up at seven, but she didn't sound the least bit weary; her usual cheerful tone sounded only a little bit forced.

"I'll drive Melissa to school this morning," she offered.

"No. I'll take her." If this was my last day, I was going to spend as much of it with my daughter as possible.

Mom's tone was a little more serious when she answered. "Of course, dear. You know what's right."

She went out to pick up some breakfast for the growing crowd in my house, however, and promised to be back in a half hour.

Melissa came down at seven-thirty, like always, showered, dressed and prepared. She was working very hard at being normal, and wouldn't talk about anything but trick-or-treating later that day with her friends.

"Do you think we can get the ears done right after dinner?" Melissa asked.

"After dinner? How late do you think you're going to go out tonight?"

She rolled her eyes. My daughter could be captain of the Olympic eye-rolling team. "*Nobody's* going out before dinner, Mom," she protested. "We're not little kids anymore!"

At nine, they're no longer little kids?

"Fine," I told her. "You can go out after dinner. But you'll be home by eight-thirty, and that's not negotiable."

"*Eight-thirty!*" Melissa wailed. "It doesn't even get dark until six!"

"You want to negotiate down to eight?"

She folded her arms and attached her chin to her chest. "Fine. Eight-thirty."

I drove her to school, and she was silent the whole way there. She got out without so much as a kiss and walked into the school without a backward glance.

I certainly hoped *that* wasn't a last.

I started to get out of the car to run after her, and—I don't know, tell her to take the day off from school?—when Ned Barnes spotted me from the parking lot and stopped me dead just by walking over to me.

"How are you holding up?" he asked.

"I'm still standing," I said.

"Would it be all right if I came to the house tonight?" he asked. "I can help hand out Halloween candy or something."

I tried to think of excuses. If Ned was the killer, it would probably be a bad idea to invite him over. On the other hand, Tony and Jeannie would already be there, as would my less-alive tenants.

"I don't know," I said.

"Alison. Please."

Maybe he *wasn't* a homicidal maniac. I nodded my agreement.

"Great." Ned's smile, truly a work of art, made suspecting him very difficult. "I'll bring something for dessert." Uh-oh.

But the *real* shock of the morning came on the ride home when my cell phone rang, the call coming from a number I did not recognize. Worried that it might be the killer, I pulled over. Wouldn't want to cause an accident. I'm a responsible driver.

"Hello? Is this Alison Kerby?" a woman's voice asked. She didn't sound very threatening.

"That depends," I answered.

"This is Bianca Valessy. I'm Adam Morris's assistant?" She'd gotten my note! "Yes, Bianca," I said.

"I read your note. Can you meet me?"

That posed a difficult question. If Adam Morris was the person threatening me, he might try to lure me to a particular spot where he could do me harm. Or Bianca herself could be the killer, innocuous though her voice sounded. "Where?" I asked.

"Someplace we can't be seen," Bianca said. That didn't sound at all positive. "I could get in a lot of trouble." Sure you could, honey. How stupid do you think I am? "Anyplace you can think of?" she asked.

"How about my house?" I asked.

Forty-four

If there's one thing you want when you're meeting with a person who could be dangerous—or representing someone dangerous—it's witnesses. Luckily, my place was packed with them.

I'd been planning this since I'd written the note to Bianca on my way to Adam Morris's office the day before. I had finally recognized her as the blonde woman who'd met Kerin Murphy at Oceanside Park and taken the appointment book. I had figured (with some help from Paul) that Bianca was probably just a messenger, not the recipient of the book, and might be persuaded to talk if my knowledge about her was revealed. So I did just that, on the back of a receipt from HouseCenter. I assumed she'd be smart enough to look up my cell phone number (I couldn't be bold enough to write it down, given that Adam Morris was in the next room) through the records on my house.

When I hadn't heard from Bianca immediately, I'd been

a little concerned that she'd shown Morris the note, but luckily, it appeared she'd spent just as sleepless a night as I had, before deciding to make the call. I was ready.

I phoned Jeannie after I got off with Bianca, and alerted her to the meeting. She and Tony were in the kitchen when I got there. They said Mom had called from her house, where she'd gone to shower and change, and would be back soon. They hadn't told her about Bianca's visit.

"Where do you want us to hide?" Jeannie asked before I'd even made it all the way inside. "We can ambush her anytime you want."

"I don't want you to hide at all," I said. "I want you visible, to help intimidate her."

"This should help," Tony said, and opened his jacket to show me he had a gun tucked into his belt.

"Okay, that's scary," I said.

"Gotta be prepared," Tony said.

"Don't even think of using that unless she pulls out a nuclear bomb," I told him. "I don't want bullet holes in my walls."

Jeannie shook her head.

Maxie swooshed through the ceiling as we walked into the living room. "Look out!" she yelled, and darted in and out of walls, still looking for the deed.

"You didn't tell them?" I asked Jeannie, pointing around the room.

"Tell who?" She could see Maxie lift a hammer and fly it across the room, and she'd still deny anything unusual had happened. As long as Maxie didn't hand the hammer to Tony—something Tony had discovered the night before, trying once again to square out the hole in my wall. Jeannie had given him a look that could have caused frostbite. And then insisted he had made the hammer levitate.

"Forget it," I said.

I asked Maxie for Paul's whereabouts as she made

a quick circle of the living room. Jeannie walked to the kitchen, acknowledging nothing.

"Basement. He's trying the crawlspace again."

"Would you zip down there and ask him to come up?" I requested. "I need both of you."

"Oh yes, ma'am!" She groaned like the annoyed teenager my daughter would be in four years and disappeared into the floorboards.

Jeannie returned to arrange lawn chairs in the front room, and Tony checked his gun for at least the third time to make sure it was loaded.

Paul rose up through the floor and accidentally through Tony, who shuddered and looked around, no doubt worried that Maxie was striking again. I shook my head to reassure him.

"What's going on?" Paul said, professional demeanor at the forefront.

There was a loud knock on the door (despite the fact that the doorbell was perfectly functional). "This is," I told Paul, and hurried to let Bianca inside.

"This is what?" Jeannie asked.

Tony and Jeannie rushed toward the door as she came in, and Bianca's eyes widened. She looked terrified.

"I can't talk with all these people here," she said as Paul floated near and Maxie rose up from the basement.

You have no idea, I thought.

"They're my friends," I told her. "You can trust them. Please, have a seat."

That proposed something of a dilemma, as I had only the old, dusty lawn chairs to offer. I actually took a towel from the downstairs bathroom and spread it over a chair for Bianca, who was eyeing the house warily.

"I hear there are ghosts here," she said.

"Oh, that's just people talking around town," I said. "It's just silly stories."

"No kidding," Jeannie said out of the corner of her mouth.

I pressed on. "Now, you said you had something important to tell me?" I asked Bianca.

"I read your note saying I should tell you if I knew something about this house," she said. "I've seen you in Adam's office. You're not afraid of him."

Well, I was afraid of *somebody*, but I couldn't be sure it was Adam Morris. "That's right," I told her.

"Well, I do know something. I know a lot."

I waited, but she seemed to need some prodding to go on. Luckily, Jeannie was in the room. "So tell us," she said, a little heatedly.

"See, here's the thing," Bianca said. "Adam wants this house way more than he's letting on. He came into town all set to take this whole section and make a real big project out of it, you know, beachfront property, lots of condos and big houses to sell to rich people. He's been working on it for years. And all the other owners of all the other houses sold out to him right away, because he was offering good prices in a bad real estate market."

"But the Prestons sold to Maxie before he knew it, and then Kitty Malone wouldn't sell, right?"

"Well, not the Prestons—that was just bad luck," Bianca answered. "Adam's agent in the area, Ms. Wright? He didn't contact her until a month after they sold the house to Ms. Malone. Adam dropped the ball on that. But when that owner died, and her estate still wouldn't sell, he got mad. He stopped seeing Ms. Wright, just cut her off entirely."

"Adam Morris was seeing Terry Wright?" It was news to me.

"Oh yeah. Among . . . others," she answered. "He's lucky his wife is back in Nebraska."

"His wife?" Tony said. "The guy's married in Nebraska,

and he's having multiple affairs here in New Jersey?" He blinked a couple of times. Jeannie poked him on the arm, thinking he was expressing admiration for Adam Morris's accomplishments. "What?" he asked her.

"Yeah." Bianca was warming to the attention she was getting. "He was with Ms. Wright for a while, then the mayor for a while . . ."

"The mayor? Bridget Bostero? Harbor Haven's mayor?" Jeannie wasn't aghast—she was thrilled with the treasure trove of gossip she was receiving.

"Yeah," Bianca repeated. It appeared to be her favorite word. "He was going to finance her campaign for state assembly, but he got mad when she couldn't deliver the planning board vote, and that was it. She gets no money and no Adam."

My head was spinning. I actually felt like lying down (a concussion never really leaves you), but instead, I sat on the stairs. "Let me see if I've got this," I said. "Adam Morris was having an affair with Terry Wright. But he broke that off because he thought she failed him by not getting this house for his project. So he started seeing the mayor, thinking she could get him the house by influencing the planning board, and enticed her with an offer to put up money for a state assembly campaign."

"I'm not sure he was only seeing one of them at a time," Bianca corrected me. "And they weren't the only ones. Like the lady who got his appointment book."

"Excuse me?" Jeannie looked like she was five and it was Christmas morning. "Adam Morris was having an affair with *Kerin Murphy*?"

"Is that her name?" Bianca asked.

"Oh, this is too good!" Jeannie gushed. I was trying to wrap my mind around it.

Adam Morris had tried to use his charm on me and, frankly, I'd found him very easy to resist, so it was hard to imagine that he was such catnip to so many women. But this wasn't getting me any less killed, so I plowed on. "Okay, so all this was fine until Maxie convinced the board to vote against him. Then he withdrew the money and broke it off with Bridget."

"Yeah." Again. "Except he was getting back together with Ms. Wright before she died."

"He was?"

"Yeah. He kept calling her and sending her flowers."

"Ask her how he reacted when she died," Paul suggested, so I repeated the question.

"It was weird. He didn't really seem to care that much." There was a long silence. I know what I was thinking.

"Why are you telling me all this, Bianca?" I asked.

She looked from face to face in the room (and missed a couple she didn't know were there). "I think you need to be careful. He still wants your house, and he knows you won't sell it to him. He's tried to get this house before. He got really mad when it didn't work."

"Don't I know it," Maxie said. Paul never took his eyes off Bianca.

"I just . . . I don't know for sure, but I saw what happened the last time he got this mad, and I thought it would be wrong not to warn you."

"What happened the last time?" I asked.

"I'm not sure. But those two people died here." Bianca shuddered a little, and Maxie wasn't touching her. I checked.

"Do you think Adam Morris killed the people who died here in this house?" I asked. Paul and Maxie were similarly tensed up and leaning forward, and if they'd had breath, they'd have been holding it.

"I don't know for sure," Bianca said. "But I know he was awful mad."

That wasn't enough. Detective McElone would tell me

it wasn't enough. I'd go to her, but she'd tell me it wasn't enough.

"Why did you decide to tell me this?" I asked Bianca again.

Her eyes got watery, and she covered a tear with the back of her hand. "He told me I was the only one," she said.

Forty-five

"It's not enough," Detective Anita McElone said.

I leaned back and put my feet up on her desk, which I'm sure did not please the detective. Jeannie and I had gone directly to police headquarters when Bianca, having recovered from her misty moment of regret, reorganized herself and headed to work so as not to draw any suspicion.

"I thought you'd say that," I allowed, "but it should be enough at least to question Adam Morris. That, coupled with what we talked about the last time I was here?"

"The guy killed probably three people," Jeannie said, not having to worry too much about the niceties (what the hell, *she* didn't live in Harbor Haven). "You're a cop, right? So what's the problem?"

McElone had initially insisted that Jeannie stay out in the waiting room, but Jeannie had inched her way in a little at a time and was now standing next to the chair in which I was sitting. McElone hadn't looked happy about it, but she hadn't said anything. Until now.

"Didn't I ask you to wait outside?" she asked Jeannie.

"Yeah, but I decided the answer was *no*."

I decided to put us back on topic. I held up a finger. "One," I told the detective. "Adam Morris was having an affair with Terry Wright when she was selling my house to Maxie Malone. Two"—second finger. Hey, this was fun!—"Adam Morris was having an affair with Mayor Bostero as well as with Kerin Murphy, and offering to finance Bridget's campaign, while she was trying to push a condemnation order through the planning board. Three"—next finger—"Morris dumped each woman when she was no longer of any use to him, but, four"—finger again—"he was starting to see Terry again—just before she was killed. Five"—thumb—"he knew the kind of poison used on Terry, even though you hadn't made that information public. Six—"

Before I could put up another finger, McElone held up one of her own. "So far, what you've given me wouldn't even stand up on an episode of *Perry Mason* from nineteen fifty-nine. All the information you say you have comes from a so-called anonymous witness, and is all hearsay, anyway." It was true; Bianca had insisted that I not tell McElone her name. "Two, you don't know that any of it is true. Three, even if all that stuff about him sleeping with all those women *is* true—and I have no reason to think it is—it doesn't make him a killer, just an adulterer. Four, there's nothing tying Morris to the killings of Harrison or Malone. Five, get your feet off my desk."

I took my feet off her desk.

"Okay," I said. "So I don't have any *physical* evidence. But you have to admit, the fact that Morris was involved with all these women and that he was so desperate to get my house would at least give him a motive. Isn't that enough to investigate?"

"We *are* investigating," McElone said. "We've *been* investigating since these incidents happened. I questioned Mr. Morris myself."

"And?" I asked.

"When did you become a police consultant?" the detective asked in return. "I have no reason to tell you anything, but how about this: Adam Morris says that he left the restaurant at least a half hour before Mr. Harrison and Ms. Malone finished their dinner the night of the meeting. Most of the restaurant staff corroborates that account. And the ME says that's the wrong time frame for him to have poisoned their drinks."

I gave her my best *oh please* face. "He couldn't be lying, or have gotten someone else, like the bartender or the waiter, to do it?" I hated to cast suspicion on Ralphie, especially since I had no reason to think he had anything to do with the poisonings, but McElone was cornering me.

"We questioned the entire staff," she said. "If there's anything suspicious, we already know about it. And no one has been ruled out as a suspect."

"Not even me?" I asked.

"You?" Jeannie asked. "How can you be suspected of threatening yourself? I thought we'd gotten past this library card thing."

"We have," McElone said wearily. "Ms. Kerby is no longer a suspect in Ms. Wright's death." She looked at me. "You didn't have a motive. And we checked your cell phone records. The call you got came from a disposable cell phone, and even if we could triangulate its location, I guarantee the person who used it has discarded it and gotten another by now."

"So, how should I proceed now?" I asked.

"Until I tell you otherwise, assume you're still in danger," McElone said. "But I'm betting I'll tell you very soon to stop worrying." She smiled warmly.

"See? And I thought you didn't like me."

"I don't," she said. "But if you're not in danger, you won't be bothering me anymore."

We turned to leave. "To protect and serve," Jeannie scoffed as we walked out.

My cell phone buzzed on the way out, indicating a text message. I opened it, and the message read, "I WANT THE DEED. 2NIGHT."

I didn't even bother to go back and show it to McElone. She'd say it wasn't enough.

Forty-six

"What's our plan of action?" I asked Paul.

"We have no choice," Paul replied. "No matter who the killer is, we have nothing to bargain with if we don't find that deed."

"But we've looked everywhere," I told him. "There's no place left to explore."

Paul composed himself, and I got the impression I wasn't going to like what he had to say next. I was right. "The Prestons and Mayor Bostero were really fascinated by the hole in that wall." He pointed, as if I didn't know where the hole that had been haunting (so to speak) my thoughts was located.

"Don't even think it," I said.

"Alison, there's a very strong possibility that the document that can save your life is hidden somewhere behind one of those plaster walls, and the only way we can find out is to let in enough light for Maxie or me to look inside."

I shook my head. "That's a hole in every wall in this house, none of which I'll know how to repair."

"They'd be small holes," Paul tried.

"We wouldn't have time to be neat. We'd have to ruin every wall until we found it."

"Weigh that against waking up tomorrow morning," he said.

"I'm not afraid of . . . whoever it is," I lied. "They can't poison me if I know it's coming. I won't eat anything for the rest of the day. I'll only eat food I cook myself from now on. I'll save money. I can't destroy the house—it's the only way I can make a living, Paul."

He did whatever ghosts do that looks like sighing. "Alison, you can't live scared forever. I firmly believe that the only way to stop this is to find that deed, and the only way to do that is to break holes in each wall in this house until we find it."

"I'd rather die," I said. And at that moment, I meant it. "I will not take down months' worth of work just because something *might* be behind one of the walls. When you guys develop X-ray vision and can tell me exactly where the deed is, I'll think about it."

The argument went on for hours: I finished the urethane job, putting up and taking down barriers to keep (live) people from stepping on the floor until it dried. Jeannie made two more curtains for my bedroom, Wendy's mom gave Melissa a ride home from school, Tony called to say he'd be back after his drywall job was completed, and Maxie was holed up with the laptop doing "research," but neither Paul nor I had moved from our original positions: Paul thought taking down all the plaster walls, which could never be adequately replaced, would save my life, and I thought the possibility was just a little too iffy to warrant the damage.

Oh, and Mom called to say she'd call later.

Melissa was upstairs getting into her Mr. Spock outfit, and we expected the horde of trick-or-treaters, discreetly followed by a few mothers (including Kerin Murphy, much to my chagrin), to arrive at our house for pickup in ten minutes. I called up the stairs.

"Liss! Come on down! I want to get pictures before you leave!"

"Just a second!" the tiny voice came back. "I'm finishing up."

The typical wave of four- and five-year-olds had already been coming by trick-or-treating from pretty much the minute school let out, each one followed so closely by a parent it was hard to tell who was getting the candy. But that died down fairly quickly, and we were awaiting the second wave, which would include Melissa and her posse, shortly. The teenagers would come after nine, and I'd stiff them. Teenagers trick-or-treating. Really.

Paul, wearing black jeans and a tight black t-shirt, looked like he should be attending an extremely casual funeral or a reunion of New Yorkers from the Clinton era. But his face was serious. "Alison . . . ," he started.

I cut him off. "No more. We're done." Once again, I called upstairs. "Melissa! They'll be here any minute, and I'm going to get pictures whether it mortifies you or not!"

"One second!" More insistent.

Paul bit his upper lip and tried a different tactic. "All right, then. If we're not going to look behind the walls, where else haven't we tried yet? This is a big house; there has to be *some* area we haven't searched thoroughly."

"I can't think of anyplace," I answered. "There's no furniture in the house; each room is empty. I've been behind the tiles in the bathrooms, checked the mortar and every brick of the fireplaces, and pulled up each and every rug. There isn't an inch of this house with which I have not become intimate."

"There's something we're missing."

"Of course there is, or we would have found it by now. *Melissa!*" I ran up the stairs to move my daughter along. "You have to come down *now!*"

And I found her in her bedroom, standing in her blue *Star Trek* shirt with the insignia on the left side. Her hair had been piled up under a store-bought wig that gave her black bangs and a bowl cut with sideburns. She had on the Silly Putty ears, which for the moment actually looked pretty natural (but almost certainly would not by the fourth house).

Also, her eyebrows were half-shaved, and Maxie was kneeling next to her, applying mascara to extend them up in a diagonal line on each side.

Melissa gasped. I gasped. Maxie looked up and didn't so much as blink.

"We're not done yet," she said.

"I . . . you . . . didn't I . . . ?" I was at my most articulate.

"Looks pretty good, huh?" Maxie said.

Melissa, considerably more savvy to my expressions and the fact that I'd specifically forbidden this activity, didn't look nearly as confident. "Mom," she said. "Don't freak out."

"Don't freak *out*?" I echoed. "I told you without any question that you could not do this, and here you are with . . . with her, doing exactly what I said you couldn't!"

"Oh, chill," Maxie said. "They'll grow back."

I advanced on her, and she tried to wield a Gillette Venus safety razor as a weapon. "I don't want you near my daughter *ever* again, do you understand?" I bellowed. *"Never!"*

And I turned on my heel and left the room. Behind me, I heard sobs, but I couldn't say for sure which one of them was crying.

When push came to shove, I didn't have the guts to ground Melissa on Halloween, especially since I arrived downstairs to find at least eight of her friends, in costumes ranging from Captain Kirk to Lieutenant Uhura to Princess Jasmine (Marlee Murphy didn't get the memo), and four mothers, including Kerin Murphy, standing in my empty living room, eyes round and wide. At first, I thought they were admiring the restored beauty of the old place.

No such luck.

"Ready for the SafeOWeen?" Kerin asked, no doubt dredging up skills from a cheerleading past. The kids looked glum.

"Is your house really haunted?" Wendy, Melissa's best friend, asked. She hadn't even asked where Melissa was, and here she was inquiring after the deceased. "Can we see the ghosts?"

"Yeah!" A little girl named Sandy (I remembered her because she had been trading Melissa Twinkies for apples until I got wind of it) asked. "Where are the ghosts?"

"Do they wear sheets?" another one asked. The poor kid.

Melissa appeared at the top of the stairs. Her face registered angry, nervous and a little scared, mostly, I thought, at what vengeance I might take for her disobeying me so blatantly.

"I'm sorry, girls, there really aren't any ghosts here," I told the gathered assemblage, and in that first second, I must report that the mothers were the ones who looked the most disappointed, Kerin perhaps most of all—if I had a haunted house, she could probably put it around that I was a witch. "I know stories have been going around, but they're just stories. Like Aladdin and Princess Jasmine." I gestured to Marlee in the Jasmine costume.

"Princess Jasmine is *real*!" she insisted, and crossed her arms with great conviction.

"You're right, my mistake," I agreed. "But the ghost stories are just . . ."

And that was when Maxie appeared out of the floor, reached for "Captain Kirk's" communicator (made out of a painted-over McDonald's apple pie box) and made it "fly" across the room. She looked at me, sneered, and stuck out her tongue.

The little girl in the Kirk outfit yelled, "Hey—!" But then she stopped and realized what had happened, and her mouth dropped open.

"A ghost," said the Uhura girl.

"No, no," I told them. "This is just a big, drafty house, and sometimes the wind . . ."

"All the windows and doors are closed," Kerin said. Her smile was just a little evil. "There's no draft in here." I decided there and then to destroy her.

But Maxie wasn't finished getting her revenge. She pushed the hanging overhead light in the living room and made it sway. Then she made the communicator hover in front of Captain Kirk until the little girl understood she could take it back. And Maxie topped it off by picking up Melissa and carrying her down the stairs, then placing her gently on the floor. Melissa looked up and nodded at her.

"Thanks, Maxie," she said.

Maxie looked in my direction. "No problem, Melissa," she said. "I'll *always* be your friend."

"You can *see* them!" Wendy said to Liss. "You know their names!"

"I told you," Melissa said, very matter-of-factly.

Kerin stared at me. "There really is no explanation, is there?" she said in a cold, calculated tone.

I can't justify it. Maybe the pressures of the past few weeks just exploded out of me all at once. Maybe it was the imminent threat that I'd be deprived of my life in six hours or less. Maybe it was the scared expression on the faces of those mothers and the delighted ones on the faces of their children.

"Sure there is," I said loudly. "Yes, there *really are ghosts* in this house. Melissa and I can see them. We can talk to them. Why can't *you*?"

"Oh, there are not," one of the other moms protested. "You're just playing a Halloween trick on us."

"No, I'm not," I said. Suddenly, I felt like there was nothing left to lose—let the guesthouse idea go down the tubes. Let the rest of the town think I was insane or a "Wiccan Gone Wild." Let the fourth grade think my daughter was weird. "They're real ghosts. Real dead people, still existing in this house, and they can *never leave*. Go ahead, tell your friends! Tell your neighbors! The place is *haunted*, I tell you, *haunted*!"

Paul, attracted by the noise, floated into the front hallway and looked at the amassed children and parents, aghast. "What are you doing, Alison?" he asked.

"I'm telling the truth!" I shouted, and then I pointed at the mothers, who stood stock-still and widened their eyes to the size of Oreo cookies. "They all need to know, in case their kids want to play here! There are ghosts here, and they're not the *least bit dangerous!*"

Maxie picked up the little girl dressed as Lieutenant Sulu and swirled her around the room, something the girl (I think her name was Soyong) could not possibly have enjoyed more. She squealed with delight and clapped her hands when put back down.

Her mother, thankfully, was not present, but Kerin grabbed "Sulu" by the shoulders protectively, once she was back on solid ground.

"Any questions?" I asked.

The girls applauded mightily, and I noticed Melissa among the most arduous clappers. One of the mothers backed out the door.

As the kids each grabbed a mini Crunch bar and the remaining mom stood absolutely motionless, I pulled Kerin to one side. "I know you're sleeping with Adam Morris," I said. Mentally, I thanked Bianca for my newfound power: Kerin's eyes widened and her jaw dropped. "If you don't want that information in the hands of someone who'll use it"—why use Jeannie's name?—"you'll skip SafeOWeen and watch my daughter like a hawk door-to-door all evening, is that clear? Don't say anything, just walk away."

Kerin just walked away. Quivering.

Chattering with excitement, the girls headed out to an evening of sugar-fueled avarice. The mothers huddled together on the way out, and I knew that there was no chance I'd ever be elected PTSO president in my lifetime. If I had one.

I knelt down by Melissa before she turned. "You look wonderful, sweetie," I told her, and she gave me a hug. I made sure she took her cell phone with her, and told her to call in at half-hour intervals. I also reminded her of the eight-thirty curfew, and told her that under the circumstances, it was even more unbreakable than it would have been otherwise.

Melissa didn't argue. She was gone far too soon for my liking.

After all, it might have been a last hug.

Forty-seven

Tony got back to the house with Indian food just as the sun was setting, but I wasn't eating. Nothing had happened, and while I should have thought that was a good thing, it just made me feel that a bad end to the evening was coming closer and closer.

Occasionally, we'd get some business from trick-or-treaters, and the ones Melissa's age (and some younger) seemed to crane their necks to get a good look inside the house. Obviously, the story of the earlier part of the evening was getting around town. Some of the kids even forgot to ask for candy.

One of them yelled, "Hey, ghosts!" when he came in, but was not rewarded with a reaction. But once he turned his head, his friends could see the plastic pumpkin holding the candy fly around the room. When they shouted, he turned back, and the pumpkin was back on the chair by the door.

Odd.

Mom called at about seven-thirty, saying she wasn't a

bit worried, but wouldn't be coming tonight because she had "business to take care of." I was going to ask, but what would have been the point?

Melissa remembered to call after the first half hour, and I waited fifteen minutes after the second to call her. She was fine. I was . . . I'm not sure what I was. Nervous? Annoyed? Frustrated?

Just before eight, the doorbell rang again, and I reached for the latest bag, this one holding tiny 3 Musketeers bars (let other people's mothers worry about cavities). But I didn't need them, because it was Ned Barnes who showed up at the door, and he was carrying ingestible items from Dunkin' Donuts.

What was weird was that when I opened the door to let him in, there were maybe twenty kids, ranging from eight to sixteen or so, standing a few yards from the house.

Just staring.

They weren't coming to ask for candy. They weren't playing tricks. No toilet paper or eggs were visible.

They were just staring. I hustled Ned into the house and shut the door quickly.

"I have coffee and I have Munchkins and muffins," he announced. "Let's get this party started!"

Everybody in the house, dead and alive, looked at him as if he were truly crazy.

"All right, I was trying," Ned said. "I hoped I could distract you." I gestured for him to join us at the collapsible picnic table I'd been using as a tool table until this afternoon. He sat down opposite Tony, and Paul, hovering toward the ceiling behind him, seemed to scrutinize him especially carefully.

We ate—well, *they* ate—silently for a while. I put food on my plate, and moved it around with a fork for a while. Nobody ate anything Ned had brought. Including Ned.

"Have you heard . . . Has there been . . . ?" Ned couldn't decide how to start.

"No contact yet," I said. "No phone call, no e-mail. I've been checking." I pointed to the laptop sitting on a radiator across the room.

"How about . . . ?" His eyes lit up.

"No, we haven't found the deed." I scowled.

"You won't let us look in the most likely spot," Paul said. Of course, no one here but me heard him, and I didn't feel it necessary to relay that message.

But for some reason, that did it. I dropped my fork, which wasn't doing me much good anyway, and stood up. Everyone in the room stared at me with a different brand of concern on each face.

"I've had it," I said. "I don't believe anyone's coming after me. No one can actually expect that I've found something that no one else has been able to locate for more than a hundred years. Killing me just for *not* finding it won't do anyone any good. It would just expose what's been done before. So I'm calling it quits. I'm not worrying about it anymore. There's nothing anyone can do that can scare me now." I started to reach for a doughnut, just to be brazen.

And just as Ned stood up and moved toward me, my phone began to ring.

"You've had your time," the muffled voice from before hissed. "You need to bring the deed to McArver Cemetery now."

"I don't have it," I said with as challenging a tone as I could muster. "I never found it. I don't have a clue where it could be. So move on to your next scam, my friend. You'll get nothing out of me."

"Don't roll it up or damage it," the voice went on, not acknowledging that I'd spoken. "Bring it in exactly the state you found it."

"I *didn't* find it. You're operating on a mistaken assumption. You're being an idiot."

Paul's face animated. He'd caught something. I put the

cell phone on speaker so he—and everyone else—could hear.

"I'm not tearing my house apart anymore," I told the voice, just to keep it talking so Paul could hear more. "I've done enough damage. I need this house."

The voice went on without a direct reply. "It's not raining, so there's no need for plastic sheeting, but protect the document from the wind. No damage must come to it, or you will be extremely sorry."

"What are you going to do, poison me through the phone?" I asked. "I'm not coming."

"You are," the voice said, still without enough inflection to determine the gender of the speaker. "And you'll be there in thirty minutes."

"I had until midnight. It's only eight-fifteen." I don't know why, but I figured that any disagreement I could muster was worthwhile at this point. After all this anonymous wiseass had put me through, the least I could do was be an irritant.

"Yes, and wasn't your daughter supposed to be back by eight-thirty?"

My blood temperature dropped 20 degrees. "Who are you?" I croaked.

"She looks very cute in her *Star Trek* costume," the voice said. "But I wouldn't have done the ears with Silly Putty; it wilts. There are latex options that would offer better results. Get the deed to me in thirty minutes, Alison. McArver Cemetery. Come alone. Don't dare call the police, and don't be late." And the phone disconnected.

Forty-eight

The first thing I did was call Detective McElone (what am I, an idiot?), who assured me she'd be discreet in staking out the cemetery, but would have plenty of backup. Paul said that it didn't matter that the voice had told me not to call the cops; it was the smart move to make.

The second thing I did was call Melissa's cell phone, and got no answer. Trying to control my trembling, I dialed Kerin Murphy's cell phone number, which I'd insisted upon before she took my daughter so much as down the driveway: It, too, went straight to voice mail. I resolved to murder Kerin as soon as possible, but first, I decided to go into the basement and get the sledgehammer.

Tony, Ned and Jeannie did the same. There were enough hammers to go around. "Every wall," I said. "No exceptions until we find it."

"There are too many walls," Tony said. "We don't have time."

"Get anything that'll make a hole," I instructed. Then I ran to the front door and opened it wide.

"Who wants to help the ghosts trash the house?" I yelled.

At least a half dozen kids made war whoops and joined in. Each was issued an implement of destruction and put to work.

It doesn't take long to make a hole in a plaster wall when you don't care how much damage you're doing. Each time, we'd get just enough open to shine a flashlight inside. We worked in teams: As soon as a ghost and a light could fit inside, the wall was tested. Paul and Maxie were relatively discreet—it was easy to be in that crowd—and if Jeannie or Ned noticed things flying around or questions being asked to the ceiling, they just accepted it and moved on.

By the time we were done decimating the first floor, I had only twenty minutes left, and we had no deed of any kind, signed by any official of any municipality in any era. I had to leave in ten minutes to ensure an on-time arrival, and we had the whole second floor to do.

The thundering hordes went upstairs and I took in the damage we'd done. There would be no repairs now; I'd just have to take down the walls, all of them, and put up wall-board. It would take weeks, it wouldn't look as good, and it would make my house that much less competitive in the accommodations market.

I couldn't have cared less.

I heard the pounding on the walls from upstairs, and I hefted my sledgehammer to get upstairs and help. And then for some reason I looked across the living room and saw it, each wall demolished between studs, in a way I'd never seen it before.

The window seat. With the pressed-metal-pattern grill. Could it be?

What the hell. I had to find that deed.

I got to the window seat as quickly as I could while

dragging a five-pound sledgehammer, raised it, then remembered there was a perfectly workable hinge on the top. I opened the window seat.

Nothing.

But reaching in, it seemed the bottom panel of the seat was too high. There was room underneath. A false bottom.

Without time to be dainty, I smacked the base of the window seat with the hammer, and it buckled. And when I cleared the debris away, sure enough, there it was.

A heavy wooden box.

"Paul!" I screamed. Maxie appeared first, before I'd even gotten the whole name out of my mouth. She'd looked absolutely stricken when it appeared Melissa was in danger, and now she was practically vibrating.

"Where?" she shouted, and I pointed at the window seat. She swooped in, and came out holding the box.

Paul showed up seconds behind her, and I could hear footsteps on the staircase behind me. Ned, seeing a wooden box floating in the air by itself, made a strange sound in his throat. There were still screams and pounding from the kids upstairs.

"Open it," Paul said.

I grabbed the box out of Maxie's hands and put it on the floor. It certainly looked old enough—it was ornate and carved, with a symbol of an eagle on the top—and it was fairly heavy, but mostly from the weight of the box itself. Ned covered the distance across the room in perhaps a second, and was breathing heavily when he reached my side. He reached for the box.

"We don't have time to be in awe now," I said. "This is Melissa's life."

I opened the lid just enough to know we'd found what we'd been looking for. I nodded at Paul.

"Get on the Ghosternet," I told him. "See if anybody has seen Melissa, and if she's okay."

"Get on the *what*?" Ned asked.

Jeannie showed up behind him. "Humor her," she said. "She thinks Casper the Friendly Ghost lives here."

Ned didn't say anything, and seemed to be deciding whether to stare at me or Jeannie. He settled on me.

"I'll get Maxie to text to Tony on Jeannie's phone if there's news," Paul answered.

"How are you going to get . . ."

Paul pointed to Jeannie's cell phone. "She leaves it lying around," he said.

"I'll drive," Tony said.

"I can . . ." Ned began.

"Stay here," I told him. "Get them to stop tearing my house up. And if you don't hear from me in an hour . . ."

"I will," he said.

I stood up. As I rushed for the door with Tony leading the way, Paul shouted my name, and I turned.

"I know who it is," he said.

"I can back you up," Tony said.

We were a minute or two away from the cemetery, and not a word had been spoken since we'd gotten into the truck. I'd been examining the deed, a document not quite so grand as the Declaration of Independence, but a hell of a lot fancier than a real estate contract looks today. It would have been easy to get lost in the beauty of the document, but I was, let's say *preoccupied*, so just the sound of his voice made me jump a little. I caught my breath and said, "What do you mean, back me up?"

"I can be behind you. Be ready in case they try something. I have the gun with me."

That didn't make me feel even a little safer. "The voice said to come alone," I reminded him. "I'm not taking any chances on this."

"You called the cops."

"Yeah, because they're the cops. If one of the bad guys sees you loitering around a cemetery with no clear purpose, they'll know I brought you, and Melissa's life could be in danger. For that matter, if a police sniper sees you, *your* life will be in danger. Thanks, Tony, but no."

"They won't know I'm with you," he persisted. "I can be a trick-or-treater."

I would have laughed if my stomach hadn't been in knots. "Dressed as a contractor in his mid-thirties?" I asked.

"I have a drop cloth in the back. I can put it over my head and be a ghost."

"You'd be a ghost with paint spots all over it. Who goes out on Halloween as a Jackson Pollock ghost? Tony, thanks, really. But no. Drop me off and stick around so you can come if I call you, but otherwise, stay in the truck, okay?"

He nodded, and that was it.

Just before we got to the center of town, a text message came in from Jeannie's phone, reading, "No news." Melissa hadn't been spotted by any ghosts.

Tony dropped me off a block from McArver Cemetery, a relatively small plot in the middle of town, behind an Episcopal church. The burial ground had been used as far back as the eighteen hundreds, and no one had been interred here in more than fifty years.

It was, to say the least, a strange place to be having this meeting on Halloween night. Or perhaps the perfect place.

My breath was coming in spurts as I approached the main gate. I didn't see any sign of McElone or any other police officers, and I couldn't decide if I was alarmed by that or reassured that they'd taken precautions to be so well hidden. I decided on the latter, because the thought of going in here alone was more than I could accept right now.

I held the box with the deed in it so tightly I was afraid it would shatter in my hands.

The voice hadn't specified an area in the cemetery to

meet. I checked my watch and saw that Tony had dropped me off about three minutes before the deadline. So I started in and figured I'd head for the center, from where I could get to any spot fairly quickly.

There was a rustle in some decorative shrubs behind me, but when I turned to look, there was no one there. When I turned back, a figure in a hooded black cloak stood about fifteen feet in front of me, the bright moon behind it obscuring the face. But I could easily tell who it was.

"You can take off the hood, Bridget," I said. "I know who you are."

Paul had been right: Mayor Bridget Bostero lowered the hood on her cloak. Her eyes weren't angry, or even very intense. They were like the eyes on a fish—open, seeing, but completely unexpressive.

"You brought the deed?" she asked, in a tone as conversational as if she were inquiring about the health of my dog. I didn't have a dog. If Melissa wanted a dog, I'd get her one. Just let her be all right.

"Where is my daughter?" She could have the stupid deed. I wanted Melissa.

A laugh escaped from the mayor's mouth. "I honestly have no idea," she said. "But when she came trick-or-treating at my house looking so adorable, and said she had to be home by eight-thirty, I pushed up the timetable. I knew that would get you here no matter what."

Melissa wasn't here? She wasn't being held by people trying to blackmail me? She was safe?

"You bitch," I hissed. "Do you have any clue what you've put me through?"

"I did what was necessary, Alison. If you'd cooperated before, I wouldn't have had to do that tonight. It's really your fault." Bridget's grin was a little less jovial than before.

"I didn't have any idea where the deed was until after you called," I said. "I tore that house apart—literally— looking for it." Where the hell was McElone, already?

"Well, then, it served as an effective incentive," the mayor said. "Now hand over the deed, please."

"Just a minute," I said. "I'm trying to figure this out. You were behind all the threatening e-mails to Maxie and me, the threatening calls to the Prestons and the package to my mother's house, weren't you?"

"That's right," Bridget agreed. "But for different reasons. At first, I just wanted that woman out of the house so Adam could bulldoze it, but she talked the planning board out of it. Go figure the little tramp could be eloquent. But with you, well, Adam had cut me off, but I discovered—after all this time—that the story about Washington's deed was true. I found a copy of the record for the deed in the county clerk's office when I was there on town business. And I figured you could find it if you were given enough . . . motivation. I need that document."

"I know it's worth about a half million dollars," I said.

"Yes, but that's just part of it," Bridget responded. "Sure, I could use the money to finance my campaign, but the document itself, a tie to history? That's worth all sorts of political capital, and it could get me on the national news. The next thing you know, I'm a candidate for the senate."

"This was about getting a better position in politics?" I couldn't believe what I was hearing. "You killed Paul Harrison and Maxie Malone over that?"

Mayor Bostero shrugged. "A lot of people have died for such causes," she said. "I simply wandered over to the bar at Café Linguine just in time to add a little something to the drinks going to that table. Honestly, Ms. Malone was the target. The man—and he was adorable, by the way—was collateral damage. I couldn't be sure which drink would be placed in front of which person, so I had to poison both."

"But you had to make it look like suicide, so you went to my house—that's how you knew what the upstairs looked like—and injected them with Ambien. Only you would have had it handy in liquid form."

"I have such trouble sleeping," Bridget said with a grin.

"All that so you could get a part-time job in the New Jersey state senate?" I asked, not hiding my contempt. "Serving the people?"

I took two steps back, hoping the increased volume of our voices would attract someone. The cops *were* here, right?

"Are you counting on the police, Alison?" Mayor Bostero asked. "You shouldn't: I got on their communication system, said I was Detective McElone, and told them that the call to the cemetery was cancelled. They won't straighten it out until long after we're done here. So stop stalling. Hand over the deed."

Any incentive I had to do as she asked was gone. "No," I said.

Bridget's right hand came up, holding a gun. "Did I forget the magic word?" she asked. "I apologize. Hand over the deed, *please*."

"You're going to shoot me for it?"

"That's the general idea. You can hand it over, or I can pick it up off the ground when you fall. I'd prefer not to risk hitting the deed, but I am a pretty good shot."

My voice got louder. Maybe Tony would hear. "I think you'll *shoot* me either way," I told her. "I already know that *you killed Paul and Maxie*. You can't let me walk around."

The Mayor nodded her head approvingly. "You're right again, Alison. I am going to kill you. But first, I'd like you to please put the box down."

Instead, I held it up vertically, covering the area from my chin to my waist. "If you want to take a chance, feel free," I shouted from behind the case. "But I'll be leaving now."

I took another two steps back, and Bridget fired the gun just to my left. I could feel the air move as the bullet passed me. She had been telling the truth; she was good with a gun. I kept the case right where it was, figuring she wouldn't risk a shot into it, and I was right.

"The next bullet goes into your knee, Alison. And you will drop the box then."

Damn.

I stopped. Perhaps negotiation was the way to go. "Maybe we can work out a deal," I said. "I'll stay quiet on the murders in return for your agreement not to shoot me, and a recommendation for the guesthouse by the town's economic development commission. How's that? You can keep the money."

There was movement in the shrub behind me again.

Mayor Bostero raised the gun and took aim at the top of my head. "Nice try, Alison," she said. Before she could fire, a figure lurched out from behind the shrub. A figure the size of a man, wearing a sheet. Tony must have gone for the drop cloth in his truck after all.

He started walking toward us. Bridget, exposed with the gun in her hand, faltered—her shooting hand wavered between me and the sheet. Tony was going to get himself killed for me, and then I'd get killed on my own.

"Get out of here," I hissed at him.

"Stop," yelled the mayor. "I'll fire at you."

But Tony kept walking, and Bridget raised the gun, pointed straight at him.

"Tony, *no*," I said louder.

The mayor fired. The sheet took a hit, never so much as flinched, and kept walking toward her. She fired again, with the same result. And again.

I screamed, I think. How could I tell Jeannie I'd gotten her husband killed?

But the figure came close to me, shoulder-to-shoulder, and the familiar voice I heard as it passed—with the sensation of a warm breeze through my right elbow—was not Tony's.

"It's okay," it said. "I'm right here, baby girl."

He walked by me. And right at Bridget. She fired once more. Again, it had no effect.

The figure walked right into the mayor, and when he passed through, I could barely see an outline of him, but the sheet stayed over Bridget Bostero, and she struggled to pull it off.

That was the only opening I needed. Fueled with the fury of her confession and the pent-up anger over her having threatened my daughter, I dropped the box with the deed, dove onto the mayor and brought her to the ground. The gun fell out of her hand and skittered away.

I hit her again and again, longer than I needed to, probably, but it felt so good that I kept doing it until I rolled off her unconscious body, covered in a sheet, and started to cry.

The tears were the problem, I believe. If I had been dry-eyed, I would have seen the hand reach for the gun on the ground.

But as it was, I didn't realize what was happening until I was staring up at Adam Morris, holding it casually.

I almost laughed; I was beyond reason. "What the hell are *you* doing here?" I asked.

"You," he said. "You told the police about me. You found the appointment book. It's your fault the police are after me."

"What?"

"I knew she"—he pointed at the mayor, still prone and unmoving—"was after you. And that I could follow her and find you. To do this." He pointed the gun at me.

"The deed is there," I said, indicating the spot where I'd dropped the box.

"What deed?" he asked.

I didn't even have time to speak. He pulled back the hammer on Bridget's revolver and aimed right between my eyes. The shot rang out.

And immediately Adam Morris fell to his knees, then

flat on the ground, facedown. Behind him, Detective Anita McElone was standing, her weapon held straight out in front of her. She ran to Adam and kicked the gun away from his hand.

"Do you still actually *need* the right to remain silent?" she asked him.

"My leg," he moaned.

McElone nodded. "I imagine that smarts a bit," she said. "Be happy that's all it was." She looked at me and pointed at the other prone figure. "The mayor?" she asked.

"My *leg*," Adam insisted.

"Oh, be quiet. I'm calling for an ambulance."

Still in a state of diminishing hysterics, I nodded. "Where were you?" I finally managed.

"After she called off my officers, it took me a while to figure out what had happened," McElone said. "I'm sorry; I got here as fast as I could."

My teeth were chattering. I couldn't see anything clearly. "I could have died," I said. I hadn't been really talking to her. It was just something I said.

"I am sorry." I noticed she was breathing heavily; she must have run when she'd heard the gunshots.

"Did you see my . . ."

"I just saw the gun, and I heard the shots. Don't worry. Just let me call in for an ambulance."

I had a hard time controlling myself, and found I was crying. McElone actually held me for a few minutes until she had to talk to the EMTs and her backup.

The next thing I knew, I was back at the house, hugging Melissa so tightly I was probably the biggest threat to her health that day.

Forty-nine

"I had Adam Morris being watched," Detective Anita McElone said. "So when the officer called in and said Morris was tailing the mayor and heading for the cemetery, I realized something was wrong. Then I heard the mayor call in as me and cancel the operation."

After my brief but important reunion with Melissa, McElone had insisted I come back to the police station to make a statement, which I thought was fair. But her tone had softened, and even the look of the dreary cop house was not quite as ominous as it had seemed before.

"Why were you watching Adam Morris?" I asked. "I mean, besides the fifty-two reasons I'd already given you, all of which you'd told me were stupid."

"Morris was the last person to see Terry Wright alive," McElone answered. "His name was on the hard drive and the appointment book Bianca Valessy had." She shot me a look. "Yes, we knew about Bianca. We had plainclothes officers following Kerin Murphy after you told me about the appointment book, and after we checked Kerin's cell phone records, we traced her to Bianca. If you hadn't been meddling, we probably would have gotten there faster. Nice work."

I grimaced, then told her about what Bridget Bostero had said in the cemetery, and McElone shook her head in what would have been disbelief had she allowed herself the ability to be surprised.

"She didn't tell you anything?" I asked. "She's not still unconscious, is she? I didn't hit her *that* hard."

"No, she's awake and talking, but not about killing anybody. In fact, she tried to press assault charges against you, but I saw the gun in her hand, even though I couldn't get a clear shot at her, so no lawsuit's going to happen."

"And Adam Morris?" I asked.

"Morris will have his leg up in traction for a while," McElone said. "He's clammed up for the time being. The shooting, like any incident that involves an officer, is under review."

"If neither of them are talking . . ." I started.

"We're getting a lot of the story from Bianca." McElone grinned. "She has quite the story to tell, and she has Morris's appointment calendar and his computer schedule to back it up. She says Morris also hired a guy to break into your house twice, once to plant that one-dollar bill with the nasty note on the wall, and once to bust up the patch in your hallway. We should have him in custody in a couple of hours."

"Anyone I know?" I asked.

"You remember David Preston?" McElone couldn't hide her grin this time.

"*David Preston*? The former owner?" My jaw dropped about a foot.

"Yeah. He was on Morris's payroll as, well, I won't say an *enforcer*, he's too old and tired for that, but he does some dirty work. Turns out Preston's been doing that for decades really, for various shady characters. Did anybody really think he could raise nine kids on a NJ Transit salary? He was the one who sent you and Malone the threatening e-mails, and even called his wife with a disguised voice every once in a while to keep himself looking clean."

"Why?" I asked. "What good did that do Adam Morris?"

"The mayor saw the hole when she came 'touring' with the Prestons, the time I got you out of there against your will. I suspected both Prestons at that time, figuring they'd been trying to find this historical whatever and then got mad when they thought you'd succeeded where they'd failed. But it turns out they'd just been digging up their yard for some landscaping plan Madeline Preston couldn't ever get to work right. The mayor, however, saw the hole in the wall and figured *you* were looking for the deed. And if that's where you were looking, that's where *she* would look. She could get herself back in Adam Morris's good graces, and get her campaign going again."

I sighed a little. "Not exactly the Albert Einstein of the Jersey Shore, the mayor."

"Bostero's not as dumb as you think," McElone said. "She chose that cemetery because it's one of the few public spots in town that doesn't have some video surveillance nearby, and she almost got you to hand over a half-million-dollar piece of paper."

"What about Adam Morris?" I asked. "Did he really kill Terry Wright?"

"Yeah. They were having a relationship of some sort—it sounds like Morris was quite the ladies' man—but when he realized he wasn't getting the house, he called off their affair. Wright threatened to expose him, and he took a page from the mayor's book. Figured if it had worked for her, it would work for him."

"This is one crazy small town," I told her.

McElone rolled her eyes a little. "Tell me about it," she said.

* * *

"It was the cosmetics advice," Paul said.

The next morning, with the light of day better illuminating the backyard of my "new" house, we were taking in the morning on a bench I'd restored near the back shed, near where I was hoping someday to have a greenhouse. Right now, I just wanted to sit.

I'd gotten back from the police station at about three in the morning, and hadn't turned on the lights when I went to bed. On the way downstairs this morning, I'd been very careful to look only at the floor. Anything else would have been too depressing.

"When Mayor Bostero called last night, it was the cosmetics advice she offered, unsolicited, that gave her away," he went on. I was cold in a light jacket, but Paul was wearing a pair of jeans and a gray t-shirt. Being dead, he didn't seem to have to worry about the weather too much.

"That was it? She suggests latex ears, and you expose a killer?"

"That actually just triggered it. I really got it all at once," he said. "She'd clearly been in the house before, certainly on the night we died, when she administered the Ambien to cover her tracks. She couldn't have put that much Ambien in our drinks; we'd have noticed it. But the poison she used was a substance often found in nail polish remover, the kind of thing a beautician would have."

I smiled at him. Paul really was a nice guy, and I was sorry I hadn't known him when he was breathing. "I guess you really were a good detective after all," I said.

"I want to talk to you about that."

He didn't get the chance, because Ned Barnes appeared from the back door of the house, and waved as he walked toward us. I checked my watch and, having delivered Melissa—reluctantly, on my part—to school, I knew he should have been there, as well.

"It's my off period," he explained when he reached us, although he thought I was alone. "I only have about ten minutes, but I wanted to talk to you about something in person."

"It's the deed, isn't it?" I said.

Ned nodded. "I guess I've been pretty obvious with my obsession, haven't I?"

"You could say that."

"Well, just to put a rest to it, may I ask what you plan to do with the deed?"

I'd already made a few phone calls. "It has to be authenticated, of course, and sorry, they won't accept a fourth-grade history teacher's word. Right now it's at the New Jersey Historical Society in Newark being examined. But it seems likely that the deed is real, and if it is, I'm going to donate the deed to the New Jersey State Museum."

Ned raised his eyebrows. "Not the Smithsonian?"

"Nah. They have enough Washington stuff. Let New Jersey have a little of its own for a change."

Ned smiled. "Not many people would give up the shot at four hundred thousand dollars."

"Oh, I could sell it, but this way, I don't have to worry about it, and I get a great big deduction on my taxes for a good number of years. That'll come in handy while I try to get the guesthouse off the ground."

He gave me the grin that had been my downfall since we'd met. "You're an interesting person, Alison."

"How interesting? Enough to overlook a few . . . miscalculations?"

Ned's face lost its look of amusement. And I suddenly remembered Paul was watching, and turned to give him an irritated glance, but he was gone. "You mean that you thought I might be trying to kill you?" Ned asked. "That's a lot to overlook."

I looked at my shoes. "I didn't *really* think that," I mumbled. "I was under stress."

"And I was acting like the Captain Ahab of Revolutionary War buffs," he admitted. "But maybe we need to think about Melissa."

"Melissa?" That had taken me by surprise. "What about Melissa?"

"I think maybe it's better if her mom isn't dating her history teacher," he said. "She's going to have a hard enough time as the Ghost Girl for a while."

"I don't know," I said. "From what I could see, Ghost Girl is a pretty popular title around here. And she's Melissa—she lets nothing stand in her way most of the time."

We started walking back toward the driveway. "Nonetheless," Ned went on, "I think given what you've just been through, and what you thought I was doing, *and* the fact that I'm your daughter's teacher, maybe we need to put the brakes on. For a while."

I hate it when men use logic. "For a while," I agreed. "But there's one thing I really need to ask."

He stood straight and nodded. "Name it."

"What is *Ned* short for?" I asked.

He looked at me strangely for a moment, and squinted a little, like he was trying to decide if I was real. "Edward," he said. "Everybody knows that."

"I didn't. Where does the *N* come from?"

Ned smiled and shook his head.

I had barely waved good-bye to Ned when Paul appeared at my shoulder again.

"There's something I want to ask. Let's go inside, and—"

His abrupt manner had made me turn my head so fast, I almost put a crick in my neck. "Hold on there, Quick Draw!" I said. "I don't want to go inside. I don't want to look at all the damage we did, and the repairs I have to make. I realize it was the right thing to do, but after all the work I put in and all the expense I went through, I'm just not ready to face it. Okay? So ask what you want to ask out here."

"No, really, Alison," Paul said. "We'll just go inside for a second, and—"

Before I could protest again, my cell phone rang: Mom was calling.

"I know you're fine, but I just have to check in and make sure." She managed to apologize while not actually apologizing.

I'd filled Mom in briefly last night, but McElone had been standing right next to me, so I hadn't been able to fully explain to Mom what had happened.

"Mom, listen. There was something I didn't tell you about last night."

"What? Is Melissa okay?" Her voice immediately rose a half tone.

"Yes! Mom! Everybody's fine. It's just . . ." I turned away from Paul's inquiring eyes. "I . . . I saw Dad, I think, last night. He sort of saved my life."

There was a long silence. She must have been shocked.

"You mean . . . he didn't tell you I sent him?" she asked.

Another long pause. This time, *I* was shocked.

"You sent him?"

"Of course! You were walking into such a dangerous situation all by yourself. So I got in touch with your father and told him to get down there."

It was all crashing in on me at once. "What do you mean, you got in touch with him? You can talk to Dad whenever you want?"

"Well, not *whenever*. He sort of comes and goes. Luckily, he was around last night."

Wait a minute . . . "How did you know where to send him?" I asked my mother. "I didn't tell you where I was going."

"I was tailing you in the Viper," she said. "You didn't think I'd just sit home and wait for a phone call, did you?"

Actually, I had thought exactly that.

I signed off with Mom after having promised to bring Melissa over for dinner that weekend (and having elicited a promise that she'd explain how to get in touch with Dad). My mind was reeling with all the new information it had to process. I didn't think it could take much more.

But Paul, who had been waiting at a discreet distance while I spoke to Mom, had other ideas. He approached as soon as I put the phone back in my pocket. "Come on," he said. "I have an idea I want to discuss with you. Just come on into the house, and—"

I almost stamped my foot, something I haven't done since I was ten years old. "Did I not make myself clear?" I asked. "I'm not ready to go inside yet."

Paul's features softened, partially because of the sun coming out from behind a cloud and diluting his image. "Trust me," he implored. "Just for a second."

I gave in, as I usually do. After all, I'd have to see the mess again sooner or later, if just to assess the cost in materials, labor and time. I wondered if I could hire help on the job, and then wondered anew how the hell I'd pay for it.

Paul went straight through the door, of course, but I had to open the screen door and then the kitchen door to get inside. I stopped on the threshold and gathered myself; this wasn't going to be easy.

"Come on, Alison." I heard Paul's voice from inside.

I stepped into the kitchen, where the walls hadn't been too badly damaged, I remembered. It was probably the best place to start, but there was no getting around the fact that all the walls would have to come down and be replaced with drywall. "I don't see why we had to talk inside," I said to Paul.

And then I looked.

There wasn't so much as a tiny crack in any of the plaster. Everything was exactly as it had been before we started flinging sledgehammers around. No—it was *better*.

Small imperfections I hadn't been able to sand out for fear of opening too large a hole had been smoothed over. The paint job was perfect.

Everything was perfect in the kitchen.

I literally gasped. Then I looked at Paul, grinning and hovering around the ceiling, where my stencil work was perfectly intact. "What happened?" I asked.

"Come look inside." He beamed.

A little unsteady on my feet, I made it into the dining room. Then the living room, the sitting room, the den. . . . Every wall was absolutely pristine. Not so much as a small bump.

Even the hallway wall, where the three-foot gaping crevasse had started all this trouble. Perfect.

"How did you *do* this?" I asked Paul. "The only guys who really know plaster are . . ."

"I made a few calls," he said.

Fifty

"So this is the place all the fuss was about." **Phyllis Coates** had not seen the house since the renovations (by myself and a host of dead artists) were completed. So now, fully furnished and primped for a photo shoot two weeks after Halloween (the changing leaves making the outside shots even more appealing), it was looking as impressive as it ever would. Even the weather was cooperating, with bright mid-November afternoon sunshine flooding in through the windows.

Since Phyllis's articles on the murders, the arrests of Adam Morris and Bridget Bostero, and the promotion of Anita McElone to detective sergeant had been picked up by some national wire services and posted on the Internet, my little guesthouse had achieved a certain amount of notoriety, and I was determined to exploit it for all it was worth.

I'd hired a photographer named Spud (he swore his mother gave him the name) to take brochure pictures, and Phyllis, happy to oblige her newest advertiser with a feature article on the house in an upcoming edition of the *Chronicle*, decided to stop by and see the place for herself.

"I might call the article 'Haunted Guesthouse Open for Business,'" she joked. "Everybody's saying there are ghosts here, after all."

"What do *you* think?" I asked her.

"I've learned to believe only what I can see, and that only part of the time," Phyllis answered.

"You're a smart woman."

While I showed her the house and Spud snapped away, Phyllis filled me in on the latest news: Both Mayor Bostero (well, *former* Mayor Bostero, now that she'd been forced to resign) and Adam Morris had been arraigned, and Adam had made a plea bargain that would keep him in jail for at least ten years. Bridget Bostero, as it turned out, was hundreds of thousands of dollars in debt and couldn't make bail, which was fine with the judge, since he hadn't authorized bail to begin with.

Meanwhile, Kerin Murphy and her husband were separating while she defended herself against obstruction charges. Kerin also gave up the presidency of the PTSO "until this difficult time is behind us." I was hoping she'd move out of town, but I don't really have that kind of luck.

Phyllis asked me whether I'd be interested in writing a column for the *Chronicle*, and I declined. I had enough to do. But she encouraged me to stay in touch and, as she was leaving, promised to do so herself. She also asked if Melissa would like to deliver papers for her, and I told her to ask again in a couple of years.

Jeannie and Tony still called pretty much every day, having gotten into the habit. Jeannie's calls were especially entertaining, as she would never refer to anything the least bit unusual at my house. But whenever she came by, she was tense. When I'd ask her about it, she'd deny everything and tell me *I* was crazy.

It's nice to have friends.

Maxie, who'd been unusually quiet and often absent in the two weeks since the Halloween insanity, poked her head up through the perfectly repaired window box when Spud and Phyllis were gone. "I thought they'd be never leave," she whined.

"What do you care? They can't see you. You could have made faces at them and otherwise tried to embarrass me to your heart's content. Assuming you have a heart."

She scowled. "You're really mean to me sometimes," she said.

"I *told* you that crack about never coming near Melissa again was just me being angry," I reminded her. "I *told* you that you can talk to her whenever you want, and I'll even let you be alone in a room with her again once her eyebrows grow all the way back in."

"See? Mean."

Before I could respond, the doorbell rang, and Maxie looked a little anxious. She'd hadn't said anything, but lately she seemed to dislike seeing people she wasn't expecting, and was going outside the house less and less. I thought it was sinking in that unmasking her killer wasn't going to change her situation—she'd still be a ghost stuck in my house. So I took a deep breath before opening the door, because I didn't know how she'd react.

Maxie's mother, Kitty Malone, looked just as anxious on the other side of the threshold. But I'd told her on the phone that it was really important she come by and, after she'd protested mightily, I'd told her why. She hadn't believed me when I'd said she could speak to Maxie—and I didn't blame her—but I wore her down.

"I'm not sure about this," Kitty said, but she bravely stepped into the foyer and looked around. "Wow. This place is really beautiful."

Maxie, peeking in from the living room, looked astonished. "Oh my God," she said. "Mommy." She seemed to regress to about six years old, and she backed up a little in shock, but she didn't leave the room.

"Thank you," I told her mother. "Actually, as much as I hate to admit it, many of the best ideas were Maxie's. Like painting this room white with navy blue molding." Maxie didn't seem to hear that, because she didn't react at all—normally, she'd do a dance of victory at my admitting she was better than me at something.

Kitty's mouth opened a little. "That does sound like Maxie," she said.

I led Kitty into the living room, where Maxie seemed unable to move. She stared at her mother. And I believe I saw tears on her cheeks, but the framed painting on the wall behind Maxie, which showed through, might have obscured my view a little.

"What are you doing?" Maxie asked me.

"She wants to know why I invited you," I told Kitty. "I didn't tell Maxie you were coming."

Kitty's eyes widened. "You mean . . . she really is here?"

"In the room with us."

Kitty sat down on one of the sofas without asking, which was perfectly fine with me; I wanted her to feel at home. "Didn't she want to see me?"

Maxie fluttered down from the ceiling to her mother's side and stared into her eyes. "Tell her I always wanted to see her," she told me. "I thought she didn't want to see *me*."

I relayed the message, but Kitty's eyes narrowed a bit. "How do I know she's really there?" she asked.

It was a good question, and one that I hadn't been able to plan for in advance. But Maxie knew what to do: She flew to the small secretary I'd put in one corner, took out a pen and a pad of paper, and brought it back to the sofa.

Kitty looked with fascination as the pen, seemingly suspended in midair, wrote, "I'm here, Mommy." She ran her hand around the pen a couple of times, looking for hidden wires.

"That's Maxie's handwriting," she said. "She never could write very well in cursive." And she started to cry, but the tears were those of restoration rather than of sorrow.

Maxie ran her hand over her mother's cheek, and Kitty put her hand up to her face, having felt her daughter's presence. "Oh Maxie," she said. "My God, I've missed you."

"Me, too," came the reply, a little slower as Maxie worked on her penmanship.

"Are you okay?" Kitty asked, and I watched the pen move over the paper again.

I didn't stay to see the reply, but I heard some laughter from both of them as I walked out of the living room. I was going to head for the library, where I was still sorting some books for the shelves (I'd made sure they looked good for Spud, but they weren't properly categorized), but the doorbell rang again, and this time I was the one startled, because I wasn't expecting anyone else.

A little man of about seventy, dressed very nattily in an overcoat and a hat, stood on my doorstep and presented a business card identifying himself as Edmund Rance, representative of Senior Plus Tours.

"My company helps to provide its clients with special and unique accommodations, particularly on the New Jersey coast." (That was classy—everybody in New Jersey says "down the shore.") "We schedule as many as ten tours per season." *Holy mackerel! That could put me on the map!* "I have seen some online mentions of this house as a tourist accommodation during the spring and summer months, but I couldn't find your Web site," he said.

"Year-round accommodation," I corrected. "We're ready to accommodate people immediately, but the Web site is still under construction." After all, the photographs had just been taken today. I hadn't expected guests until April at the earliest, but I could certainly be flexible.

Rance's stern expression did not change. "May I come in and inspect the facility?" he asked. He took off his hat, an indication that a gentleman was entering the "facility."

I stood aside and gestured him in, and then I remembered the paranormal family reunion going on in my living room. How could I steer him away from such a central location?

"Would you prefer to tour the bedrooms first, Mr. Rance?" I asked, leading him away from the living room and toward the stairs.

"Any order is fine. But I do have one question, Ms. Kerby."

"Please, ask away." I'd given up the expression *shoot* on Halloween night.

"There have been rumors, both online and in the town of Harbor Haven, that undead spirits walk the halls of this house."

Oh, brother. I knew I shouldn't have let Maxie loose on those kids, and then let them all in to tear the place apart. They'd mouthed off to their tight-assed parents on Halloween. There went my ten tours a season.

"Oh, that's just silly, Mr. Rance," I told him. "People like to make up stories. There are no such things happening here."

But he looked disappointed. "There aren't?"

Now I didn't know what to say. "Um . . . no."

Rance put his hat back on. "Then I'm sorry to have wasted your time, Ms. Kerby," he said. "Thank you for your hospitality."

"Wait. I don't understand. You *want* a house with ghosts in it?"

He looked back at me, assessing. "Of course. Without some spectral experience, this is just a house by the beach, isn't it? If you don't mind my saying so."

"I don't mind at all." I turned away from Rance,

considered the personal experience going on in the living room, and shouted, "Paul!"

After an experience (including a game of "keep the hat away from the distinguished old gentleman" that Paul wouldn't have been able to pull off even a week earlier) that convinced Rance there were, indeed, spirits on the premises, I got a promise of at least five tours of four people or more each for the spring season, and more if there were "paranormal encounters" that could be verified among the guests to bolster word of mouth. Paul nodded in my direction, and I told Rance I could guarantee such visits. Then Rance, given his hat back, smiled a very distinguished smile, almost bowed a little in the direction he imagined Paul to be, and got into a black sedan for his trip back to wherever he'd come from.

Paul and I decided to give Maxie and Kitty, who were still hooting it up with laughter on a regular basis in the living room, some privacy, and took a walk in the backyard. Taking a quick peek, I could see that Kitty looked fifteen years younger, and I was thrilled to have played a part in that.

Paul, a bemused smile on his face, kept looking at me as if trying to decide on the proper time for something.

"What?" I finally said to break the tension.

"I liked being a detective with you," he blurted out.

"Well, aside from the threats to my life and my daughter, I sort of liked it, too," I said. "You're good at what you do."

"I know," Paul said, and then smiled at his audacity. "I was thinking maybe we could continue doing it."

"I beg your pardon?"

"Just every once in a while," he said, putting up his hands to slow things down, it seemed. "I'd like to take on the occasional case. To keep my mind occupied. You have no idea how dull being dead can become."

I thought about that. "I suppose not, but I'm not crazy about the danger."

"We'll only take safe cases, and only when you're not too busy. You would have to sit for an exam and get a private investigator's license, since we obviously can't use mine. But I can certainly help you with the test, and you don't have to investigate anything you don't want to. Okay?"

"Well . . ." I had to play this right.

"Well, what?" Paul was already wary.

"You need me to become a private investigator."

"Yes." He looked at me, waiting for the shoe to drop.

"I need you to supply 'paranormal experiences' to tourists."

Paul smiled. "I don't know if I can convince Maxie."

"I think it's possible the problem with Maxie will be holding her back."

Paul smiled, and we walked a bit farther. Soon, we'd have to turn around, as Paul was about to reach his border.

"Meeting you has been an interesting experience," I told him. "Don't ever tell Maxie, but I'm almost glad she dropped a bucket on my head."

"I won't tell." A pause. "I was thinking our first . . . well, *second* investigation . . ."

"Another day, Paul," I said. "Another day."

ABOUT THE AUTHOR

E. J. Copperman is a native New Jerseyan and an award-nominated screenwriter, mystery author, and freelance journalist who has written for the *New York Times, Hollywood Scriptwriter, Writer's Digest, Entertainment Weekly* and many other publications.